THE PARADISE PROJECT

THE PARADISE PROJECT

H. G. STRATMANN

Starship Press, LLC
Springfield, MO
www.starshippress.com

The Paradise Project

"Hearts in Darkness" appeared previously in *Analog Science Fiction and Fact*, March 2002.

"The Paradise Project" appeared previously in *Analog Science Fiction and Fact*, November 2007.

"The Last Temptation of Katerina Savitskaya" appeared previously in *Analog Science Fiction and Fact*, September 2008.

"Wilderness Were Paradise Enow" appeared previously in *Analog Science Fiction and Fact*, December 2009.

"Thus Spake the Aliens" appeared previously in *Analog Science Fiction and Fact*, January/February 2010.

ISBN-13: 978-0-9790480-5-0

LCCN: 2010909078

Cover image: Hubble Space Telescope image of Mars, courtesy of NASA.

Published by
Starship Press, LLC
4319 S. National, 135
Springfield, MO 65810-2607
www.starshippress.com

DEDICATION

To my wife Maryellen, whose love has been
my greatest source of inspiration.

ABOUT THE AUTHOR

Henry G. Stratmann, M.D., F.A.C.C., F.A.C.P., F.C.C.P. is Clinical Professor of Medicine at St. Louis University in St. Louis, Missouri. He is board-certified in Internal Medicine and in the specialties of Cardiovascular Disease and Nuclear Cardiology.

Henry has been a cardiologist for more than twenty-eight years. He has either authored or coauthored over seventy peer-reviewed scientific publications. He and Maryellen, his wife and a fellow physician, have also coauthored a book for the general public, *Sex and Your Heart Health: A Cardiologist Tells All.*

A lifelong reader of science fiction, Henry is a frequent contributor of both stories and science fact articles to *Analog Science Fiction and Fact.* He is a longstanding member of the Science Fiction and Fantasy Writers of America.

Henry lives with Maryellen and their two teenage sons in the Missouri Ozarks.

PREFACE

The stories collected here form an accidental novel. The first one, "Hearts in Darkness," was conceived and printed as a stand-alone story. "The Paradise Project" also started out as an isolated work. However, while writing it I realized both stories could be linked together in characters and themes. The three other stories in this series were planned from the beginning as sequels. They describe the aftermath of events depicted in "The Paradise Project."

I intentionally wrote these stories with flawed heroes but no clear-cut villains. The conflict and drama arise from how my characters react when confronted by extremely challenging situations. They want to do the right thing but aren't sure what the right thing to do really is. Even worse, they must make their choices while under enormous physical and psychological stress. An overarching theme of these stories is how we as individuals and a species deal with no-win situations in which all our choices are bad—when we can only decide what and how much we will lose.

Finally, watch for all the allusions I've included in these stories. You will find many references to pop culture, philosophy, music, theology, and literature within them, including the literary works cited in their titles. These allusions help deepen each story by invoking additional ideas and images.

Table of Contents

Hearts in Darkness

So we'll go no more a-roving
So late into the night,
Though the heart be still as loving,
And the moon be still as bright.

George Gordon, Lord Byron

"**V**alentina is wearing makeup."

Stone stoically watched the needle jab his arm, sending dusky blood spurting into a red-stoppered glass tube. The cardiologist locked his feet against a low horizontal rod welded to the Destiny module's side, then coldly shrugged. "So?"

Morita slid the needle from Stone's vein and pressed an alcohol pad against it, grabbing his crewmate's arm to keep from floating away. The biologist smirked, "You should see her. All dolled up and dressed like a Victoria's Secret model. A wet dream come true."

Stone frowned. "Boris might not appreciate you talking about her like that."

"I think he likes it when somebody ogles Vali. Isn't that what a trophy wife's for? To show off what you get to screw?"

"I wouldn't know."

"Too bad." Morita poked the needle into a sugar cube-sized styrofoam block. He pushed off from the "floor" and darted toward the sample centrifuge-analyzer rack at the other end of the cylindrical module, his shaggy black hair trailing behind him like a rocket's exhaust trail.

Keeping his feet secure, Stone briefly applied pressure to the venipuncture site, discarded the crimson alcohol pad properly into a plastic waste bag, then rolled down his gray jumpsuit's sleeve. Stretching his lean nearly two-meter tall frame toward a nearby laptop, he tried studying graphs comparing his five crewmates' muscle mass and bone densiometry measurements to his own during these last four months on the station. But he kept wondering who Vali was getting "dolled up" for.

She shouldn't even *be* here. It was uncommon for someone's first trip into space to be a six-month tour on the International Space Station. It was unheard of for anyone to join a crew they'd never trained with on Earth—and for good reason.

Maybe it was just another symptom of how sick the Russians' space program was. For over twenty years they'd extorted most of the cash to build their modules and keep Progress supply ships coming to the station from NASA and the other partners. Now the Russian Space Agency even threatened to withdraw from the ISS and SPLISH-SPLASH if they didn't get more bribe money. They didn't realize nobody *needed* them anymore—

Morita said, "I'm downloading your results."

He floated over, his sallow ferret-like face peering over Stone's shoulder at the data scrolling onto the laptop's screen. "It looks like you're a successful lab rat. Wish my serum calcium and phosphorus were as good as yours. At least *you* won't topple over and break a leg when we go home."

Stone ignored him, fingering one of the paired form-fitting devices hooked behind his ears. The icy steel-gray metal vibrated as its microgyros sent pulses through his mastoid bone to his vestibular nerve. To medical researchers in Houston, he was merely "Subject No. 6" in their Dedicated Universal Countermeasures to Microgravity experiment—designed to keep his body anatomically and physiologically similar to its "normal" state in 1 g.

Those "vestibular stabilizers" he wore supplemented signals from his inner ears' semicircular canals and otolith system so that, whenever he turned his head or moved, his brain received the same body orientation and position information it was used to getting on Earth. Thin, lightweight, microprocessor-controlled negative-pressure "trousers" over his jumpsuit kept body fluids from shifting from his lower to his upper body—preventing the facial puffiness and nasal congestion that still plagued his unenhanced colleagues. His "special" diet included potassium citrate, antioxidants, and equally delicious nutritional supplements.

And there were those delightful injectable medicines. Erythropoietin, to keep red blood cell mass from falling. The latest cysteamine derivative and other radioprotectants, to reduce cell damage from higher levels of radiation than any terrestrial worker faced. New genetically engineered osteoblast stimulating factors and "myocyte stabilizers," to keep gravity-deprived lower extremity bones from demineralizing and weakening, and muscles from atrophying.

On Earth, he hated to take aspirin. In space, he was the poster boy for polypharmacy.

Morita squinted at the series of musculoskeletal data graphs. "Hell, your numbers aren't any different from when we launched! Hmm...I still have the second-best readings. But poor Boris! At the rate he's losing bone and muscle mass, he'll wind up a 99-pound weakling. Must be doing...*other* things besides exercising."

"He spends as much time on the bicycle and treadmill as you."

"Yeah, but he's nearly twice as old as me. Maybe he needs to exercise twice as long too. At his age, it must take a lot longer and more effort to do everything."

Morita tensed his bare biceps in a Charles Atlas pose. "Do you think Vali prefers men with big muscles?"

Stone's glare seemed to physically push the biologist away. Morita blinked and disappeared through the far hatch. "If you don't need me, I'm going to TransHab for a snack."

15

"I don't need you."

Now truly alone in the dimly lit Destiny lab module, Stone didn't try concentrating on his regular duties. Maybe he was worrying about Boris and Vali for nothing. Maybe his suspicions were paranoid fantasies generated by a mind isolated too long.

Or maybe they *were* real, and the station was an orbiting time bomb. He might be the only person on board who realized how dangerous the problem was—or even recognized it as a problem.

The problem of sex in space.

Stone grit his teeth. No choice but to discuss it with LeBeau. As commander, he was ultimately responsible for everyone on the station.

The physician disengaged his feet from the restraining bar and cautiously pulled himself several meters into the adjoining Unity node. But despite moving carefully, the empty module spun nauseatingly around him.

He quickly locked his feet beneath another bar, then waited for his surroundings and stomach to settle down. *Stupid VSs!* His crewmates' neurovestibular systems had adapted long ago to microgravity. They could somersault, float, or swim like dolphins with impunity.

But if *he* tried any acrobatics, his unadapted brain suddenly thought it was whirling on a manic merry-go-round. Right now it didn't help that—theoretically—he wouldn't have the problems standing and walking they'd have readjusting to Earth's gravity after landing. Still—if his misery showed the VSs could help prevent the first person setting foot on Mars from unheroically falling on his or her face on worldwide TV after months of "weightlessness," it was worth it.

The small observation window beside him showed that the station was moving back into Earth's shadow. As he watched the tediously familiar scene, a last glint of sunlight disappeared behind the planet's edge—plunging it back into night. Like the opening of *2001* played in reverse, though several days shy of twenty years too late. His mind played a fragment of Strauss's *Also Sprach Zarathustra*—its rumbling chords and rising trumpet exultantly proclaiming the birth of the *übermensch* and the death of God.

Stone's haggard face reflected faintly in the window. His stubbly beard was more salt than pepper, and his utilitarian Mercury Seven-style crewcut accentuated the gray metastasizing through his thinning brown hair. Reminders he was in his mid-forties—and the best years of his life were past.

He sighed. What do you *after* your dreams come true? Was getting into space worth all those years of work—or sacrificing all his other needs and those of the people he loved? Right now, instead of drifting like a lonely island in the uncaring void, dealing with diseased attitudes and behaviors that were probably incurable, he could be doing something easier. Like standing in a busy ICU saving the life of somebody with an acute MI.

Stone shook himself. *Remember all those lectures you give astronaut trainees about how common depression and feelings of isolation are toward the end of a half-year tour here on the station? Physician, heal thyself!*

Still nauseated, he pulled himself into the jug-shaped TransHab module's central tunnel. "Down" past the deserted Crew Health Care Area, its treadmill and stationary bicycle standing unused. Down through its middle section, with the equally empty six small compartments of the crew quarters.

As he descended into the galley at the module's far end, Stone heard two men snickering.

"Maybe he should hang a sign on the hatch to Zvezda. 'When the module's rocking, don't come knocking.'"

"The last time they sealed it off, you could hear her moaning all the way to Unity! Maybe she should change her name to 'Polly Orgasmic'."

"The way she's made up, she must really be hot. If Boris can't get it up, one of us young studs might get lucky—"

As Stone emerged into the dark galley it went silent. Morita and Newkirk floated near the expansive table that dominated the module, each clutching a long snack bar. They grinned sheepishly at him—like two junior high students caught thumbing through a contraband girlie magazine by the school principal.

Stone glared, "Where's LeBeau?"

Morita wadded his food wrapper into a ball and let it float beside him like a miniature moon. "Beats me. Why don't you raise him on the intercom?"

"I need to talk to him—in private."

Newkirk raised bushy raccoon-like eyebrows. "About what?"

"I said, it's private!"

Morita yawned. "He's probably in the Columbus lab."

Stone snatched Morita's discarded food wrapper and placed it in a disposal unit. The other two men silently floated away to the opposite side of the galley, the cylindrical module's central tunnel separating them from his sight. He heard them whispering and snickering again. His ears picked out the word "stone" from their otherwise unintelligible babble. Then Newkirk starting humming off-key an ancient Simon and Garfunkel tune—"I Am A Rock." More laughter.

Stone peered out an observation window at the night-shrouded Earth. *Won't it ever be day again?* He gazed longingly at one of the station's two Crew Return Vehicles, shaped liked a miniature version of the long-defunct Shuttle with its wings' tips bent up, docked tantalizingly close by. A set of solar arrays attached to the ISS, functionally useless now in Earth's shadow, seemed to waft and cool the small white vehicle like a huge fan. He wished he were in it—preparing to go home and escape from his worries.

Disgusted and sick, Stone climbed back into the Unity node. He dragged himself once again through the Destiny lab module, then entered the Harmony node, and finally crawled into the Columbus laboratory module.

LeBeau looked up from a crystallography experiment—his face first flashing a leer, then disappointment. "Oh, it's you."

"Do you have a minute?"

"No—well, what do you want?"

Stone moistened his lips. "I'm worried about Vali."

"Why? Is she ill?"

"No, she's very healthy. I'm worried about the effect she's having on the rest of the crew's morale—and maybe their safety."

The muscular Frenchman tossed back a leonine mane of blond hair and squinted suspiciously. "Explain."

"She shouldn't *be* here. It's standard operating procedure for crews to train with each other for months before going into space. That way everyone learns to work as a team to complete mission objectives—and, just as important, they see how well they get along together. If there are any serious personality clashes among the crew—if they find they hate each other's guts—better to find out before they leave Earth so interpersonal conflicts can be resolved or crew rosters changed than after they get up here!"

"I've seen no problems. Except for Vali, the rest of us have known each other for years. We've all been on missions with each other before being selected for the station."

Stone frowned. "Yes, *five* of us have worked together long enough to smooth out any psychological 'rough edges' we might've had at first. Same with Golda Verchinski, who was supposed to come up with you and Boris last month—instead of a freshly trained novice."

"Are you saying Vali isn't qualified to be here?"

"From what I've seen of her work, she seems reasonably competent. Medically, including all the times I've checked her, she's in excellent health. But that doesn't explain why she was 'promoted' over considerably more experienced cosmonauts we've already worked with."

LeBeau snickered. "It's elementary, my dear doctor. Vali slept her way to the top."

Stone suddenly felt dizzy—then realized his feet had worked free of the restraining bar he'd reflexively secured himself with upon entering the lab module. He grabbed one of the experiment racks lining the module and rooted himself back to its side, resisting an urge to vomit. A pink-eyed albino mouse examined him curiously from its enclosed plastic cage inside the rack—wondering what all the fuss was about.

Pale and sweating, Stone muttered, "You're kidding. Not even the Russians would sink that low!"

The commander grinned. "She bed-hopped through dozens of low-level bureaucrats in their space agency. When they finished with her, they introduced her to their bosses. Then those middle managers opened doors for her to meet *their* superiors—until she got 'access' to the cosmonauts themselves.

"I'm surprised Boris married her. Why buy the cow when you're getting the milk for free? What Vali got was her doting husband pulling strings for permission to bring her along with him."

LeBeau smirked. "And Boris still gets his milk. Have you noticed Vali showers in TransHab every other day, instead of weekly like the rest of us? She's very adept at slathering soap and water over her entire body, then suctioning them from her bare skin. Then she puts on a negligee and makeup for a rendezvous with Boris in one of the Russian modules."

"So I've heard."

"I hope you're not shocked, doctor. I've noticed some Americans seem puritanical about such matters. At least officially, or when they don't have the opportunity—or courage—to freely express themselves sexually. We Europeans tend to be more sophisticated, more adult in these areas."

Stone hardened. "I've been a physician for twenty years. Nothing dealing with human biology—including sexual activity—shocks or offends me anymore. I'm not interested in making moral judgments about what other people do—or acting as censor over their personal lives. If we were on Earth, this wouldn't be an issue except to Boris and Vali.

"But we're *not* on Earth. All six of us are locked up on this station. We can't get away from each other—or our problems. Still, I am bothered when people do stupid things. And when those stupid things might endanger the health and safety of the crew, I *have* to make it my business!"

The commander chuckled. "Are you saying it's unhealthy for Boris and Vali to make love?"

"No. Based on their medical records and the exams I've given them, there's no obvious health risk to it. I'm a bit concerned Boris's exercise tolerance has dropped lower than expected recently. But he's still better conditioned than most terrestrial sixty-two-year-old men—and should be up to the relatively mild physical demands of having sex.

"And Vali's very fit—as you'd expect in someone twenty-nine years old with excellent preflight health. The chance of her becoming pregnant—which *would* be a major health hazard in space, both for her and for the embryo—is infinitesimal. Boris had a vasectomy when he was forty. Interestingly, *she* had a tubal ligation three years ago. She's nulliparous, and didn't have any medical reason for it—except, from what you've told me, the obvious one."

Stone frowned. "It's not like they're the first people who've done it in space. NASA has kept a 'Don't ask, don't tell' wrap on this for years. The last thing they need is another proposal to slash their budget from hypocritical demagogues in Congress demanding to know why billions were being spent on 'hanky-panky in the high frontier.'"

"But there are anecdotal reports in the files. Problem is, even if those experiences felt good for the participants, scientifically they're worthless. No way to control for their natural tendency to exaggerate the successes—and downplay the failures. With more men and women staying off Earth for longer times, we need to conduct formal studies of how effective and safe sex is in space, just as we've done for every other aspect of human biology. Until that happens, the unofficial policy is still 'Be careful, be discreet'—and don't get too distracted and injure yourself or a partner by floating into an instrument rack and hitting your head."

LeBeau snorted. "When they approve those studies, sign me up! But if Boris and Vali are careful, why do you say it's a problem?"

"It's not just them I'm worried about. *Because* Morita and Newkirk haven't trained or worked with Vali before, they might see her more as a potential sexual partner than a colleague. It's impossible to maintain conventional levels of modesty on the station, and they've had plenty of opportunities to see she's very…attractive. Plus, they're both in their early thirties, heterosexual—and been forced to remain celibate for over four months. You don't need a medical degree to see they might be pretty horny by now!"

"How serious you make it sound! Those stirrings are perfectly natural. As long as they don't *rape* her, it's none of my business—or yours!—even if she decides to 'relieve' them."

Stone glared at him frigidly. "That's *exactly* what I'm afraid of. *You* know about that incident here two years ago. *That* crew didn't have any 'problems' either until Stevens caught his wife practicing zero-gee sexual gymnastics with their commander. He was lucky Stevens only managed to slash his thighs with a knife before the others stopped him. Just think what a PR nightmare it would have been if he'd cut off the parts of Lecoque's body he was aiming for—and forced an emergency evacuation to Earth for medical treatment! I don't want Boris going on a rampage against Morita or Newkirk as the cuckolded husband—or, even if he just *thinks* one of them is getting it on with his wife, reenacting the starring role in *Othello!*"

The commander smiled smugly. "Perhaps you're citing the wrong play. Boris might be like the husband in *Mandragola*. But I don't suppose you know what I'm talking about."

Stone stiffened. "Just because I'm a physician doesn't mean I read only medical literature. I'm familiar with Machiavelli—especially his nonfiction. My opinion of human nature is as realistic as his."

"Oh? I noticed you didn't mention *you've* been on the station as long as Morita and Newkirk—and are just as sexually 'deprived.' With all those physicals you give us, you see Vali naked more often than Boris! A psychiatrist might think you're projecting your own repressed lusts for her onto them. Or perhaps you're an Alceste—a self-righteous hater of humanity and their weaknesses. Though I doubt that you're well-read enough to understand *that* allusion!"

Stone stared frostily at LeBeau. "Let's not get personal about this. You're the commander, and I've reported a potential crew problem to you. It's your responsibility to do something about it."

"To me, there *is* no problem. If you still think so, talk to Boris yourself before you confront anyone else—especially Vali. That's all I have to say on the matter—*doctor*."

"If *you* won't, I'll speak to Boris. And believe me, for everyone's sake I hope I'm wrong about this!"

As Stone crawled "up" the lab's side like a poisoned ant, he sneered back over his shoulder, "By the way, I've read Molière's plays too—and I'm *not* a misanthrope!"

Disgusted with himself, Stone pulled himself toward the Russian end of the station. *LeBeau acts like a pompous pseudointellectual jerk—and do you keep your cool and act professionally? No, you act like a bigger jerk!*

No point waiting to talk with Boris. *Somebody* had to take responsibility. *Just wish it wasn't me.*

As he passed back through the Unity module, Stone peered again through the observation window. Some 400 kilometers below, Europe and northern Africa lay cloudless in sable night. He gazed wistfully at Cairo—wondering if Naseer was home now with his family.

Strange how one's perception of people can change. When they'd started training together eighteen months ago, the station's pudgy previous commander seemed stern and unsociable. But, while working together here over the last three months of the Egyptian's tour, they'd discovered a surprising number of common interests. Like a passion for classical literature and music.

Rose and Edith, the other veterans of the prior crew, provided more than intellectual companionship. The two grandmothers—charter and sole members of the Shannon Lucid Fan Club—had taken the three "youngsters" under their wings when they arrived here four months ago. They'd nursed Morita and Newkirk, suffering from bad cases of Space Adaptation Syndrome, during the pair's first miserable days on the station. Fellow physician Edith—a pulmonologist, and DUCM "Subject No. 5"—was a special mentor to him, using her experiences to help him cope with his tribulations as the project's latest guinea pig.

He'd rarely felt lonely those first three months on the station. The exhilaration of finally living here and a time-absorbing work schedule kept his mind healthily occupied. And whenever he felt himself missing his wife and kids, he could commiserate with Naseer, Rose, or Edith. They'd been married even longer than him, with many children (and grandchildren) of their own to miss.

When it was time for his three friends to go home a month ago, the four of them had a private party in the brightly decorated Destiny module. Ignoring his vertigo, he had danced a whirling microgravity tarantella with Rose and Edith while Naseer incongruously piped the

Preludio from Bach's Partita No. 3 in E Major, BWV 1006, on his soprano recorder. Rose invited him to her granddaughter's Maryellen's confirmation in five months—followed by a family feast showcased by her special homemade lasagna, a recipe handed down through generations of Sicilian ancestors. Not to be outdone, Edith extracted his promise to attend her oldest grandson's bar mitzvah. "And," she said, "if your VSs keep making you sick, take this medicine." He'd laughed at the label on the tube of food paste she handed him.

Chicken soup.

Cloistered in the gloomy module, Stone heard muffled voices drift up from the depths of TransHab. Two simpering male ones—and a single tittering female. Grimly hoping that Boris wasn't "down" there, he slid through the circular hatch into the Zarya module.

The first of the station's components to reach orbit was now little used and belied the English version of its name, "Dawn." Only tiny warning lights illuminated its musty interior. Stuttering air circulation fans uselessly cooled the few racks lining its dark walls holding, like tombstones, dead electronic equipment from long defunct experiments.

Preparing to penetrate deeper into this technological graveyard, Stone grimly wished Virgil was here to guide him. He slid through another hatch into the equally dark, empty Zvezda module. Scattered display panels glowed dimly with faint signs of electrical life. The amount of scientific work the Russians still supported here and in their research modules was pathetic. As much as he and the others grumbled about how *their* work had been scaled back to fund SPLISH-SPLASH, this was far worse.

Then he heard a sharp clank and several rumbling curses in Russian behind the closed entrance to the CRV attached to the far end of Zvezda.

What's he doing in there? Stone rapped politely on the hatch.

It opened. Boris boomed, "Some company! Come in, come in, my friend!"

Grabbing the physician's arm, Boris yanked him into the nine-meter-long CRV. Dizzy again, Stone tried focusing his eyes on the tangled rainbow-colored wires floating like a hydra's tentacles from the craft's large instrument console.

Boris grinned. "Don't mind the mess. The communications system failed when Newkirk tested it last shift. He asked me to fix it."

He pointed to a big chunk of electronic components rotating uncomfortably close to Stone's head. It reminded him of the install-it-yourself car stereo system he'd tried—unsuccessfully—to put in his old '13 Ford minivan.

"Uh—Boris, I thought only Newkirk and LeBeau were certified to repair the CRVs."

The Russian twisted two bare wires together—then cursed as a jolt of electricity lanced his fingertips. "They are. But, with little else to do, I've reviewed the repair manuals and had them teach me everything they know. When I was on Mir long ago, it was a slow shift if we didn't have several repairs like this. Another few hours work, and this craft will be better than new."

He slapped Stone on the back—rocking the doctor back and forth from where he'd secured his feet like his son's old Bernie the Dinosaur punching bag toy. "Don't worry, my friend. If we must leave the station before then, there's still the other vehicle. And as long as the automatic navigation system is working, who needs to communicate with Earth during a descent? Besides, there's never been an emergency evacuation."

First time for everything. Stone shivered, remembering when his main parachute didn't deploy properly during a training jump last year. As reliable as these pale wide-bodied successors to the venerable X-38 were supposed to be, the idea of trusting his life to a parafoil was not at all appetizing. *They* didn't have a dependable reserve chute to prevent you from splattering into fertilizer when you hit the ground instead of limping away with only bruises.

As Boris wound gobs of electrical tape around a power cable, Stone hesitated. Doctors shouldn't be at a loss for words with patients. But this problem needed a friend's help—and he doubted Boris really considered him "my friend."

Stone rasped, "I need to talk to you about something."

"Please talk."

"It's about your wife."

Boris convulsed as if a cattle prod had shocked his privates. "Is she hurt?"

"No, it's about…are there any problems between you and Vali? Anything I can help with?"

The Russian's face sagged into a melancholy smile. "No. Nothing you—or I—can do."

He sighed. "Do you think Vali is—attractive? Sexy?"

Stone stammered, "She's very…nice. A fine scientist and a great asset to the station. You're lucky to be married to her."

And, a nasty voice inside his head whispered, *her teeth are really straight too. Great interview skills, doctor!*

Boris nodded. "She *is* attractive. Too attractive for *me*."

Stone winced as the Russian's eyes burned into him. "Look at me, my friend. Once I was young and handsome. The best MIG pilot in Afghanistan. A Hero of the U.S.S.R. The prettiest women in the Motherland had to 'take a number' for my favors. Even in the dark years after those fools Gorbachev and Yeltsin destroyed our country, my good looks still brought me as many women as I could undress. The night I returned from my first tour on Mir, before rising from my bed I serviced *three* so young they were almost virgins. But later, for too many years women only 'respected' me as a space hero—and I almost always slept alone."

The Russian's lined face seemed to cave in. "Look at me—and see why. I'm now over sixty. My jowls sag, my eyes are baggy. See my wrinkled forehead—the whiskers that make me look like Father Frost! Despite all the exercise I do, my strength is failing. The only reason I'm here is because young, virile cosmonauts have no use for this old 'trash can.' No, *they* are now the lions in their prime—clawing their way to be selected to build the first permanent base on Luna, your 'South Polar Lunar Ice Sustained Habitation.' *They* will extract water from regolith and the ice deposits in Shackleton Crater to create more liquid oxygen and hydrogen fuel for their rockets. *They* will pilot your foolishly named 'Staged Prototype Luna-to-Ares Shuttle and Habitation' on to Mars.

"Let the old men, the used up men, have *this* orbiting relic for their home—and grave!"

Boris grinned like a death's-head. "Lucky to be married to Vali? Lucky to have someone less than half my age—so beautiful, so passionate—for a wife? Lucky, yes. But cursed too."

He laid a bear-like hand on the physician's shoulder. "Thank you, my friend. There's nothing you can tell me I don't already know. Whatever Vali does with other men, I will endure—and enjoy whatever happiness she chooses to give *me*."

"Isn't there anything I can do to help?"

"No. Except…perhaps as a doctor."

Boris pointed to the center of his chest. "I had pain here the last time I exercised on the treadmill. Maybe you can give me a pill for it?"

"What kind of pain?"

"Just a pain. A pulled muscle."

Finally dealing with something he *was* comfortable with, Stone answered, "It might be something else. Is it a sharp pain? Dull? Pressure?"

"Yes, it's a—never mind. It's not that bad."

"Boris, I need to know. It's probably nothing serious, but you better come back with me to the Health Care Area so I can check you over."

"Later, my friend. After I finish my work here, I'll let you do doctor things to me."

After more fruitless cajoling of his suddenly taciturn crewmate, Stone gave up. Trying to get Boris to cooperate when he didn't want to was as futile as making the bankrupt, ever-shrinking Russian Federation into a world power again.

"If you need anything, call me on the intercom."

Boris nodded.

Retracing his path, Stone paused in the Unity module to let his stomach catch up with the rest of him. Below, deep in TransHab, a third male voice, bubbling in lascivious French, elicited tinkling feminine laughter. *Why am I not surprised.*

Disgusted in spite of himself, the doctor crawled back to the gloomy Destiny lab module, closed its hatch, and opened the small locker protecting his stash of books and personal effects. Ignoring his pocket edition of Byron's poetry and miniature copies of Cicero's *On Moral Duties* and Seneca's *Epistulae morales*, Stone removed a portable media player and strapped it to his arm. Careful not to disturb his VSs, he placed a headset over his ears and searched through his music collection.

Mahler's Seventh Symphony? Way too bombastic. One of Haydn's "Sun" string quartets? Not even the C Major could brighten his spirits.

Mozart. Nobody can stay depressed listening to Mozart. He frowned at a playlist containing several serenades—No. 6 in D Major, K. 239, and No. 13 in G Major, K. 525. No, his mood was dark enough already.

Die Zauberflöte was the piece he selected on the player. *At least it has a happy ending.*

But even the opera's sprightly overture couldn't dispel his disenchantment with his crewmates. If it didn't bother Boris whether one of the others seduced Vali—or vice versa—and there were no medical issues involved, it was none of his business what happened between consenting adults.

Still—the monumental *stupidity* of it all irritated him. A marriage of convenience like Boris and Vali had wasn't really a marriage at all—

merely a business agreement between two independent contractors that included sex as one of the terms. There might be a modicum of mutual caring—but no real love or desire to truly share their lives, pleasures, and pains together.

And what about all the others? He'd met LeBeau's wife and their doll-like five-year-old twin daughters last year. At least Morita and Newkirk—each married about a year—didn't have any kids to be potential innocent victims of adultery and divorce. Did they think that, if their "loved" ones didn't discover what happened, it *didn't* happen? That being here in space—cut off from the rest of humanity—made nothing they did here "real"?

Maybe that explained why those two felt no shame treating Vali like first prize in an emotionally bankrupt sexual competition. Or maybe they shared LeBeau's "sophisticated" attitudes about sex. There was nothing sophisticated about using another person as just a *thing* to satisfy your own pleasure. It was merely the unbridled self-centeredness of the three-year-old—the blind unthinking hormonal insanity of adolescence—coupled with the power and ability to rationalize of an adult.

Loving another person meant caring about them for *their* sake, not just as a vehicle for your own selfish gratification. Love was *hard*.

But sex *without* that kind of love was easy. Anybody with the proper anatomy and hormones could do *that*. No thought, no brain required—except to figure out how to get the belusted into bed. Using one's reasoning powers, not as arbiter of the passions, but as their slave.

Humean, all-too-Humean.

No, he felt sorry for people whose desires stopped at such a shallow, superficial level. They wouldn't understand that sex with someone you truly loved—someone you'd committed your life to unreservedly—was far more pleasurable than sex with just another person's *body*, no matter how physically attractive.

Explaining the difference would be like describing Bach's Mass in

B Minor to someone deaf from birth. Some things you could only understand by having felt and experienced them. Even trying to explain what real love was would probably just shut their minds tighter against the idea. It'd sound like he was preaching at them. And nobody likes to be preached at—even if the sermon is a good one.

As the aria "Der Vogelfänger bin ich ja" warbled in his ears, Stone extracted a well-worn photograph from his locker. An accommodating passerby had snapped the four of them with the White House in the background during their family vacation last spring. Donna's gleaming smile beamed back at him from the glorious sunshine of that long ago day. His wife's arm was wrapped warm and close around his waist—always supporting him with her love.

Mary, their thirteen-year-old, looked glowingly back at him with her own special affection. She was blossoming into a lovely young woman, with honey-brown hair like her mother's. Soon he'd be supplanted as the most important man in her life. Before leaving Earth, he had lost count of the times "Johnny"—the boy she called her "angel"—had telephoned his daughter. Without meaning to, he'd metamorphosed into the comically overprotective father of ancient sitcoms.

Eleven-year-old Jeff's eyes were bright with mischief. Sometimes the boy was exasperating—especially on school nights when homework that should've taken thirty minutes stretched to four hours of constant cajoling. But it was still nice being a parent. Was it only eight months ago he'd been proudly introduced to a classroom of awestruck fifth-graders as "My Dad, the Astronaut"?

Tenderly holding his family in his hands, Stone cursed himself. *He* was guilty of worse infidelity than the extramarital quickies the others might be contemplating. *He'd* betrayed his wife by selfishly pursuing the one dream they didn't share.

It wasn't supposed to be that way. Before they'd gotten married right after graduating from medical school together, he and Donna agreed how they would start their lives as husband and wife. After she had finished her pediatrics residency and he his cardiology fellowship together in Houston, they'd go into private practice and start their family. Everything went according to plan—until one of their visits to the nearby Johnson Space Center when, partly as a joke, he'd picked up and mailed in an application form for astronaut training.

He wasn't accepted—not yet—but they wrote back encouraging him to enroll in their newest program training physicians as specialists in space medicine. It meant more years of study, less money than private practice when he finished—and many arguments with Donna. But finally, after convincing her this was really what he wanted to do, she had shown her love by sacrificing her own needs for his.

And so, as his wife's pediatric practice became busier and the kids were born, gradually he'd stepped closer to living his boyhood fantasy. While Donna often functioned as a single parent during his long hours at JSC and trips away from home, he'd acted as medical consultant for manned missions, taught astronauts—and finally became one himself. Especially this year, preparing for this tour on the ISS, he'd only been moonlighting as a husband and father.

Even now a parasitic part of his psyche still clung to the hope he'd be selected for SPLISH-SPLASH. Although he wouldn't be the first person to set foot on the Moon, being the twentieth would be good enough. Except—it'd mean more precious, vanishing time away from those who needed him. Even if Donna agreed to that too, was it right for him to keep their marriage an afterthought in his life? Was living out his private dream worth the price?

Meanwhile, a bullet-sized meteoroid flashed out of the void unnoticed. It missed his lonely module by several meters before plunging down toward the darkened world below and ending its eons-old life as a transcendental streak of light across the starlit night sky.

Stone jerked as if he'd been struck—twisting away from the unexpected pressure on his left shoulder. He tore off his headphones, leaving them floating beside him as they played a tinny version of "Alles fühlt der Liebe Freuden."

"I didn't mean to startle you!"

She was a phantom of angelic delight, gently wafting before his bedazzled sight. Her supple legs were bound tightly in black fishnet stockings, their warmth palpable this near him. The frilled edge of a radiantly raven-hued diaphanous negligee fluttered just beneath her slim waist. Its silk and satin molded her upper body into a thrilling landscape of taut flesh, gentle curves, and rounded breasts constrained and accented by the fabric's sensuous embrace.

Valentina smiled at him invitingly with full vermillion lips, parted to reveal a hint of brilliant white teeth. Her cheeks were delicately dusted with rouge to bring out their natural vitality. Green-tinted eyes shone like scintillating twin suns, surrounded by a dark corona of finely tapered eyelashes. A slow descent of blue-blushed eyelids sent them into brief eclipse, only to shine again in torrid glory. Cascading ebony hair was tamed and woven into a complex braid coiled behind her head.

Lithely floating in front of him, Vali caressed his damp forehead with the soft sure tips of a pianist's fingers. "I've been looking for you."

Stone vibrated in sympathy with her dulcet soprano tones. "I've just been...thinking."

An autumnal sadness shaded her face. "You must be lonely here."

"I manage."

Her bright eyes pored deep into his, as if reading the diary of his soul. "It's wrong for you to be so alone. Deprived of warmth and light, like a monk in a dirty cell."

Vali gently squeezed his clammy hand. "Come with me, and let me heal you."

Stone gazed back at her—stunned to see his own loneliness reflected in her eyes. The exquisitely enticing perfume she wore flooded his senses, a springtime blend of lilacs and honeysuckle. His face prickled with the summer heat of her body gliding so close to his. Her mouth melted into a coaxing smile. With a sweep of his arms he could thrust her against him—sear his frozen wintery body against her fiery heart, and quench so many pains in an incandescent moment of passion.

But his feet stayed fixed in the module's metal rung—resisting Vali's butterfly-delicate tug. Too much of him recoiled in bittersweet horror.

It's me *she wants!*

"No."

Instantly the spell shattered like a crystal goblet. Vali stared at him with innocent wonder. Then she noticed the picture clutched tightly like a talisman in his hands. She gazed wistfully at it. "Is that your family?"

"Yes."

"Your wife seems very—nice."

Stone glanced down at the frumpy, bespectacled middle-aged woman in the photograph. An overweight matron of average height, dressed unattractively in shorts and a plain white blouse, with dirt-colored brown hair beginning to streak with gray.

"She is."

"You're very lucky."

Floating free, Vali arched her back, flexed her knees and let her thighs fall to either side. "If you change your mind, I'll be waiting for you in TransHab."

Stone didn't move.

Long after she glided out of the module her perfume lingered in his nostrils. Eventually it dissipated enough for his mind to clear. A terrible pressure filled his chest and groin as he put that family picture away. Still trembling, he placed the headphones floating nearby back on his ears. The florid coloratura aria "Der Hölle Rache" pierced his brain.

Stone savagely stabbed the player's "Stop" button. He'd had enough of the Queen of the Night already. A swift review of the player's menu brought the opening strains of another opera—*Fidelio.*

Outside, Earth lay cold and still in unending darkness.

Much later, in the stillness of the first faint trumpet call announcing the arrival of Don Fernando at the prison-fortress, Stone heard a muffled voice over the intercom. He removed his headphones.

"—need you! Stone, come here!"

He pushed a button. "What do you want?"

"It's Boris! He's sick! We need you in the galley *now!*"

"On my way."

The nausea returned as Stone hurriedly pulled himself through the intervening passages. Ashen and sweating, he plunged rapidly down into TransHab—

And fell into a Hieronymous Bosch painting. Faceless naked bodies tumbled chaotically around him in semidarkness. The acrid smell of sweat and other body odors overwhelmed him. For a disorienting moment he didn't know where he was or what was happening.

Gradually his brain created order from this nightmare. The blurred faces focused into those of his five crewmates—their clothing scattered like drifting clouds around the claustrophobic module. Vali's wadded-up negligee brushed his arm. Then its owner, dressed only in shredded fishnet stockings, floated forward to face him. Again his senses reeled, stunned by the Praxitilean beauty of her flawless figure.

Another instant and that compartment of his mind crashed shut like a bulkhead. Instead of the man's desire to touch and kiss those roseate nipples nearly touching his face, the physician saw only two suspended masses of glandular adipose tissue.

Lipstick smeared over her cheeks, her hair braid half unknotted, Vali motioned him toward the elderly grimacing figure hunched over the zero-gee toilet. Boris was pale, diaphoretic, and gasping for air. His brick-like fist was pressed against his sternum.

"Boris, what's the matter?"

The Russian looked up at Stone miserably. "There's a terrible pressure in my chest. It won't go away!"

"When did it start?"

"About ten minutes ago, right after my turn with—"

Vali hovered close to Stone, a worried expression darkening her face. A loose strand of her hair tickled his cheek. The doctor coldly nudged her away with a flick of his shoulder—sending her gliding away from him and his patient.

His eyes tracked down Newkirk, drifting nude nearby. "Get the portable oxygen setup!" He turned and glared at Morita, who'd snatched his underpants from mid-air and was struggling back into them.

"Get over here!"

The station's other Crew Medical Officer gave up on redressing and obeyed, his twisted undergarment hanging around his left ankle like a white flag.

Stone shouted, "We've got to get Boris to the Health Care Area. Go there and get the backboard!"

Morita replied, "Can't we just float him there now?"

"Don't want to risk it. Once he's wrapped on the backboard, we won't have to worry he might get confused from hypoxia and start fighting us."

Stone checked Boris's radial pulse, and frowned. The Russian looked at him pleadingly. "Is it something serious, my friend?"

"I don't know. I hope not. But I'm not taking any chances."

Morita returned, his underpants now worn properly. He stood the long backboard he'd brought upright, then Boris painfully stretched himself out to help them position him against it. Soon long cloth flaps enfolded most of his body, secured by velcro straps. Newkirk brought a clear plastic mask and tubing connected to a small oxygen tank. Stone positioned the mask on Boris's face and turned the oxygen flow to four liters/minute. After several breaths the latter said, "I feel better."

"Good."

As Stone opened his mouth to tell the others to start moving Boris, something wet splattered against his left cheek. He wiped it away, then rubbed the viscous droplets with his fingertips until he realized what it was.

Semen. More globules floated nearby.

He gritted his teeth at LeBeau, cowering silently at the far end of the module. "Get a handvac and suck that stuff up before somebody breathes it in and chokes on it!"

Stone watched as Morita and Newkirk pulled Boris "up" two levels to TransHab's medical suite. They secured the backboard to a wall, leaving his arms free and accessible. As Morita reconnected the mask to a larger oxygen supply from a wall outlet, Stone clipped a pulse oximeter to Boris's left index finger and wound a crackling blood pressure cuff around his upper right arm.

The Russian winced as Morita shaved mounds of gray hair off his chest and applied sticky white electrode patches to its raw skin, and then to each arm and leg. He watched Stone frown at the flaming red numbers a nearby screen displayed. "What do they mean, my friend?"

Blood pressure 115/60. Heart rate 110. Respirations 20. O_2 saturation 96%. Nothing critical—but not entirely normal either.

"Don't talk. I need to listen to your lungs and heart."

Thirty seconds later Stone removed the stethoscope from his ears. *Lungs clear. No murmurs or gallops, but many irregular beats.* He barked at Morita, "Get him hooked up to the monitor!"

The latter hurriedly attached the last wire to the electrode patches. A rapid high-pitched "beep, beep" echoed in the module in time with a bouncing green line on an LCD screen. Stone's forehead furrowed. *Lots of PVCs.*

"Get an EKG. Then start an IV with D$_5$NS at KVO."

Morita pushed a button on the console, then wrapped a tourniquet around Boris's left arm. Stone watched a twelve-lead electrocardiogram displaying the electrical activity of the Russian's heart play out on the screen. He scowled, "That doesn't look right. Check the leads."

Morita pressed the electrode patches and jiggled the wires stuck to Boris's skin. "Seem OK to me."

"Print a hard copy."

Glossy paper divided into tiny pink boxes rolled slowly out from a printer. Stone snatched the paper, stared in disbelief at the pattern of blue squiggles on it—and felt sick. He released the EKG, letting the Russian's potential death warrant drift away. "Get that IV in *now!*"

Morita swabbed Boris's forearm with an alcohol pad and jabbed a plump vein with a thin needle. He grunted with satisfaction as a bead of ruddy blood formed at its free end, slipped a short plastic catheter over the needle into Boris's vein, and connected it to the clear IV tubing and bag suspended beside him.

Stone rummaged through a drawer of medical supplies and yelled at Morita, "Pump the pressure bag up! That fluid's not going to flow without gravity!"

The latter squeezed a black rubber bulb repeatedly, sending air into a sealed bladder surrounding the bag of IV fluids. It compressed the bag—forcing the dextrose and saline solution into Boris's bloodstream.

Stone turned to Newkirk. "Patch me through to a flight surgeon!"

Kicking his naked legs, the other man disappeared as he headed toward a communication console. Boris winced as Stone ripped several electrode patches from his chest, slapped on two considerably larger ones in their place, and reapplied the smaller patches around them. "Is your chest still hurting, Boris?"

"Some."

"Open your mouth."

Stone placed a tiny white tablet under the Russian's tongue.

The latter grimaced. "That pill burned."

"It's supposed to! Now chew this aspirin tablet."

Boris massaged his chest—wondering how mere aspirin could ease the terrible pain there.

Newkirk's voice boomed at Stone from the intercom. "JSC's on the line. Mina Osler is the flight surgeon on duty. They'll patch you through to her in a minute."

Stone grunted. "Good, she's an internist. She'll understand what's going on."

As Stone connected a cable between the two large patches on Boris's chest and the defibrillator, Vali floated into the module. She'd dressed back into standard-issue blue top and shorts. Stone deliberately ignored her as he reached for a preloaded syringe of morphine. She glided beside her husband and stroked his grizzled cheek with wifely concern. "Feeling better?"

Boris grinned weakly. "Don't worry, my love. Dr. Stone's taking good care of me. I'm feeling fine now…"

His eyes rolled back, lower jaw slack. The shrill alarm tones from the EKG monitor made every conscious eye in the room twist toward it.

"*Get away from him!*" Vali cringed at Stone's order, but she moved away as he hastily set the defibrillator to 200 joules. He shouted at Morita, "Check his carotid!"

The defibrillator squealed as Stone stabbed the "Charge" button.

Morita's fingers kneaded the side of Boris's neck. "I can't feel any pulse!"

"Then get back!"

Morita pushed off the module's side, grabbing Vali's arm as he went and dragging her away with his momentum. "What's wrong?" she stammered.

39

Stone checked the monitor again—making sure the jagged chaotic complexes racing across it were unchanged. Though the others were well away from Boris he reflexively recited, "I'm clear, you're clear, everybody's clear!" Then he pushed the defibrillator buttons.

Boris's body convulsed as a pulse of electric current arced through his chest—arms flailing upward in a gesture of supplication and staying there. Stone sighed thankfully as sinus rhythm reappeared on the monitor. His fingers moved to the Russian's neck.

Stone sighed. "Good pulse. Looks like he's breathing OK and his O$_2$ sat looks all right."

Morita moved back towards the cardiologist. "Should we start CPR or intubate him?"

Before Stone could reply, Boris shook his head and snorted. "Did I fall asleep?"

He winced at Stone. "The skin on my chest feels like it's on fire."

The physician waited to reply until he'd made another blood pressure measurement and saw it was acceptable. "I'll give you something for it."

Vali tentatively floated back toward them. "What did you do to Boris?"

Stone sneered at her. *What kind of medical training did they give you?*

Newkirk's voice returned over the intercom. "Osler's on the line."

"Stone here. Mina, are you there?"

"Yes, what's going on?"

"Boris developed angina about twenty minutes ago. We moved him to the Health Care Area and got an EKG. I'm transmitting it now."

A moment later Osler exclaimed, "Holy Mother of God! How is he doing?"

"He's alert, vital signs are OK. We'll set up the full telemedicine link with you so you can get our readings."

"What have you given him so far?"

"One sublingual nitroglycerin and a chewable 325 mg aspirin tablet. He just went into VT at a rate of about 300 and lost his pulse, but came out of it with one shock. I'll load him with amiodarone."

"What about giving him tenecteplase? "

"I don't know yet. Let's get another EKG and see if his ST segments are coming down before we decide on thrombolytics. Based on how he does, we'll have to think about evacuating him."

Osler groaned. "Don't even *mention* that right now, you've got to stabilize him first! I can't believe this is even happening. There was nothing in the medical records that the Russians sent us to indicate Boris was having any problems preflight. Was he doing anything unusual before it happened?"

Stone glared at Morita and Vali—coldly reading the fear and pleading on their faces. *Yes, he and the rest of these so-called professionals were having an orgy!*

"He was...performing a mild to moderate level of exertion. Maybe 4 or 5 METs."

He pressed a button. "Here's the next EKG."

Stone's heartbeat slowed a bit as he studied the paper the printer spat out. Osler said, "Looks better—no more 'tombstoning'—but he's still got nearly 2 mm ST elevations in V_1 through V_5."

"His heart rate and blood pressure are still good enough for morphine and IV metoprolol. Let's try them before we go with tenecteplase."

"OK. I'll contact the Russians to see how they want him treated—and about evacuating him."

"Fine."

As Morita finished administering the medications Stone ordered, Vali said, "What's wrong with Boris?"

The cardiologist ignored her. "Is your chest pain better, Boris?"

"Yes. But what is wrong with me?"

"You're having a myocardial infarction—a heart attack. Your EKGs indicate a blood clot is blocking the artery that supplies blood to the front of your heart. That's why you've had chest pain and went into the abnormal heart rhythm—ventricular tachycardia—we had to shock you out of."

"How could that be, with all the exams and tests you and the other doctors have done on me?"

The Russian paled. "Could…what we were doing a little while ago have caused it?"

Morita and Vali cringed as Stone sneered at them, his voice like ice. "What do *you* think?"

Then, to Boris, "We're trying to decide which medications are best for you. One of them might dissolve the clot. But it'll also increase your chance of bleeding elsewhere in your body—and our supply of blood substitute is limited. If we were at a hospital on Earth, you'd be getting a coronary angiogram right now instead. I'd thread a long thin tube through an arm or leg artery up to your heart and open the blocked heart artery by inflating a small balloon inside it. Then I'd insert a tiny tube—a stent—to keep the artery open."

Vali whispered, "Will he be all right if he doesn't have that done?"

Stone focused on his patient. "I'll do the best I can with everything I have here. I hope it's enough."

Stabilize and transfer. That medical mantra was scarred deeply into Stone's memories. Many ages ago, during his cardiology training, he'd spent countless weekends moonlighting in ERs at small community hospitals in rural Texas. Patching together and pumping medications into mangled auto accident victims barely clinging to life, until they were finally stable enough to survive the airlift to an urban medical center with the specialists and equipment needed to give them definitive treatment—and save their lives.

Stabilize and transfer. A fine principle—usually. But when reaching that lifesaving care meant a fiery descent from orbit and then suddenly thrusting a fragile heart back into the stress of 1 g—maybe it was better to leave bad enough alone.

Osler returned and finished her update. "Everybody down here— including the Russians—agree you should give Boris tenecteplase and enoxaparin and then, if he's reasonably stable, get him down here to JSC ASAP. We can have him at St. Luke's forty minutes after you land."

Stone said, "It might be the lesser of two evils to keep him here. If he has more VT or goes into cardiogenic shock while we're deorbiting—"

"I know. But if he stays on the station, you don't have all the medicines and equipment you need to treat those problems *there* either! Still—you're in the best position to see how he's doing. I'm afraid you get the final call about when—or if—we try getting him home. I'll sign off and get everything ready here, in case you do decide to bring him down."

Stone sighed. *Not that I want that responsibility.* "Okay."

Vali held her husband's hand as Morita drew the blood samples Stone ordered. After the biologist left to analyze the specimens, the physician injected several more medicines into his patient. Finally he said, "Boris, we have to decide now. If we keep you here, and a couple hours from now you have more chest pain, or even—"

"Die?"

Stone nodded. "If that happened, we'll wish we'd evacuated you. But if we send you down on the CRV, and you have problems en route—"

"Then, my friend, you'll curse yourself for doing *that*."

The Russian shrugged resignedly. "You're the doctor. Tell me what you think is best, and I'll do it."

"Medically, it's too close to call. *If* we get you safely to a hospital on Earth, your chances of getting through this will be better than they are now. But that's a big 'if.' And it's *your* life at stake, so I need to know what *you* want to try."

Boris placed a hand on the doctor's shoulder. "If you think it's better for me to go to Earth, then that's where we must go."

As Stone began "That's not what I said—", an unexpected voice interrupted him.

"Newkirk's getting the CRV ready."

LeBeau, attired in a fresh jumpsuit, had recovered his usual jauntiness. "He said it'll take at least four hours to finish repairing the communications system Boris was working on, so you'll use the other vehicle."

"I still haven't decided whether Boris should be evacuated."

"Well, decide now. You'll need to leave the station in thirty minutes to be in the best position to deorbit and land at JSC. If not, you'll have to wait another orbit before you're in prime position to leave again."

Stone hesitated. During his career he'd had to make many quick life-and-death decisions on critically ill patients when there wasn't enough information to tell him what the best one was. The scientist in him hated extrapolating beyond the data points. But sometimes you had to make a leap of faith—and go with what your *instincts* told you was right.

Finally he said, "Let's do it."

"Good. You'll only need one person to go with you and Boris, to pilot the CRV."

"Morita can't go. With me gone, he'll be your only fully trained CMO."

"And I, as mission commander, should stay too."

"Then Newkirk's the logical choice—"

"*No!*"

Vali and Boris shouted the word simultaneously. The latter said, "I want her with me, otherwise I won't go!"

Stone turned to LeBeau. "Newkirk's better qualified. If we have any major problems with our systems in-flight, he's fully trained to make repairs. She isn't."

Vali protested, "But Boris needs me with him! I'm his wife!"

"Yes, I won't go without her!"

Stone snorted. *How touching. Such a devoted couple.* "Whatever. She can come along for the ride—*if* Newkirk comes too."

The commander stroked his chin. "There's no need for four people to leave. I'm more familiar with Vali's training than you. I believe she's perfectly qualified to pilot the CRV. And *I* understand why she wants to go."

"*My* first concern is getting my patient safely back to Earth. Let's see what JSC says—"

LeBeau waved his hand impatiently. "There's no time for that. *I* am in charge here. We'll do it my way!"

Stone swallowed his rage and forced himself to think. He glanced at the monitor, then at Boris—the innocent victim caught in the middle of this senseless argument. Fighting LeBeau's pigheaded idea would waste too much time. Appealing to their bosses at the Johnson Space Center could also take too long—even if they agreed with him, the first opportunity to deorbit might be lost. And if Boris took a turn for the worse during those precious minutes before their next chance to evacuate him—

The doctor shouted, "Have it your way! Let's get Boris to the CRV *now!*"

The hatch above Stone clanked shut. Though the dimly lit CRV held only three of the six people it was designed to accommodate, he still felt claustrophobic—like they'd just sealed his tomb.

Boris was strapped into one of the three seats forming the back row of the vehicle. Its nearly five-meter-wide interior was a comforting hospital-white. Special compartments and attachments in the CRV's rear held the medical supplies and portable equipment needed to support his patient on the way down.

Stone increased the infusion rate of Boris's D_5NS, then he checked the wires and tubes tethering the Russian to a monitor and defibrillator plugged into the craft's power system. *Vital signs look good, EKG's almost back to normal. No Q waves yet. So far—so good.*

Boris smiled at him. "Don't worry, my friend. We'll all be fine."

Wish I could believe that. "The way things are looking now, the tenecteplase I gave you might have at least partially dissolved the blood clot blocking your heart artery."

"And I feel almost well enough to go back on duty! Maybe we don't need to leave—"

"It's not that simple. For the next twenty-four hours, even with the amiodarone you're getting, that abnormal heart rhythm we shocked you for has a good chance of recurring. And for the next couple *days* there's another serious risk. Most likely you had a small blockage—a plaque—in your left anterior descending artery that was too mild to show up on routine tests. It ruptured, and blood clotted over that injured area."

"Like it does on your skin, when you cut yourself?"

"Something like that. But because your ruptured plaque still hasn't healed, until it does *another* blood clot could form there—giving you more chest pain and heart damage."

"So I could still die."

"Not if I can help it!"

Stone withdrew a liter bottle of Astroade from a supply chest and pulled himself dizzily toward the front of the CRV.

"Drink this."

Vali, strapped into the middle of the three front row seats, frowned at the computer screens and data displays on the instrument console before her. "In a minute. I need to study these readings first—"

Stone thrust the bottle at her. "Take it!"

"But why—"

"You lost about a liter of fluid from your bloodstream after entering microgravity. Some of the remaining fluid shifted from your lower to your upper body. If you don't replenish it, after we land Earth's gravity will pull too much blood back to your legs when you stand. Then your brain won't get enough blood—and you might pass out."

Vali took the bottle and pressed her lipstick-smeared mouth around its nozzle. She squeezed it and gulped down its contents. "Why aren't you drinking any?"

Stone scowled and patted his upper thigh. "Because *my* body's still adapted to 1 g. These negative-pressure trousers I'm wearing kept me from losing that fluid. I'll just have to neutralize the pressure after we deorbit."

In a shadowy recess of his mind a shrill voice sneered, *I wasn't any- thing special to you! You wanted the others too!*

From the console LeBeau's voice crackled, "Two minutes till dis- engagement."

Stone strapped himself in beside Boris, leaving Vali alone in the front row. As the seconds ticked by, shame at his thoughts and beha- vior seeped into his mind—melting some of his anger. Of course it didn't matter whether Newkirk or Vali came. The CRV's reentry se- quence was fully computer-controlled and automatic. Its inertial navi- gation system used data from Global Positioning System satellites or transmitted from the ground to direct the craft to the right place in orbit, fire the Deorbit Propulsion Stage's engines to slow it for reentry, then jettison the DPS.

Their unpowered vehicle would then glide down like one of the old Shuttles until, at an altitude of about five kilometers, it deployed two secondary parachutes and a large parafoil to slow it down. Then the Navigation Guidance and Control System would guide the parafoil autonomously—turning it as needed to keep them on course to a runway at JSC. Finally they'd slide to a soft pinpoint touchdown on the craft's retractable landing skids.

All routine, all perfectly safe. Because the electronic systems in CRVs never failed. And parachutes always deployed properly.

"One minute to disengagement."

Stone wriggled in his seat—trying to think happy thoughts. In another hour or so, he'd be home. Hopefully the family liaison people at JSC knew where to reach Donna to tell her what was happening. She and the kids, now halfway through their Christmas vacation, were out of town in Cincinnati visiting her parents.

But maybe it was better if she *didn't* hear he was returning early. During their telephone link several days ago, Donna said a blizzard had made the city's Christmas all too white. Knowing her, no matter how bad or dangerous the weather was, she'd try flying—or, if the airport was shut down, maybe even driving back to Houston to be with him. *Her* chance of getting hurt or killed in an accident on the way there might be more than his.

Think something happier. Shortly after they landed, Boris would be tucked safely into a comfy ICU bed at St. Luke's. There he'd have all of the doctors, nurses, and state-of-the-art medical care he needed to get well—and wouldn't be only *his* responsibility any more.

Except—this was Boris's farewell to space. Whatever caused his MI, they'd never clear him to fly again.

And—maybe—it was his farewell too. Back home with his family after all these long months, this time he might not be able to rationalize leaving them again. Maybe it was finally time to renounce Luna, his harsh mistress.

A melody from *Dr. Zhivago* waltzed through his mind as the CRV silently separated from the ISS. The small OLED display on the wall beside him showed a shielded minicamera's view of their windowless craft moving slowly away from the huge, dark, spider-like structure.

Stone saw Boris stare transfixed at the screen. A tear trickled down the burly Russian's cheek as he murmured, "Farewell."

Vali turned around to look at her husband. Her eyes misted over. "I'm sorry, my love!"

Squirming uncomfortably, Stone studied the monitor showing his patient's vital signs and EKG. For many long minutes a profound quiet enveloped the cabin, punctuated only by the faint chatter Vali kept up with JSC, and gentle vibrations as thrusters fired and maneuvered the CRV into position for its deorbit burn. The ISS dwindled in size, then disappeared from the screen. Now it was just the three of them—alone in a lifeboat bobbing in the vast black ocean of space. The cardiologist chuckled grimly at his memory of Alfred Hitchcock's cameo in a newspaper weight-loss ad.

Vali murmured, "Deorbit burn in ten seconds."

Stone glanced worriedly at Boris. In theory, the deceleration forces during the DPS's big burn should put little additional strain on the Russian's cardiovascular system. Neither should the slightly more than 1 g they would experience during reentry itself. But, in his present condition, even what would normally be a trivial stress might prove life-threatening.

"Five seconds...two...one..."

Stone braced himself for a rumble and shove that never came. Instead he heard a sharp *SNAP!*—and the lights went out.

In the terrifying darkness Stone reflexively placed his palm over his heart—checking if he was still alive. The curses in Russian bellowed beside him, the "beeps" and dimly lit screens and displays of his medical equipment—now the CRV's only illumination—finally reassured him of his continued existence.

At least for now.

Vali was first to shout what they all recognized. "We've had a total power failure!"

Stone felt Boris try to lunge forward before being stopped by his seat restraint. The Russian roared, "There is a flashlight in that compartment on the left side of the console!"

After long seconds of metallic clanking from the CRV's front, Vali exclaimed, "I found it!"

Boris yelled back at the wavering light that clicked on in front of him, "Check our batteries!"

Then Stone smelled it. An acrid smell—like burnt insulation. Not a good sign.

Next it was Vali's turn to spit curses in Russian. "The batteries—they all look charred, like they shorted out!"

Boris called back, "All of them? Impossible!"

"But they are!"

"I must see them!"

Stone squelched his flashback of scenes from *Apollo 13* when the shadowy figure beside him tried to tear off the tubes and wires attached to his body. "Boris, stop it! If you don't lie still you could die!"

"If we don't get power back, doctor, we're *all* going to die!"

Suppressing his medical reflexes, Stone grumbled, "All right. But let me disconnect you the *right* way. If you yank out your IV lines we'll be swimming in blood—*your* blood!"

The Russian waited impatiently until the physician finished, then rocketed forward. Stone shut off his medical equipment, the glowing lines and numbers on their displays now meaningless with no patient attached, and followed more cautiously—guided by the flashlight darting frantically in front of him.

Boris moaned, "This is bad."

Stone dimly saw him attach a multimeter to the bank of batteries that supplied the craft's electrical power. Then Boris pronounced his diagnosis.

"They're all dead."

Then so are we. With a clinical detachment that surprised even him, Stone pictured himself dead. Dealing with death and dying so long as a doctor numbed some of the regret he felt for himself.

But he grieved for those he loved. Having a dead "hero" for their husband and father might bring them slight consolation. But what about all the "might-have-beens"—the birthdays, holidays, even the experiences most taken for granted, like feeling his wife pressed warmly against him on a leisurely Sunday morning after they'd made love, that he wouldn't be there to share?

Vali whispered, "Is there anything we can do?"

Her husband murmured, "We have one chance—"

His flashlight flailed wildly in the darkness for a while. Finally he yelped, "Good! The spare battery modules are fully charged! Vali, help me replace these bad ones!"

Stone sighed. Thank goodness for NASA's obsessive insistence on redundancy—even for components that no one realistically expected to fail completely.

Except—he was a doctor, not an engineer, but he vaguely recalled something from those basic courses on the CRV even he'd had to take.

"Boris, do we have enough spare batteries to replace *all* the ones that are dead?"

A pause. "No. Only two of them."

"Do we have enough power for the systems we need to get down in one piece?"

"That is what we must talk about…"

In the near-darkness, clustered around the glowing flashlight like teenage campers telling ghost stories, the three of them floated in the center of the CRV and—almost literally—put their heads together.

Boris began, "I'm not sure, but I think we have just enough battery capacity to reach Earth—if we're careful how we use it. We *have* to fire the DPS, we *have* to use our navigation system to plot our location—and the computer *has* to release the parachutes at the right time."

Vali nodded. "You and I trained to maneuver the parafoil with manual controls if the NGCS failed. That would save a little power."

Stone added, "The life-support system. Normally we'd have enough supplies and power for nine hours with a full crew. With only three of us, our oxygen supply will last longer. But, without an operating thermal control system, over the next few hours it'll get uncomfortably hot and cold in here."

Boris laughed. "*I* don't intend to be up here a few hours from now! I estimate we'll be in the right orbital position to try another deorbit burn in about one hour."

Vali frowned. "What about communications? Shouldn't we try to contact the space center, or the station? They could give us advice."

Her husband shook his head. "If we had enough power to spare, I would. But we don't—and I doubt they could help us anyway."

"What about returning to the station?"

Boris looked at Stone, and sighed. "All this time, our orbit has been slowly decaying. We're too far away from and lower than the station now to rendezvous with it. And it'd do no good if they came to us in the other CRV. These craft are not designed to dock together—and we don't have the suits for an EVA!"

Stone shrugged. "At least now we have a plan."

"Except...I wonder if—"

Both men turned their heads in Vali's direction.

"Doctor, didn't you say a blood clot blocked an artery in Boris's heart and deprived it of blood?"

"Yes."

"Well, that reminds me of how our batteries suddenly failed and shut down our power."

"I suppose, but—"

"Don't you see? Maybe, just as that blocked artery damaged Boris's heart, whatever destroyed our batteries—perhaps it was a short circuit, Boris?—also damaged a computer or other system that we need to get home. Maybe your giving medicines that partly dissolved the clot is like us using these replacement batteries."

Boris nodded. "Do you understand what she's saying, my friend? You said the same problem that blocked my heart's artery could happen again. And if whatever damaged the original batteries destroys these replacement ones too..."

Stone said nothing. There was nothing to say.

Stone watched anxiously as his two crewmates, sitting beside him in the front row of seats, applied power just long enough to run diagnostics on each of the craft's critical systems. As each computer and display flared briefly to life and Boris murmured approvingly, the doctor breathed another sigh of relief. If any critical system didn't work—couldn't be repaired—well, it would take only one weak link in the chain to kill them.

As he waited for their last flicker of hope to be extinguished, Stone remembered something the Machiavelli-reading LeBeau said. *Newkirk's getting the CRV ready.* Now he wondered if that preparation might've included—sabotage. How convenient, if the one person who could have squealed about their extracurricular sexual activities suffocated in space—

Boris's forehead beaded with sweat. "Now for the last test—our navigation system."

Stone shivered—but not simply from fear. With their heaters not working, he could see Boris's breath. Based on how cold the cabin was, they must've been in Earth's shadow for a while.

But he felt warmer when Vali exclaimed, "It works!"

Her husband kissed her cheek, then whooped as numbers flashed on the console's screen. "The GPS is showing our position! At least now we know where we're lost!"

Vali's fingers flew over a small keyboard. She exclaimed, "In sixteen minutes, we'll be in the right place to fire our engines!"

"Now we know everything we need to!"

Boris flicked a switch, and the cabin went dark again until Vali turned on their flashlight. He said, "We'll reactivate these systems three minutes before we reach our deorbit point. That will—I hope—give us sufficient time to make sure everything is still working and to update our readings, while wasting as little precious power as possible."

Stone interjected, "How far away are we from the terminator, Boris?"

"We've already passed it. Though we cannot see it, the Sun is shining on us!"

"Good. Then it should start warming up in here soon."

"Let's hope it does not get *too* warm. If our deorbit engines don't fire properly, or we reenter the atmosphere at the wrong speed or angle—"

Stone completed the sentence silently. *We burn up.*

He said, "Boris, let me hook you back up to the monitor and defibrillator."

"I'm afraid I can't do that, my friend. I may need to move around quickly to check the batteries again if anything goes wrong during our descent. I cannot have your medical devices weighing me down like anchors!"

"But your body is going to be stressed during deceleration and reentry. If I can't monitor your blood pressure, EKG, and other data, I won't be able to treat you effectively!"

The Russian shrugged. "I must take that chance. Your medicines have done a wonderful job. I feel fine now!"

"*Feeling* fine doesn't necessarily mean you *are* fine. Back on the station you were 'feeling fine' too just before you went into VT! If we hadn't already connected you to the defibrillator and shocked you immediately—"

Boris shrugged. "I suppose I'd be dead now. Perhaps it would have been better if I'd died on the station. At least then Vali and you would still be there—and safe."

In the darkness Stone heard Vali, seated to his left, lean away from him toward her husband. He only heard the kiss she gave Boris. "Don't say that, my love!"

Boris murmured soothingly to her, then raised his voice. "There's something you *can* do for me, doctor."

He angled the flashlight so it gently illuminated Valentina's face. Her makeup was nearly rubbed off, and her hair was a tangled mess floating haphazardly behind her. The grimy jumpsuit she wore flattened and neutered her figure.

Stone went rigid as Boris continued. "I know, my friend, you've been angry at Vali. You don't approve of certain ways she's chosen to live her life. Not because, as that fool LeBeau thinks, you have no human feelings. No, though you hide it well beneath that hard doctorly crust, you care very much about people—perhaps too much. It hurts, even angers you when they do things to themselves you think are harmful— or that won't make them as happy and healthy as they could be. And it frustrates you when you can't help them see or do what you believe could bring them much greater joy and fulfillment.

"Perhaps Vali and I have sacrificed things we shouldn't have—like a warm, loving home, with children scurrying about. Perhaps the ways we choose to soothe and quench our loneliness aren't the best. But, if we are to pursue our greatest love, we must be faithful only to it."

Boris delicately nudged Vali's cheek away from him, until she was looking at Stone. "Tell him, my beloved. Tell him why you made love to me, and all those others on Earth."

Stone stiffened as the woman beside him hesitated. Then she murmured, "Because I *had* to. It was the only way I could get into space. When I was a little girl growing up near Kursk, I'd go out on cloudless nights and look up at the round bright Moon hanging over the wheat fields. I'd dream about being the first Russian, the first woman to stand on it—to look back at the tiny Earth hanging suspended in velvet, and see how far I'd come, how much I'd achieved!"

Her eyes shimmered with starlight and the vast wondrous expanses of the universe. They reminded Stone of the seven-year-old boy from Illinois that he'd once been—squinting through the blurry eyepiece of a rickety department store telescope, straining beneath a cold night sky to glimpse the canals of Mars.

Boris smiled. "You see, my friend, we all have something more in common than just sharing this predicament. And if we survive this, I want you to do something for me."

"What?"

"*Don't* do or say anything that will keep Vali from living her dream! There will be many questions about what everyone was doing when my heart failed me. If you tell them the truth, it will cause a scandal, with shame and disgrace for the rest of us. Perhaps their space agencies will eventually forgive our three absent 'friends' on the station, and let them go back into space—if only for missions no one else wants.

"My government will not be so understanding. It doesn't matter what happens to me. My body has failed me, and I can never fly into space again. But it would break whatever is left of my heart if Vali were to be, as you say, 'blackballed.' For *her* to stay bound to Earth for the rest of her life would be death by lingering, perpetual torture."

Boris chuckled dryly and pressed his fist over his breastbone. "Humor a dying man. Grant his last request—promise me you won't say or do anything that could hurt Vali!"

Stone hesitated. "There are other issues involved, Boris. Lying about what happened might make things worse."

"I am not asking you to lie, but merely be…discrete about what you say."

"I'll—do the best I can."

Boris sighed. "I suppose that is the most any of us can be asked to do."

Minutes later, at Boris's signal, Vali flicked the first switch. One after another, a firecracker cascade of glowing computer screens and readouts illumined the console.

Although, like everyone assigned to the ISS, he'd been trained to operate the CRV, Stone let the two Russians do it. Watching them work, Boris—and yes, Vali too—clearly knew what they were doing. His efforts were better directed toward observing Boris—alert for the first sign his patient was taking a turn for the worse.

Vali murmured, "Deorbit burn in thirty seconds."

We hope. Stone watched Boris point to a vertical bar meter on the console. "We all must watch this meter very carefully. See how it's glowing just a little into the yellow area? Even now you see it creeping down toward the red, as we deplete our batteries' power. To conserve it, we must shut off each system as soon as it has done its job and is no longer needed. For if this meter stops glowing before we reach the ground—"

Splat. As he leaned back, Stone felt like he was sitting in a dentist's chair. A flashback of that family vacation to Yellowstone two years ago made him squirm more. Driving at night through a lonely stretch of Wyoming, he'd shaken off his highway hypnosis to realize that the minivan's gas gauge was pointing perilously close to "E." With no artificial lights behind or ahead of them under that cold starry sky, he could only hope—or pray—there was a gas station just beyond the black horizon. And while the kids slept in back, he and Donna discovered their cell phone's battery was dead—with no replacement or way to recharge it in their vehicle.

Whether divine providence or merely luck, they'd made it to that lonely ramshackle gas station driving only on fumes and will power. Even paying six dollars a gallon beat being stranded in the middle of nowhere—with slim prospects of rescue. Maybe his idea of wiring the

Hearts in Darkness

cell phone directly to the car's battery with jumper cables might've worked. More likely the phone would've just been fried—

"Five seconds…two…one…"

Stone braced himself for the console to go dark again. But instead an invisible mattress pressed him back into his seat. The craft rumbled around them like a runaway vibrating bed as he heard Vali recite, "De-orbit burn 25% complete…50%…75%…complete!"

The mattress vanished. Boris muttered, "Now let us pray this clever computer jettisons our engines!"

As if in answer the craft jerked forward slightly, and a green light lit on the console. As Boris blurted "Thank you, dear God!", Vali flipped several switches and reported, "Everything is shut down except the navigation system."

Her husband frowned at the meter. "Perhaps I thanked the Almighty too soon. We're deeper into the red than I hoped."

As the CRV performed its preprogrammed turn and plunged into the atmosphere, three pairs of eyes stared anxiously at the solitary lit display on the console. Watching their altitude and distance to the landing site decrease, seeing the meter dim—and hoping the thin lifeline they clung to wouldn't snap.

Stone listened as Vali slowly counted out numbers. "Altitude 100 kilometers…90…" Then he glanced at Boris—and his own heart skipped a beat. The other man was pale and diaphoretic. His breath came in gasps, and his fist rested on his chest.

"Boris, what's wrong?"

The Russian exhaled a huge sigh. "We did our best. But…"

His moist finger stroked the meter. Only a sliver of red at the bottom warmed his fingertip.

Vali stopped counting and clutched her husband's hand as he said, "The batteries will probably be exhausted about the time our parafoil must deploy. If they fail before it does—"

Stone interrupted. "The parafoil *won't* deploy, and—no pun intended—we drop like a stone. Of course, if we're lucky, they fail after the parafoil is out. Except—with no navigation system to tell us our location, we'll be flying blind. Not that it'd matter anyway—with no electricity for the automatic or manual systems, we can't steer the parafoil and control where we land. Let's hope we don't take out a chunk of downtown Houston with us."

The two Russians' eyes widened at their crewmate. The doctor sighed. "Sorry. I shouldn't have said that."

Boris groaned. "But it *is* the truth."

Vali brushed perspiration from her husband's forehead. "If we only had another battery…"

Boris didn't reply. His face was ashen—and it seemed he might not live long enough to matter how he reached the ground. Stone grimaced, thinking it wouldn't have made any difference if he'd talked his patient into hooking him back up to the defibrillator—

Suddenly he shouted, "Wait, we do have more batteries!"

Vali screamed *"What?"* followed instantly by Boris's *"Where?"*

Stone replied, "I use portable medical equipment so much, I take for granted they have backup power systems inside them for when they aren't plugged in! Your monitor and defibrillator—*they* have good-sized batteries inside them!"

Doubt shaded the newfound hope on Vali's face. "But are they the right kind of batteries? Will they work?"

Suddenly rejuvenated, Boris replied grimly, "I'll *make* them work!"

As Vali resumed her countdown ("Altitude 50 kilometers…40…") Stone unstrapped himself and followed Boris to the back of the CRV. That end of the craft now was—and *felt*—tilted downward as Earth's gravity brought weight back to their bodies. As Stone held the increasingly heavy devices, Boris unscrewed their back panels and ripped out their small but powerful batteries.

Struggling "up" to the front of the craft, Boris laid on the floor beside the left side of the console and braced himself against a wall. Stone held the precious batteries while the other man fumbled for cables and tools. As he watched Boris's hands flying inside the tight compartment, pausing only to snatch another battery from him, he seemed to catch fleeting images of Mir in the Russian's eyes.

Vali's murmured "Altitude 20 kilometers…" was interrupted by a thundering voice below her. "Any change on the meter?"

A pause. "No. Ten kilometers—"

Boris cursed, and jiggled a cable. "Now is it changing?"

"No…wait, the reading's higher!"

Stone glanced up too. There *was* more red showing—but not much.

Boris wiped his brow and accepted the doctor's helping hand to pull him up. "Nothing more we can do. Let's hope it is enough."

They strapped themselves in on either side of Vali. She murmured, "Altitude 6 kilometers…"

Stone felt himself jerked upward as the CRV rocked. Vali shouted, "Drogue chutes deployed!"

A bigger lurch turned his stomach upside down. Through his nausea Stone heard Vali cry, "Parafoil out!"

A faint voice on the cabin's opposite side said, "Shut down the automatic guidance system and use manual controls. They need less power."

Vali obeyed, using their position display to guide her as she steered the parafoil to keep them on course. She whispered, "Ten kilometers from target…9…8…"

Stone pictured the huge fluorescent orange parachute now unfurled above them—hopefully carrying their dead weight safely down to Ellington Field. Belatedly he wondered if JSC knew they were coming in. They'd been out of communication for nearly two hours—

A groan interrupted Stone's reverie. Boris was lying back in his seat, eyes closed. "Boris, are you all right?"

No response.

Not now! As Stone struggled free of his seat's restraints in the bobbing craft, Vali's concentration wavered from her task. "What are you doing?"

"I have to help Boris!"

Feet spread wide for balance, the doctor twisted around and behind the row of seats—using their backs for support as he fought to reach his patient. Falling back, pulling himself forward in the swaying ship with Sisyphean tenacity, he stretched to get close enough to see if Boris was breathing—if he still had a pulse.

But what if he didn't have one? Doing CPR was impossible when he couldn't even get a stable foothold! There was no monitor to guide his treatment, no medicines to give, no defibrillator to shock the Russian out of VT—!

Stripped of his technology, skills, and reason, Stone grabbed Boris with both hands and shook him violently. Drowning out Vali's quiet "Five hundred meters...100...", the doctor screamed, "Damn it, Boris, don't you dare die on me now! Vali needs you! You've got to stay alive for her!"

Then a terrible crash sent Stone spiraling forward—and the lights went out again.

Some time later the doctor's head slowly stopped spinning. Alone in the still, silent darkness, he wiggled his toes and fingers to see if they moved—and tried to figure out what was pressing on his neck and back.

A flashlight beamed in Stone's direction—showing him that he was wedged into the CRV's nose.

Vali called, "Are you all right, doctor?"

Bruised and battered, Stone rolled free of the tight space and stood up shakily. "I'm fine, I have to get to Boris—!"

Then he heard a weak but clear voice—speaking words he'd heard *ad nauseam* from the back of the minivan on so many family trips.

Boris said, "Are we there yet?"

Stone lurched toward the other man—then realized the CRV didn't seem to be moving. "I guess we are."

"Vali, could you hand the good doctor your flashlight? I want him to check why we lost power when our landing skids hit. I must not have done a good enough job wiring the batteries, and one of my cables broke loose."

His wife whispered, "You did a wonderful job, my love."

She smiled. "Listen! Do you hear them?"

Still woozy, Stone dimly heard voices and a siren outside the craft. Wobbling forward, he released the CRV's side hatch.

Dry tepid air and the stabbing beam of a searchlight cutting through the ebbing twilight greeted him as the door came free. The first person he recognized sprinting toward the vehicle, white coat flapping, was Mina Osler. Surprisingly spry for a sixty-five-year-old grandmother, she grinned at him and said, "Dr. Livingstone, I presume?"

Ignoring the welcoming brown hand she extended, Stone waved toward the interior of the vehicle. "Boris needs help right away. We had to cannibalize our equipment getting down here, and he's not even hooked up to a defibrillator!"

Mina's face instantly turned as grimly professional as his was. She called behind her, "Get that stretcher over here *now*!"

Feeling much too dizzy to help, Stone stepped tentatively outside to the runway to let the paramedics have more room to work inside the craft. He watched them load Boris onto the stretcher and, under Mina's careful scrutiny, hook him back up to a battery of life support equipment and IVs.

Vali stepped out of the CRV and stood close beside him. Her full lips formed a grateful smile.

"Thank you," she said, "for everything you did to help Boris. And for being our friend."

A smile flitted across Stone's face before dying stillborn. He shrugged. "You're welcome."

The stretcher clanked against the side of the CRV's hatch as the paramedics carried Boris outside. As they passed he grinned and waved at Stone. "Thank you, my friend. And remember what we talked about on the way down!"

Vali held her husband's hand lovingly as she walked beside the rolling stretcher toward the waiting life support vehicle. Stone started to stagger after them until Mina's voice stopped him.

"Where do you think *you're* going?"

"I have to ride to the hospital with Boris."

"No, you don't. He's not *your* patient anymore. In fact, ever since you landed, *you've* been *mine*!"

Her chuckle died as she looked more closely at him in the fading dusk. "You don't look so good."

As the world spun dizzyingly around him, Stone slumped to the concrete runway and stretched out supine on its comforting coolness. "I don't *feel* so good. Better tell the DUCM people they still have some work to do on their readaptation experiment."

Mina's moonlike face—the dusky shade of a penumbral eclipse—bobbed in front of him. "Here's what's wrong!"

She ripped off the long-forgotten VSs from behind his ears and fiddled with a valve at his waist. "You were supposed to remove these things and turn off your negative-pressure trousers when you deorbited! Keeping them on in 1 g was making you orthostatic and a real neurovestibular mess!"

"Sorry. I got distracted."

As Mina called for another stretcher, Stone saw the nearly full Moon rising brightly above the eastern horizon. As he watched, the silvery orb seemed to recede into the blackening sky and vanish from his grasp. But though he mourned its loss, like Antaeus reborn he felt the Earth's strength flow back into him.

For better or worse, he was home to stay.

Stone lay on his back, alone and shivering on top of an old lumpy bed at the hospital—staring up through blackness at the unseen ceiling. The door to this small room was slightly ajar. Only the faintest hint of fluorescent light filtered through from the empty silent corridor outside. On a nearby nightstand, "6:28 AM" glowed in fiery red.

He'd probably used this room years ago when he was on call as a resident here at St. Luke's. But he didn't remember it. And right now, enveloped in a cold black nothingness he hoped would last forever, he didn't want to remember anything.

Minutes later the clock radio near him came to life. Faint symphonic music from a local FM station assaulted his ears.

Sounds late Romantic. Tchaikovsky?

He sighed. *Doesn't matter. Nothing matters anymore.*

The door to the room creaked halfway open. Dim light from the corridor created the shadowy outline of a chair beside his bed. A tiny window behind the chair showed only darkest night.

A somber figure entered, then sat in the chair. As the music played softly in the background, Vali spoke.

"I can't believe he's dead."

Stiffly, painfully, Stone sat up on the side of the bed and faced her. "I'm sorry. We're all sorry it happened."

"He was laughing and joking in the ambulance."

"All the doctors who treated him are experts. They did everything it was humanly and medically possible to do before calling the code."

"He was still smiling when they put him in his hospital bed. I was sitting beside him, stroking his cheek when—"

Vali sighed. "After everything we went through—Boris still died."

"We all talked about this late last night, after it happened. Sometimes you do the best you can—and it's still not enough."

"If you'd been here, maybe you could have done something to save him."

Stone shook his head. "Even if I'd argued Mina into letting me come here sooner from the JSC infirmary when we heard Boris was doing worse, it wouldn't have mattered."

They sat silently, oblivious to the tumultuous orchestral score whirling quietly from the radio.

Vali whispered, "What will you do now?"

"Learn to live without doing everything I wanted to do with my life. Devote my *full* time and love to where it should have been all along—with my wife and kids. I've said my farewell to space too."

Her voice turned icy. "That's not what I meant! What will you tell your superiors about what we were doing on the station when Boris had his heart attack?"

Stone hesitated. "The truth. They need to know everything that happened."

"*Why?* Boris asked you not to! All it will do is ruin his reputation, hurt the others' careers—and punish me!"

"I don't *want* anybody to be hurt. But this goes beyond our personal concerns. On Earth, the chance of someone as fit as Boris having an MI during sex is about one in a million. And yet—on the station, it *did* happen! Maybe—no, *probably* it was a coincidence, and would've happened even if he hadn't been doing it, or under such stressful conditions for him.

"But I don't *know* that—because there's no good data on how risky sex in space actually is. That's something we *need* to know, to protect all the men and women who'll travel there in the future. Maybe, if what happened to Boris can teach us how to keep *them* safe—maybe his death will have some meaning. I wouldn't be doing my duty as a doctor if I kept back any facts that could be medically relevant—that might prevent someone else from dying!"

Vali's words dripped acid. "Don't preach at me! All *I* know is you're destroying *my* life! *You* still have your family, your career as a doctor. I've sacrificed *everything* else to go into space—and *you're* tearing it away from me!"

Stone shook his head desperately. "I don't *want* that to happen! I realize now how much you've given up—that you need and *deserve* to go back to space more than I do! But I have to do the right thing."

"And you're sure it's the right thing to do."

A terrible weight pressed on Stone's chest. "No, I'm *not* sure. It's just—as best I can tell—what I *have* to do. Believe me, Vali, I don't *want* to do it!"

Valentina rose from the chair and stood in front of him, her face scarlet and ugly with rage. She hissed, "All you care about is your 'duty'! If you were a *real* man, with any human feelings, you would have made love to me with everyone else. Maybe, if you'd been in TransHab when Boris became sick, you could have begun treating him sooner and he would still be alive!"

Her palm swung like a scythe and slapped his cheek viciously. She laughed at the thread of blood trickling from his mouth. "See, you don't even react! You *are* a rock—a stone!"

Vali made a tight fist, drew it back to strike his other cheek—

And tumbled back into the chair like a broken puppet.

"How dare you hit my husband!"

Stone looked up to see his wife towering menacingly over Vali—ready to shove her again if she dared to rise.

Vali stared at the other woman's face for a long moment before recognizing it. She pointed an accusing finger at Stone. "He killed my husband!"

66

Donna sat down beside Stone and wrapped a supportive arm around his waist. Her voice was low and firm. "No, he didn't. I don't know everything that happened on the station. But I know my husband *cares* about other people. He always tries his best to help them, no matter how much it hurts or costs *him*. He's the most loving man I've ever known—and if you don't see that too, you don't understand him at all!"

Vali gazed at the two lovers sitting close together on the bed—and began to weep. Her heartrending sobs faded away as she rose and ran from the room, into the darkness without.

No one noticed the music on the radio end with a whirlwind of crashing cymbals, blaring brass, and thundering timpani. The announcer's quiet words ("That was Tchaikovsky's symphonic poem, *Francesca da Rimini*. Now we hear Haydn's String Quartet in B-flat Major, op. 76, no. 4.") went unheard.

Donna whispered, "I flew down here as soon as they told me what was happening and the airport reopened. The kids wanted to come with me, but I thought it'd be better if they weren't here if…something happened to you—"

Stone crumbled into his wife's embrace, desperately warming himself with her love. His cheek, still stinging from the blow he'd taken, pressed soothingly against Donna's. A tear trickled from the corner of his eye, and met one of hers.

"I did the best I could, Donna."

"I know you did, Alex. I know."

As the soulful opening melody of the "Sunrise" quartet shimmered in the room, the first rays of dawn filtered through its tiny window. Their golden glow enfolded two broken hearts beating again as one, caressed by light.

The Paradise Project

"RUN!"

Martin Slayton glimpsed the panic and fear on Katerina's face as she turned and ran back toward the habitation module. His startled cry "What's the matter?" went unanswered as her slim figure raced toward the rusty plain they'd just crossed.

Martin shivered as a cool breeze riffled his close-cropped black hair. The vast slab of steel-gray metal he stood on was even more unsettling and empty in the silence created by his fiancée's sudden flight. He frowned at the Cyrillic letters engraved in the alien metal at his feet, struggling to translate those words with the little Russian he knew. What message did they contain that could frighten Katerina into abandoning him?

Giving up, Martin scrutinized the other blocks of writing on the platform. Each of the nearby meter-wide squares etched into its surface like a gigantic chessboard contained words in a different language. If Katerina was right and this artifact really was a huge version of the Rosetta Stone, one of these squares had to be in a language he could read.

He stepped forward slowly, studying the squares—and then he spied the one in English. As his lips mouthed the words inside the square, Martin's expression twisted with fear and panic.

He ran.

Martin sprinted fifty meters before his boots leapt off the metal slab onto a patch of bare damp soil. He slipped and nearly fell before he regained traction and crunched onto rocky ground. His feet splashed through puddles of rainwater and trampled delicate lichen-like plants, fleeing from the unseen terrors spawned by his own imagination.

His lungs burning in the dry air and legs cramping, Martin finally saw Katerina's blue jumpsuit wavering far in the distance. His long strides brought him ever closer to her as the Sun, only slightly smaller and dimmer than seen from Earth, glared mockingly down on him from a rose-tinged sky.

Suddenly he was twelve years old again, watching a scary movie from the early 1950s about another twelve-year-old boy. Both of them were running from nightmarish monsters as a montage of memories flashed through their minds. The scent of death invaded Martin's brain as he remembered...

"I always wanted to go to Mars. I never thought Mars would come to me!"

A warm wet Florida wind gently wafted Katerina Savitskaya's long auburn hair as she spoke, her hazel eyes elevated toward the clear moonless night sky. Her pose reminded Martin of Botticelli's "Birth of Venus." The aquamarine shorts and halter top wrapped around her nicely rounded thirty-two-year-old figure added only a modicum of modesty to the picture.

Martin, more conservatively attired in his light NASA uniform, handed his slightly shorter companion a pair of high-powered image-stabilizing binoculars. He said, "Let's hope we're seeing Mars even closer in three weeks."

Far away across the empty field, pale lights illuminated the towering Ares VII rocket. In two days it would fling both of them to a rendezvous with the fourth planet. He and Katerina had been earthbound since their trip to the Lunar South Polar base at Shackleton Crater in '33. Though six months overdue, this first manned mission to Mars was now ready to launch. The engineers had finally managed to modify the habitation module to set its two-person crew on a world radically different from the one for which the module was originally designed.

But Martin wasn't complaining. The time Katerina and he had spent together more than compensated for the rigors of these last two years of training. Their interest in each other had long ago exceeded the organizational need to maintain cordial relations between his NASA and her Russian Space Agency. They were both the same age, never been married, and in love with space and each other.

Not that they always thought alike. His opinion of the Russian Orthodox Reawakening of the '10s that had helped shaped her worldview was tepid at best. While he respected Katerina's religious beliefs, her old-fashioned moral standards played havoc with his libido. She insisted on waiting until this mission was over and a traditional church marriage ceremony when they returned to Earth before granting him the perks of a wedding night. But compared to the decades he hoped they'd have together to make up for lost time, another year was worth the wait.

In the still of the night Katerina gazed upward and focused the binoculars on a brilliant crimson beacon high in the heavens. Starlight glinted off the three-barred cross, nearly as long as her hand, that she wore suspended by a braided gold chain around her neck. Besides its long middle crossbeam, the heavy golden cross had a small horizontal bar near its top and an even shorter slanted bar close to its bottom.

Katerina's relic was a sacred heirloom several hundred years old, preserved and protected by her grandmother during the darkest hours of the previous century. The nonagenarian had thoughtfully sent the cross to her beloved granddaughter from St. Petersburg last month to help safeguard Katerina on her coming journey to a new world.

A smile flickered on Katerina's lips as she held the binoculars fixed on Mars. She murmured, "I think I can see the canals."

"I thought I saw them too. At least we have a better chance of being right than Schiaparelli or Lowell. They saw canals that weren't there. We know there really are ones now."

"Have you heard if the orbiters have spotted any new canals carrying water from the Boreal Ocean?"

"No. We can ask about it at the briefing tomorrow."

The scent of freshly cut grass wafted towards them from the field bordering the faraway launch pad. Katerina lowered her binoculars and whispered, "I wonder what the air will smell like on Mars."

"Probably bland. There's too little plant life and the humidity's fairly low. Unless the aliens decide to spray the whole atmosphere with a humongous can of air freshener to give it the scent of violets and lavender. Considering what they've done so far, I wouldn't bet against it!"

Katerina smiled back at him. Now they could afford to joke about Mars. But ten years ago, in the year 2025, Earth seemed on the eve of destruction.

At first the public ignored or laughed at the frenzied reports radiating from observatories and space agencies around the world. A planet leaving its orbit and spiraling sunward toward Earth? That only happened in cheap sci-fi. In real life it could only be a prank by a 21st century version of Orson Welles.

But as time passed and that ruddy glow in the sky gradually blazed ever brighter like a plunging fireball, humanity could no longer doubt the evidence of its own eyes. Few people were reassured by the experts who'd calculated that the runaway world wouldn't collide with Earth. Even when Mars gently settled into its new circular orbit 157 million kilometers from the Sun, a mere 7 million kilometers farther than the Earth's average distance, the riots and apocalyptic panic continued. It was a long time before it dawned on an emotionally exhausted human race that doomsday really was postponed.

The unknown force that repositioned the fourth planet also dragged its two tiny moons and small retinue of orbiters along for the ride, adjusting their orbits appropriately as Mars underwent a miraculous metamorphosis. Month after month orbiters both old and newly arrived continued to beam back astounding pictures of a lifeless world laboring to be resurrected.

But the violent changes on the planet's surface could only partly be explained by natural means. Both polar ice caps melted far more quickly than was predicted from the greater warmth of the Sun alone. In the vast lowlands of the northern polar region, the Boreal Ocean formed and sent liquid water cascading into ancient riverbeds. The frozen carbon dioxide blanketing the south pole rapidly sublimated, allowing the water ice beneath to melt and flow into the highlands and craters of the southern hemisphere.

Other changes went even further beyond any known areology. One day a web-like pattern of deep furrows began to appear, as if some invisible giant as large as Voltaire's Micromegas were running its fingertips through the soil. Data from the orbiters suggested those furrows were created by a focused beam of intense heat from some unknown source that was slicing through the planet's crust, vaporizing its nitrate-containing rocks and liberating nitrogen and oxygen into the atmosphere. Soon those "canals" crisscrossed the planet, bringing water from both the Boreal Ocean and the crater lakes of the south to its parched lands.

Later, patches of green streaked the Martian landscape, as if unseen hands were planting a garden in its newly moist soil. But no earthly plant could use carbon dioxide rapidly enough through photosynthesis to account for the huge quantities of free oxygen flooding the planet's atmosphere. And no known science could explain how the planet's gravity and magnetic field had changed.

Humanity gradually accepted in awed wonder what was happening to its new next-door neighbor in space. But the great questions of "how" and "why" it was happening remained unanswered.

Katerina sighed. "Why do you think the aliens haven't shown themselves yet?"

"Maybe they're just modest."

"Martin, be serious!"

"Okay. Humanity is beneath the notice of aliens whose technology is so advanced they can move planets as easily as we use a bulldozer to move a mound of earth. Have you ever introduced yourself to the inhabitants of an anthill?"

"But they must know about us. Otherwise, why would they make Mars such a perfect place for humans to live?"

Martin frowned. "It worries me that what you said isn't quite true. I don't understand why, if our shy aliens really had us in mind, they didn't fully terraform the planet. If they can somehow alter a whole world's gravity, why did they increase it to only 0.91 g and not make it the same as Earth's?"

"Perhaps that's to give us a little spring in our step when we run. Besides, that level of gravity is enough to minimize any bone or muscle loss. And it makes it a bit easier to take off from Mars."

"Maybe. But they also didn't get the atmosphere quite right either. The carbon dioxide level is OK, but there's a bit too little nitrogen and the atmospheric pressure at 'sea level' is only 95% of what it is on Earth."

Katerina laughed. "But the percentage of oxygen in the atmosphere is 25%—high enough to make the partial pressure of oxygen similar to what we're breathing now!"

She rumpled his hair. "Martin, sometimes you're too skeptical. What's that expression—'You shouldn't look a gift horse in the mouth.' These aliens have reduced the orbital energy and angular momentum of Mars by astronomical amounts. They've turned the planet from a waterless wasteland with a thin unbreathable atmosphere to one nearly as nice as our own. They've given it an ozone layer and a magnetic field strong enough to keep us safe from ultraviolet rays and solar radiation. They were even thoughtful enough to create north and south magnetic poles so we can use a compass. And you're complaining that they didn't get things 'right' down to a few decimal places!"

Her fiancé brushed his hand forward across the top of his head. "I still wonder, though. What's in it for them? And what if they don't want any uninvited guests?"

"After all the good they've done, you still think these aliens might be hostile? If they were, they could have swatted Earth into the Sun as easily as one of those baseball players you like so much hits a home run!"

Katerina shook her head. "I think the reason we haven't seen them yet is that they're expecting us to show how interested we are in what they've done. They want to see if we're willing to make the effort to go to Mars and visit them."

Martin gazed across the field at the brightly lit rocket. "I hope you're right. And I'm glad enough people in the world agree with you."

Katerina took his hand and clasped it tightly. Far above them the starry heavens listened patiently to their questions, but kept its secrets hidden behind a silent twinkling smile. Martin's eyes drifted to Venus. The second planet hung suspended high in the west, its familiar golden brightness unchanged from his childhood. Unlike Mars, that world seemed a beacon of normalcy in a changing Solar System.

Except it wasn't. Whatever unknown power had remodeled Mars had also elected to send Venus drifting out to a new orbit 143 million kilometers from the Sun. Despite its dramatically closer distance to Earth, the planet was no brighter because its crushing carbon dioxide atmosphere and sulfuric acid clouds were dissipating and reflecting less sunlight. No one could explain where the vast quantities of hydrogen needed to start the torrential rains drenching its cooling flat surface had come from, or how so much oxygen was being liberated. Nonetheless, the instruments on the Vespucci orbiter clearly showed the shallow ocean of scalding but liquid water covering most of its previously searing arid landmass.

Those same superhuman forces had also made Earth's sister world spin like a tilted top with a new day just over 25 hours long. Though no one could predict exactly how long it would take, someday a reborn Venus would be as hospitable as the new Mars was now and ready for human exploration.

Martin sighed. That adventure was for another time and another crew. He and Katerina had their own planet to worry about first…

The wind shrieked by Martin's ears like the wordless chorus of Invaders from Mars. *Pain lanced through his chest with every panted breath as he ran, too terrified to glance back at what might be pursuing him. Visions of the recycled Martian war machines from* Robinson Crusoe on Mars *swooping down at any second made his back prickle, waiting for the searing caress of a heat ray to incinerate him.*

Maybe, if they could reach the return vehicle in time, there was an infinitesimal chance they might get back into orbit again before it was too late. As he slowly gained on Katerina's speeding figure, Martin prayed that at least she would survive long enough to tell their tale. Though their own lives may be lost, if she could only warn their fellow humans never to come here again, perhaps there would be no more dying.

Martin's boots pounded the dust of what might be his grave, his nostrils clogged with the sickening smell of a funeral wreath. His eyes caught the sunlit glint of metal in the distance. Not much farther now—

A horrifying thought made him stumble. He righted himself just in time to avoid tumbling into the sand and kept on running. What if the habitation module Katerina and he were fast approaching was no longer a safe haven? Maybe, just as hope was daring to trickle back into their hearts, some thing was already there—waiting patiently to hear their final screams.

Somewhere behind him in the distance a brass band seemed to play a faint, heavenly tune. The music in his mind turned ever more dissonant, swelling ever louder in a glacially slow crescendo like a distorted symphony by Charles Ives. No matter what was waiting for them ahead, there was no turning back...

"What is that thing?"

Martin floated over and squinted at the tiny dark blur that Katerina pointed out on the monitor. He shrugged. "I don't know. But it certainly wasn't there before we entered orbit."

His crewmate tapped on the keyboard secured in front of her. "Let me see if I can enhance it."

The set of cine images they'd just received from the high-resolution camera on the Mars Scout Orbiter froze into a still frame. Katerina zoomed in on the mysterious object and superimposed a calibration grid over the image. "Whatever it is, it's big—about a hundred meters square. We'll have to get radar readings to see how tall it is, but it seems fairly flat.

"And it's about three kilometers south of our landing site."

Martin shook his head. "Somehow I doubt the fact it's appeared at that location is a coincidence."

He gently pushed himself towards the other side of the craft, peering down through a viewplate. A gibbous Mars wheeled slowly beneath them some four hundred kilometers away, its canals and narrow rivers glistening in the sunlight. Their soon-to-be landing site at 39° 8' N and 84° 30' W was nearly directly below, not too far from towering Olympus Mons and near the shore of the shallow Boreal Ocean. He squinted but couldn't spot the mystery object nearby.

Martin sighed. Soon it would be time to earn his pay. So far their mission had gone nearly exactly as scripted. They'd roared off the launch pad into a cloudless cerulean sky, silently exulting as the view through the cabin window turned black and their bodies struggled against the seat restraints that kept them from floating free.

As their craft raced away from Earth, it was comforting to know that souvenirs of the home planet waited patiently for them at the other end of the journey. A fully fueled Mars ascent vehicle using the latest single-stage-to-orbit technology sat on the dusty plain near their landing site. That vehicle had used an aerobrake and parachute system similar to the one they would employ to land the habitation module that would be their home for the next year.

When their sojourn on Mars was over, the ascent vehicle would blast them back into orbit. There it would rendezvous with the waiting Earth return vehicle for the homeward trip to the Lunar South Polar base. After weeks of medical tests in quarantine to make sure they didn't harbor any alien pathogens acquired during their stay on Mars, they would finally get a hero-and-heroine's welcome on Earth.

But all that lay far ahead. After the exhilaration of the launch, the next two weeks of their flight were mostly routine, even boring. There were hours of exercise on the small treadmill, brief meals, and restless "nights" of dreamless sleep. Routine maintenance on their vessel, periodic communications with Earth, and observations of the rapidly waxing ruddy orb that was their destination filled most of their days.

The only real trouble they had during the flight was manmade. It happened during a press conference held a week before they reached Mars. The time delay between sending and receiving signals over millions of kilometers made holding real-time question and answer sessions difficult but doable. A minor TV news anchor, apparently interested in boosting his ratings, started with a seemingly innocent query about how they spent their free time in space.

Katerina replied, "We really don't have much free time. I like to read romance novels and books on philosophy, while Martin prefers science fiction. He also brought along a collection of old science fiction movies, especially ones about Mars and Martians, that he's wanted me to watch with him. I told him I'd do it if he let me play my classical music over the ship's intercom system. His tastes in music are strictly 21st century, but at least I'm getting him to tolerate my favorite 20th century American and Russian composers. By the time we reach Mars, he'll be an expert on Hovhaness, Ives, and Shostakovich."

After a long delay they heard a snicker. "That sounds so intellectual. I'd expect a healthy young engaged couple like you to entertain each other in more physical ways. You two have been compared to the new Adam and Eve, and they were given a divine command to 'be fruitful and multiply.' Besides, everybody knows what goes on in those orbital motels—"

The transmission suddenly cut off, mercifully ended by some alert individual at Mission Control. Martin looked at Katerina. Her face was redder than the planet they were approaching. She muttered a furious stream of words in her native language that would have burned their idiotic interlocutor's ears if he'd heard them.

Martin discreetly said nothing. Learning foreign languages wasn't his forte, and he'd never been able to achieve more than a basic ability to speak and read Russian. But he had enough imagination to translate what Katerina was saying into their pungent four-letter Anglo-Saxon equivalents.

She probably only felt insulted, while those snide insinuations about their personal lives only made him feel depressed. The embarrassing truth was that their love life was currently confined to handholding and an occasional chaste peck on the cheek. Katerina's religious beliefs were strong enough to keep her firmly virginal for now. He loved her too much to pressure her into doing anything she didn't want to do.

And there were pragmatic reasons for keeping their physical relationship nearly platonic for the time being. Whenever some lustful fantasy started to percolate up in his brain or elsewhere, all he had to do was remember those mandatory NASA "Thou shalt not!" lectures to squelch it. He recalled the bullet points all too well.

No form of birth control short of sterilization is 100% effective. A pregnancy on your mission would be a disaster. He couldn't argue with that. By necessity their medical training and resources were limited—enough to take care of the expected range of minor injuries and emergencies but not any obstetrical ones.

Your cumulative radiation exposure in deep space will be far less than on the six month-plus voyage to Mars originally planned in the last century. However, it is still great enough to temporarily damage your sperm cells and to produce potentially serious mutations in offspring. It was some consolation that the family jewels would be at full health again several months after their time in space was over. But for now they had to stay in cold storage.

Someday, if you prove that Mars is a safe place to live, it will be natural and necessary for men and women to conceive and deliver the first babies born on a new world. But that time is not on this first mission. All right, he understood the difference between being an explorer and a colonist. Perhaps, if Katerina and he lived long enough, they could be both.

Remember that incident on the International Space Station in late 2020. People who seemed just as professional and competent as you let their sexual urges outweigh their judgment, with disastrous results. Hearing the details of that public relations fiasco and its terrible consequences for the individuals involved was a powerful warning for anyone wanting to stay in the space program.

Sometimes those cautionary sex-ed classes for space travelers seemed to border on the scare tactics he'd heard were once used in mid-20th century high schools. Still, Martin was grateful to the person who gave those lectures. That well-respected physician had convinced the Russians to keep Katerina on this mission when they discovered she and Martin were engaged. The Russian Space Agency wanted to replace her, arguing that their personal feelings for each other might disrupt and endanger the mission.

The head of NASA's space medicine program used his considerable influence and reputation to dissuade the RSA. That cardiologist told its officials he trusted Katerina and her husband-to-be to act strictly like professionals on the mission. The Russians accepted his advice as authoritative. They knew that, on the subject of sex in space, no one had more expertise than Dr. Alexander Stone.

After their aborted press conference, Katerina seemed unusually moody. When Martin woke up from his next sleep period he found her in the science lab, praying in front of several flat colorful icons. They were attached by sticky magnetic strips on their backs to the metal door of the small locker where she stored her collection of books and personal items. Lively choral music played softly in the background as she floated in the lab, hair streaming behind her like an angel descending from heaven.

Katerina kissed the icon representing her namesake, the wise and persuasive St. Catherine of Alexandria. Finally, after ritually using the first three fingers of her right hand to touch her forehead, breastbone, right shoulder, and left side, she finished her solitary ceremony.

Martin moved quietly toward her. "Are you all right?"

Katerina wheeled slowly around to face him. "I'm not sure."

His next question was an awkward attempt to change the subject. "I like that music you're playing. What is it?"

"Haydn's oratorio *The Creation*."

Katerina turned a troubled look toward him. "Martin, what if there *aren't* any aliens?"

"What do you mean? Planets don't change orbits and terraform on their own!"

"Of course not. But what if, instead of aliens, the power doing it is actually...divine."

Martin rolled his eyes. "Don't tell me you're buying into what those crackpot religious groups were saying when we left—that what's happened to Mars and Venus is the ultimate proof of 'Intelligent Design.' The 'Hand of God' reaching down from heaven and creating a new Eden or two for us. *They're* calling us the new Adam and Eve too. Not that I'd mind it too much if you didn't, but when I get to our Martian 'paradise' I intend to keep my clothes on. And it's a good thing I don't like apples!"

His smug smile disappeared. The glare on his crewmate's face told him he'd been too sarcastic with his skepticism.

Katerina floated away from him. "Don't be so pompous! If you don't believe in miracles, you won't recognize one when you see it! I think we probably will find aliens waiting for us on Mars. God almost never breaks the laws of nature He created, and He only does it then when it's for a very special reason.

"But perhaps God is using the aliens as His instruments to help us save ourselves. With all the terrible things we humans are doing to Earth and to each other, maybe we're being given a second chance to do things right. Colonizing Mars won't directly solve problems like war, global warming, or overpopulation. But, if we're careful, it can be a symbol of how humanity can work together and inspire us to be much better than we seem."

Martin lowered his voice diplomatically. "Well, if I'm willing to believe in aliens with godlike powers, maybe I shouldn't be so critical if you take it a step further and think a real deity is involved. And I agree that whatever happens when we get to Mars will be a turning point in history."

His eyebrows arched. "I can't believe I said that. It's a scary thought—that what the two of us do could make or break the human race."

His fiancée's eyes softened. She eased back toward him and planted a delicate kiss on his cheek. "Have a little faith, and I think we'll do all right…"

Katerina's voice murmuring again beside him snapped him back to the present. She said, "The radar readings are now in on that…artifact. There's no way to tell how far down it goes into the ground, but it's only about ten centimeters higher than the terrain around it."

She rubbed her chin. "Maybe it's a platform of some kind, or the top of a huge underground building. It's even big enough to be a landing pad for us or…someone else."

Katerina sighed. "We'll see what the experts back home think about these images and readings, and what they want us to do. What do you think that structure down there is, Martin?"

He stared at the monitor uneasily.

"Let's hope it's a welcome mat."

"Katerina!"

Martin tried to shout a warning to her as she veered toward the habitation module instead of the ascent vehicle. But his cry emerged as only a dry rasp from a throat parched from continuous exhausted running. He watched helplessly from a hundred meters away as she entered the module. His ears strained to hear her screams as he forced his body onwards.

But even if he reached her side, what could he do to save her? They had no weapons, no means of defense. To creatures powerful enough to move planets, the effort needed to destroy a human body was miniscule. The lives of Katerina and him must be no more than motes of dust to such beings—too insignificant to be even noticed when those lives were brushed out of existence.

At least the two of them could die together—a tiny consolation, but the only one they might have…

"Zubrin Base established. Habitat One, the first human dwelling on Mars, has landed!"

Martin unbuckled his restraining straps and waited excitedly for a few seconds as Katerina did the same. Though wobbly from their first taste of near-normal gravity after three weeks, they hugged and kissed in a brief whirling dance around the cabin.

Finally remembering the wall-mounted surveillance camera transmitting their every action back to billions of people on Earth, they disengaged and resumed a semiprofessional demeanor. But before they did, Martin whispered in his fiancée's ear, "Won't that give the media something to write about!"

They quickly checked the habitation module's systems and looked for any signs of damage within the interior. The module, based on a classic design, was shaped like a large tin can about nine meters in diameter and five meters tall. It contained multiple wedge-shaped compartments on two decks, including a science lab, storage areas for food and equipment, and a communications center. A narrow central cylinder with small doorways and metal rungs allowed easy access to every section.

Then, as the world watched with about a minute's delay, the two of them prepared to step into history. After releasing several latches, Martin turned a small crank that made the external hatch pivot downward at its base. When its far end touched the ground the hatch served as a ramp allowing easy passage between the module, elevated a meter above the surface on multiple stubby landing legs, and the outside.

NASA and the Russian Space Agency had argued for months about which of their members should be the first to set foot on Mars. They couldn't agree whether the nation who'd first landed a craft on Mars or the one that had taken the first close-up pictures of the planet would have that honor. Neither wanted to risk a simple coin toss to decide.

Finally they chose the easiest method possible. At the count of three, with their arms locked, Martin and Katerina made a brief simultaneous jump from the far end of the ramp onto the surface. Together they both solemnly intoned their single scripted line.

"Humanity has a new home."

Then, their duty to their employers and posterity done, they reserved a mystical moment for themselves. Standing hand in hand on the rusty soil of Mars, they surveyed their surroundings with childlike wonder, soaking in its awesome sights. All around them in that brightening Martian dawn, across the panoramic rock-strewn ochre plain to a disorientingly close horizon, there was a solemn silence. No rustle of the wind through trees, no chirping of birds—it was as if they were the only worshipers in a great empty cathedral. A warm breeze, puffing gently like the bellows of some ancient organ, completed the sacred ambience.

It seemed fitting that the first spontaneous words by a human being standing on the surface of Mars should be a song of praise to the divine. A lilting soprano voice gently sang, "A new created world springs up at God's command."

The second extemporaneous sentence was scored for a considerably less melodic baritone. "What do you know, the air really does smell a little like violets and lavender!"

They completed their checklist of other scheduled tasks as quickly as possible. After shutting off the internal surveillance cameras to conserve power and visually inspecting the module's exterior, they trotted half a kilometer to the north where the Mars ascent vehicle rested. The once white exterior of the craft, shaped like a blunted cone pointing towards the heavens, was covered with a fine coating of reddish dust. Its outside hatch squeaked in a pitiful plea for lubrication as Martin entered the vehicle.

After temporarily powering up the main console, he quickly tested the craft's systems and checked the fuel pressure readings. Satisfied with the results, he emerged back into the sunlight and locked the hatch. He grinned when he saw Katerina. She was gazing dreamily at the horizon, her long hair rippling alluringly in the warm Martian breeze.

That gorgeous avatar of Dejah Thoris turned and smiled coyly at him. "I still can't believe we're really here. It's magical—like we're living in a fairy tale."

The expression of awestruck innocence on Katerina's face made Martin's heart ache with love for her. Then he shook himself back to reality. He grunted, "You're right, but let's not get too carried away. We still have a job to do."

He turned around and ran his index finger over the Martian dirt covering the high-tech spacecraft's exterior.

Katerina peeked over his shoulder—and then laughed at what he'd written.

WASH ME.

The two of them held hands as they retraced their steps. As a beaming Sun reached its zenith in the coral-tinted sky, they reentered the habitation module and had a quick lunch of dehydrated food together. Then they prepared for the only task not on their original schedule.

While Katerina went to radio Mission Control for final instructions, Martin tested the handheld transceiver that would maintain their radio link to the module. The latter's transponder would relay the transceiver's signal to an orbiter and from there to Earth.

Katerina rejoined him near the open module's hatchway. Her heavy cross dangled from the gold chain she'd just fastened around her neck. She flashed the precious golden band of diamond-studded jewelry on her left ring finger at Martin and said, "I'm so happy my engagement ring fits me again. I hated not being able to wear it on the trip here because my fingers were too puffy. It's amazing how a few hours out of microgravity can shift fluids from your upper body back to your legs, where it belongs!"

"My ring probably fits again too. Do you want me to go put it on?"

Katerina shook her head. "No need to do that. I'll be with you to fight off any little green Martian hussies we meet who can't see you're already taken!"

She slipped her right hand into the grip strap of a video camera and checked its battery status. Then, as they walked back into the welcoming afternoon sunlight, Martin said, "It's over three kilometers to our target. Do you want to unpack the rover from the module? I'll even let you drive."

"No, assembling and prepping it would take several hours. It'll take us less time to walk, and I want to find out what that artifact is as soon as possible. Besides, it's such a beautiful day!"

They set out toward the south at a brisk pace. At first the vast silence around them, broken only by the crunch of their footsteps, was vaguely unnerving. But soon Martin let himself be soothed by the enchanted world around them. As their hike continued, he almost expected Tweel to come leaping over a nearby mound of sand and land on his beak beside them, or to see a distant cloud of dust as a thoat galloped by.

Every few minutes Martin unclipped the transceiver on his belt and keyed it to send a brief continuous wave signal in Morse code back to the habitation module. It was just enough to let the folks back home know they were safe. A few brief answering tones from the transponder at the module confirmed their signal was received.

It wasn't long before they encountered their first alien life form. The small plants scattered beneath the shadow of a low rocky ridge were scrubby and a sickly shade of green. On Earth they would have been mistaken for a common weed and never given a second look.

Katerina turned on the video camera and recorded the small patch of vegetation from multiple angles and distances. Meanwhile, Martin bent over and dug his hand into the loose moist soil. The light umber-colored dirt sifting through his fingers didn't look too much different from the kind he'd harrowed as a child growing up on the family fields in the Missouri Ozarks.

The former farm boy thought of those packets of seeds for beans, corn, and wheat back at the habitation module and dreamed of vast fields of crops swaying in the breeze. He chuckled at a vision of his future self wearing blue bib overalls and holding a pitchfork while Katerina stood beside him in her gingham dress, looking out together over their Martian green acres.

Katerina knelt down beside the present day's lonely bit of greenery, brushing it gently with her palm. Then she shook her head and stood up. "We can collect a specimen on the way back. These plants obviously aren't native to Mars. They must have been planted by whoever did the other landscaping on this planet."

A disturbing thought popped into Martin's mind. "I wonder if the aliens introduced any animal life here too."

Katerina fingered the gold cross hanging from her neck. "If they did, let's hope we see it before it sees us—and that it isn't too big and hungry."

They encountered several other types of small mossy and lichen-like vegetation as they cautiously continued their odyssey. Martin became so absorbed in scanning the plain for any other signs of life, either flora or fauna, that for several minutes he didn't realize they had a serious problem.

He stopped. "Wait a second."

Katerina turned around. "What's wrong?"

Martin pressed the transmit button on the transceiver again. Only a faint crackle of static came from it in answer. "We've lost contact with the module."

He switched to voice mode. "Mission Control, we're en route to the artifact."

He glanced at the combination watch-compass-pedometer on his wrist. "Current position is 1.62 kilometers due south of the habitation module. Please confirm reception."

They waited anxiously as his watch soundlessly counted the seconds. As it neared the minimum time of around two minutes before they could expect a reply, he and Katerina held their ears close to the transceiver.

Four minutes after his transmission, Martin repeated the message. Again they waited.

Five minutes later, as they listened to the soft static hissing from the transceiver, a faint wind rustled their matching blue jumpsuits and blew a light patina of dust over their boots. A cooling shadow fell over them as the Sun, slowly sinking toward the horizon, slid behind the only cloud in the sky.

Katerina whispered, "What do you think the problem is?"

"I don't know. The transceiver seems to be working. There might be something wrong with the transponder back at the habitation module—but that could be anything from a circuit board going bad to aliens pushing the power button to 'Off.'

"Whatever's wrong, we're out of contact with Earth."

Small orange-tinged rocks crunched beneath Martin's boots as he paced in a small circle. He muttered, "The safe thing would be to go back to the module. That's what our bosses would want us to do. But, if we're not willing to take a calculated risk for a good cause, we shouldn't be here. Think of all the astronomical discoveries that would never have been made if NASA hadn't reversed its decision to cancel a last service call on Hubble thirty years ago."

Katerina interrupted his soliloquy. "And the stakes here are so much greater. I think we should keep heading south toward the artifact."

Martin stared down at his feet uncertainly. Finally he whispered, "Let's do it."

They moved slower now, alert for any signs they weren't alone. Martin periodically stopped to try the transceiver again, pointing its stubby rubber ducky antenna back in the direction of the habitation module. Every attempt brought only increasingly louder bursts of static from the transceiver as they neared their goal. Katerina used those brief pauses to sweep her video camera slowly across the landscape, making a record of their journey to upload back to Earth when they returned to the module.

They spotted the edge of the artifact when it was about fifty meters away. Martin grabbed Katerina's arm and stopped her. He whispered, "Wait. That thing could be dangerous. Maybe only one of us should investigate it, while the other one stays here and records what happens."

Katerina gently disengaged his hand. "Since I'm the one holding the video camera, I won't ask who you had in mind for the dangerous job. We can either stand here arguing all day about who does what, or just keep going together. Which will it be?"

The withering look on her face quickly decided the issue. They pressed onward together.

The soil bordering the artifact was suspiciously flat and smooth. The landscape they had just traversed had been littered with sharp rocks ranging in size from tiny pebbles to a few as big as basketballs. But all those rocks were missing within a straight swath of ground extending about ten meters out from the extraterrestrial object's edge. Looking down at that bare area around the artifact, Martin remembered he'd once compared the aliens' ability to move planets to humans using a bulldozer. Here, it looked like the aliens had used a conventional-sized bulldozer themselves to clear and level the ground—but one that didn't leave any track marks behind.

Their footprints pressed softly into the bare damp ground, dotted with tiny mud puddles, as they cautiously approached the artifact. When they reached its edge, Katerina panned her video camera along the closest section of the artifact while Martin studied the steel-gray metal's glassy flat surface. The object was larger than a football field.

An eyeball estimate confirmed their radar readings from orbit that it was about ten centimeters thick. A series of shallow parallel grooves etched into its surface divided it into squares about a meter on a side, in a pattern resembling a checkerboard.

Most of the squares near the edge of the artifact contained wildly different sets of symbols and colorful abstract pictures. One square held a series of fluorescent orange marks in a spiraling pattern that could be part of an alien alphabet, while the ones adjacent to it held what looked like entirely different letters in a rainbow of clashing colors. Scattered squares held intricate, vertigo-inducing geometric patterns that, Martin thought, resembled pictures he'd seen of crop circles.

Several squares seemed blank. When he squinted at one of them closely, however, it contained faint lettering he suspected would be much brighter if viewed under ultraviolet light. Another empty square actually seemed to produce a faint scent that kept changing with every cautious whiff he took. One moment it had the aroma of baking bread, the next a fruity perfume, then the repellent smell of rotten eggs. A third square produced a faint musical warble at the very upper edge of human hearing.

Martin looked up from his perusal of those peculiar squares to see Katerina edge closer to the artifact and raise one boot—

"Don't step on it!"

He grabbed Katerina's jumpsuit from behind near the base of her neck, nearly pulling his crewmate backwards into an undignified tumble onto her backside. She steadied himself against Martin, then turned around angrily. "Why not, Martin? Do you think it's booby-trapped? If the aliens were hostile, they're so powerful they could have destroyed us long ago. They don't *need* to resort to a complicated trap like something from one of your Flash Gordon serials!"

Martin started to defend those classic science fiction movies he'd shown her on the trip here as more helpful than she gave them credit for. But the expression on her face told him she wasn't in the mood for him to point out that the artifact resembled a giant-sized dark monolith lying on its back.

Instead he replied, "This thing might be dangerous even if the aliens don't mean to deliberately hurt us. Maybe it's some kind of machine that generates a force field or an electrical charge, like a high voltage transformer, that's strong enough to electrocute whoever touches it. For all we know, it could be a teleportation device that's activated when you stand on it. The place you'd wind up might not have a breathable atmosphere or could kill you in some other way."

Katerina looked at him dubiously. "Let's see if you're right."

She walked back across the bare area of ground and returned with a baseball-sized rock in her hand. Before Martin could speak she threw it like a fastball across the artifact. It skidded along the metal surface and came to rest.

"What did you do that for?"

Katerina shrugged. "Well, at least the rock didn't disintegrate or set off any alarm bells."

"At least none that we can hear! I—"

He stopped, looking at the rock. It was slithering rapidly back toward them across the surface of the artifact. A few seconds later, the stone plopped softly to the ground at their feet.

Both of them took a step back from the once again inanimate rock. Martin cautiously examined the suspiciously pristine surface of the artifact. "Maybe it generates some kind of electrostatic field to keep it clean and free of dust and debris. Or maybe it has an electromagnetic field and the rock was ferromagnetic enough to—heck, I don't know what happened!"

He turned his transceiver back on and turned down the squelch control. A loud burst of static erupted from its speaker. The static grew fainter and louder as he slowly swept the transceiver's antenna from side to side in the direction of the alien metal.

Martin said, "Whatever this thing is, it's generating an electrical field. That's why we lost contact with the habitation module. Something on this artifact is producing so much electromagnetic interference that we can't get a signal to or from the transponder back at the base. Funny thing is, the source of the interference across this artifact is spotty—stronger in some directions than others."

"Why is that?"

"I don't know. Maybe there's more than one power source on or beneath its surface."

Martin set the transceiver to scan through a wide range of frequencies and signal modes. Between 824 MHz and 894 MHz its speaker emitted a variety of low, warbling signals like an ancient theremin. Scanning lower through the UHF and VHF bands produced a cacophony of similarly strange, modulated sounds.

He turned the transceiver off and clipped it to his belt. "I wonder if there are transmitters buried under some of these squares."

"Why would the aliens do that?"

"Well, unless we go for a stroll out on this thing, we'll never find out."

He sighed, thinking aloud again. "The safest thing to do is to go back to the module and bring back our multimeter, high voltage probe meter, and a short metal rod. Then we stick the rod into the wet soil here, clip the high voltage probe's ground lead to the rod, and touch the business end of the probe to the surface of the artifact. That should complete the circuit and give a rough reading of how much voltage is running through this thing.

"If the reading is low enough, we use the multimeter to get more accurate measurements of how much voltage and current is present. It's the only way to tell if this alien contraption has enough power running through it to fry us if we touch it and get grounded somehow."

Katerina shook her head. "No. If we go back to the module, you'll feel obligated to check with Mission Control about what to do next. It's their duty to be cautious and to keep us safe. While they're taking hours or days to decide what's the least dangerous thing to do, you'll do your duty by waiting for their decision.

"And while all of you are doing the 'right' and prudent thing, we'll be wasting time and accomplishing nothing. I can't prove it to you, but I feel we'll regret it if we don't find out as soon as possible what this platform is and why the aliens put it here."

Katerina handed Martin the video camera, then unclasped the gold chain around her neck. She slid the golden three-barred cross down to one end of the chain and carefully made a small loop enclosing the relic. Slipping her engagement ring off her finger, she tied it to the other end of the long chain. Then she knelt down beside the alien artifact and stuck the bottom end of the cross into the soft wet soil.

Martin wrinkled his forehead. "What are you doing?"

With the cross fixed securely upright in the soil like its archetype on Calvary, Katerina stood up. She said, "You're not the only one who's had training in electrical engineering. Gold is an excellent conductor of electricity. My cross acts as a ground, so to see if there really is high voltage in this alien metal all I have to do to complete the circuit is this—"

She leaned over, dangled the free end of her chain over the surface of the artifact, and then let the chain fall. As her gold ring touched the artifact—

Katerina smiled triumphantly. "See? Nothing happened. If there were enough high voltage present, we should have seen at least a big spark when the two metals touched. If the voltage were great enough it might even melt the gold. Now we know it's reasonably safe to step on this platform."

Martin leaned forward cautiously, studying the ring and the section of the chain lying inertly on the artifact's surface. "Maybe—but I'm still not convinced it's safe enough to try. There may be parts of this thing that are electrified or dangerous in some other way. I want to find out what this is all about as much as you do, but I don't want either of us to get hurt or killed trying. The only reasonable thing to do is to go back to the module and check with Mission Control."

As he was talking Katerina knelt down again. She swiped at the part of her chain dangling in midair between the cross and the alien platform, whipping the free end of the chain off it and onto the ground. Then she pulled the cross from the ground and reverently cleaned the dirt from its end with her fingers.

After putting the ring back on and readjusting her chain until it and the relic hung from her neck again, Katerina said, "By the way, Martin, perhaps you didn't notice that for an instant I was part of the circuit too when my fingers touched the chain. I didn't feel a shock."

"You—that was stupid! You could have been killed!"

Katerina's face darkened. "Maybe it was stupid. Maybe I could have been killed. And you're right, the safest and most reasonable thing to do would be to leave here and do what you said.

"But sometimes thinking and analyzing aren't enough. Occasionally you have to go beyond reason alone and do what you *feel* is right. Perhaps once in a lifetime, when the stakes are as high as they are now, you have to put your very life on the line and rely on faith. You're a good man, Martin, and I love you. If something bad happens to me, and you want to know why, when you return to the module read those books I brought with me. Especially the one by Kierkegaard."

"Who? Oh, you mean—*don't!*"

Before he could stop her, Katerina made the sign of the cross, took one small step toward the alien platform—and made a giant leap onto its surface.

Martin made a choking sound, waiting in petrified helpless horror for the woman he loved to die in a shower of sparks, contorting in agony as electricity clamped and seared her entire body. His brain and training screamed at him to stay back from the platform and not become a second victim but they weren't enough to keep him from impulsively jumping onto it to pull her off and save her—

Katerina turned around just in time to dodge his hurtling form. As he lunged for her again she barely sidestepped his flailing arms.

"Martin, stop that! You're going to fall and hurt yourself!"

Martin glared at her, ready to start yelling, "That was the stupidest thing I've ever seen anyone do!" But then, glancing down at his own boots on top of the platform, he realized that he was just as stupid as her—and just as alive. Observing the look of relief on Katerina's face she couldn't entirely conceal, he also saw her faith wasn't blind at all. And it was very courageous.

Katerina sidled closer to him. "May I have my video camera back? I'd like to record as much of the surface of this object as I can."

Martin handed the video camera to her, then peered uneasily down at his feet. Here, with them both standing about five meters from the edge of the platform, he could see more of the strange squares. Most seemed, like the ones they'd examined before, to contain cryptic writing in no known language.

But other squares were uniquely alien. One held a hypnotizing swirl of colors that seemed to swell like a tide from the warmth of the infrared through the visible spectrum to the ultraviolet, then recede back again in a kaleidoscope of garish hues. Another was pitch black—like a hole into nothingness. That one he avoided approaching too close, in case it really was a one-way trip into the abyss. A third square rumbled menacingly when he stepped on it, becoming quiescent again as he quickly twisted his leg back onto firmer territory.

Slowly, carefully, they treaded on toward the center of the metal platform. Martin glanced back to see the dust and mud from their footprints eddy up from its surface. That dirt shot across and off the edge of the artifact as if blown by a strong wind—except there wasn't any wind. He hoped this alien object they were walking on was smart enough to realize that Katerina and he weren't merely large pieces of flotsam.

Katerina wandered a little ahead of Martin as he stopped to test a blank mauve-colored square with his transceiver. The square was transmitting an amplitude modulated signal at 700 kHz. It almost sounded like someone was speaking words in a foreign language—

"Martin, come here!"

Clipping the transceiver to his belt, he ran to Katerina's side and followed her finger pointing toward a square at her feet. She exclaimed, "Those look like Chinese characters!"

Katerina pointed again. "And the letters in that square are definitely Greek!"

She turned her video camera back on and then aimed it down at the squares. "How many languages do you know besides English?"

"You know how bad my Russian is. Otherwise, I took two years of Spanish in high school and read a book called 'French for Morons' once."

Katerina walked slowly away from him, eyes and camera fixed downward. "I'm fluent in both those languages as well as German and Dutch. I can also at least read a number of Slavic languages."

She stopped. "This square has Arabic characters! I bet if we look long enough we'll find squares with every major language on Earth!"

Martin frowned. "But if you're right, this whole artifact might be the equivalent of—"

"The Rosetta Stone? Exactly! Every square must hold the same message in a different language, so whoever came here would be able to read it no matter what their native tongue was!"

"Sounds plausible. But how do you explain all those weird squares we've found here? The ones with all the funny squiggles, smells, and sounds?"

Katerina walked slowly ahead of him. "I can think of an explanation, but that would mean—"

She stopped suddenly, her eye pressed to the video camera's viewfinder as its lens stared long and hard at the square at her feet. When she didn't say anything for a while, Martin trotted to her side, saw the letters within the square—and recognized them.

Before he could speak, Martin jerked as a single chilling word from Katerina roared in his ears.

"RUN!"

Martin bounded up the ramp of the habitation module and swung his head wildly from side to side, looking for Katerina. He screamed her name again as he threw himself through the nearest compartments of the module, barely daring to breathe for fear he might catch the nauseating aroma of burning flesh. *Please, God, let her be safe—*

He found her sitting in the communications compartment, rapidly attaching a cable between the video camera and a monitor. His explosive sigh of relief quickly turned to puzzled anger. "What are you doing?"

Katerina finished plugging the short silver cable into the monitor and turned on the video camera. Flashing images of the squares on the platform they'd just fled raced in reverse across the monitor screen until she hit the "Pause" button. She yelled, "Don't ask questions! Check to see if anyone or anything, like a spaceship, is approaching us!"

The frantic expression on her face matched his own—and what she said made sense. Martin dropped into the compartment's other chair and activated the radar and optical surveillance system. His hands raced over the controls, searching in the late afternoon sunlight for any movement in the sky or on the ground near the habitation module. Then he switched to the radar and camera aboard the Scout orbiter overhead.

He shouted, "No sign of anything nearby!"

"Thank God! Maybe it's not too late!"

Katerina tore her gaze from the monitor and adjusted their rack-mounted main transceiver. With a tense voice she slowly spoke a few sentences in Russian into its microphone. Then she pressed several switches and swiveled around to face Martin.

She sighed, "There. I've set it to transmit the message I just recorded continuously. Now all we can do is wait for a response."

Martin yelled, "What do you mean, 'wait'? You've sent the distress signal, now we've got to run to the ascent vehicle and blast back into orbit before it's too late!"

"What are you talking about? I'm not sending a distress signal. I'm transmitting a message to the aliens."

Martin's jaw dropped. "Are you out of your mind? Do you *want* them to find out we're here and kill us?"

"Kill us?"

Katerina pointed at the still frame on the monitor screen. It showed a close-up of the square with Cyrillic characters within it. "I know your Russian isn't very good, but I thought you'd eventually be able to read what this says."

"I couldn't make out any of it! But right after you ran away I found the square written in English! It must contain the same message as yours!"

"I'm sure it did. But why do you think—wait, did you read the entire message?"

"I read enough of it to know why you ran away—and that you were in danger!"

Katerina glared at him. "You thought I was afraid—"

Her face softened. "And you thought I was in danger and were coming to rescue me. I don't know whether to slap you or kiss you!"

Katerina leaned forward and brushed her lips against her fiancé's bristly cheek. "If you'd read the whole message, you'd know why I ran away. And you'd know that *we* aren't in danger—but the human race is!"

She glanced at the empty radar screen beside him and then settled back into her chair. "When I read the message I knew every second counted. There was no time to argue with you about what it meant. I knew you'd follow me back—and you did, even if it was for the wrong reason. And while I was running back here I thought about everything the aliens have done and why they've been so mysterious.

"These aliens aren't just experts at planetary engineering. They're masters of human psychology. If they'd simply landed on Earth and shown themselves, everyone's focus would have been on them and not on what they were doing to Mars."

Katerina's eyes darkened. "Instead, the aliens were devilishly clever. What they did motivated us to go to Mars far more effectively than any speech. They stayed in the background and put on a show for us. All the incredible things they've done to this planet were designed to make us watch Mars and think about Mars. They aroused our curiosity and made enough people finally realize how important Mars is as a second chance for humanity. By living here, we increase the odds of the human race surviving despite all the foolish things we've done to ourselves and to Earth. Without Mars, we may have no future.

"The aliens dangled those hopes and dreams in front of us without saying a word. They showed us just enough to let our imaginations fill in the blanks without having to tell us anything. Now that they've manipulated us to come here in person, they're increasing the pressure on us to want to stay here. They want us to feel so excited about living here, make us so afraid we'll lose the planet, that we'll do anything and pay any price to *possess* Mars!"

Martin shouted, "That doesn't make any sense! Why would these aliens lure us here, build up our hopes of colonizing Mars—and then threaten to destroy us?

"Martin, what did the message in your square say?"

"It was at the top of the square, all in big blue letters. 'This world is the property of Interstellar Development, Inc. Unauthorized use of this planet is forbidden. Trespassers will be disintegrated.'"

Katerina shook her head. "Oh, these aliens are fiendishly subtle. They even shaded the messages for each of us."

She gestured to the Russian words on the monitor. "My square reads, 'This world is under the jurisdiction of the State Committee on Planetary Construction Policy. Authorized personnel only. Trespassers will be shot.'"

"Disintegrated, shot, what's the difference? Either way we're just as dead!"

"Oh, Martin, if you'd only read the rest of the message, you would have saved yourself so much unnecessary worry! It's the part that said *we* aren't in danger!"

Katerina brought her fingertip close to the monitor screen. "I put the recording on the monitor to make sure I remembered what it said correctly. Roughly translated, the words at the bottom of this square say, 'Open planet—today only. If you like what you see, call us on 1420 MHz for more information on how this world can be yours.' The message I'm transmitting is asking for that information."

"I don't get it. Are you saying 'open planet' means we're temporarily invited to be here? And if they really want to talk with us, why did the aliens put that message to contact them on just some of the squares? I can understand them doing ones in Chinese or Arabic if they didn't know what languages we spoke. But why did they make all those weird squares with the psychedelic lights and funny smells and sounds?"

Katerina's face darkened. "I think I know—and it explains why the gravity, atmosphere, and average temperatures here were modified to be similar to but *not* the same as we have on Earth. Those strange squares could even be just a trick to put more pressure on us. But if they are a real threat, the future of the human race is at stake!

"I believe *all* the squares on that artifact contain the same message. Some of them are meant to be read by human beings, but others are in languages spoken or sensed by creatures who *aren't* from Earth. The environment that Mars has now must be close enough to their own worlds' to be as comfortable for them as it is for us."

She sighed in frustration at the blank look on her crewmate's face. "Don't you see, Martin? That artifact is a gigantic 'For Sale' sign! We humans may be first in line because we live in the neighborhood, but the aliens who renovated Mars are advertising it to potential customers from *other* worlds too! That's why it's important we get our bid in and close the sale as soon as possible—before some *thing* else buys Mars!"

Martin stared at her. Finally he said, "What you're saying almost makes sense. But if you're right, we still have a major problem. The aliens who made your 'sign' are incredibly powerful and scientifically advanced. They can move and reshape entire worlds. What could we puny, primitive humans have that they might take as payment for an entire planet?"

"I don't know, and that worries me. Let's just hope you and I can negotiate a price that's acceptable to them and to our leaders back home."

"I have a better idea. I still think we're in danger, but I'm willing to take time to contact Mission Control and get an official decision on whether we should stay or leave. In return, I want you to promise me that if there's any sign of trouble, we should both get out of here as fast as—"

Martin stopped talking. There was a faint rhythmic thudding noise outside. It sounded like heavy footsteps on the ramp leading into the open entrance of the habitation module.

He looked back at the radar screen, then quickly rechecked all of the module's internal surveillance cameras. The thing from another world that his instruments said wasn't there crept closer and closer through the module with a steadily louder, ponderous gait. Now Martin could hear the low-pitched swoosh of breathing, as deep and dark as a great whale's call in the ocean depths, coming ever nearer.

Katerina clutched the cross suspended from her neck with her right hand and raised her left index finger to her lips. She whispered to him, "Be still." Martin studied the nervously calm expression on her face as she sat waiting. He tried his best to imitate it.

A hulking oddly shaped shadow fell across the entrance to the communications compartment. As the shadow's creator slunk into sight Martin struggled furiously to make sense of the impossible image reflecting off his eyes. Then the monster from the Interstellar Development corporation projected words into his mind that seemed to be spoken in the friendly tenor of a TV game show host.

It said, *Let us make a deal.*

The Last Temptation of Katerina Savitskaya

The Eternal Feminine leads us upward.
Johann Wolfgang von Goethe

I t was a warm rainy morning on Mars.

Katerina Savitskaya, the first and only woman on the Red Planet, stood barefoot in the open entrance of the habitation module and took a deep breath of the lightly lavender-scented air around her. A moist Martian breeze gently brushed her cheek like a lover's kiss. She fingered the end of her long freshly shampooed auburn hair, watching raindrops splatter the dusty ochre ground outside and kick up miniature craters like a shower of micrometeorites.

Several meters above her head, the rain pinged softly against the flat metal roof of the planet's lone human dwelling. The habitation module had been her home here for nearly three neomartian months. Though more spacious than the compact apartment in St. Petersburg where she had grown up, the module was dwarfed by the vast desert-like plain surrounding her.

Katerina sighed, cheered by the stillness and solitude of the dawn. Mission Control had radioed a work schedule for today that included a trek northeast to the shore of the Boreal Ocean. She silently asked God if this was the day there would be a second close encounter with the enigmatic aliens who'd terraformed Mars.

Suddenly the shapely young cosmonaut sensed something large sneaking up behind her from inside the module. Before she could turn around a pair of long hairy arms wrapped themselves tightly like tentacles around her waist. She shivered as hot wet lips with fetid breath nuzzled her throat—

"Happy birthday, Katerina!"

Martin Slayton, the first and only man on Mars, stepped back and grinned goofily at his fiancée. A maroon baseball cap with both NASA's insignia and the pale intertwined letters "S" and "L" sewn on it covered his black crew cut hair. He wore the crimson pullover shirt emblazoned on the front with "St. Louis Cardinals 2035 World Series Champions" she'd bought for him late last October, shortly before they'd rocketed away from Earth. Dingy white shorts and dirty black hiking boots completed his non-regulation spacesuit.

Katerina kissed his bristly cheek. Then she sniffed his mouth and wrinkled her nose. "Have you brushed yet?"

Her husband-to-be sheepishly ran his tongue over filmy teeth. "Sorry. I was so eager to be the first to congratulate you on your special day that I neglected my oral hygiene."

"Well, you're too late. Someone else already congratulated me."

Martin blinked. "Don't tell me *they* came and brought you a birthday cake."

"Considering how unpredictable the aliens are, it wouldn't have surprised me if they had. No, your rival for my affections is the dashing Harvey Schlocknagel."

Martin struck a heroic pose. "Well, I could fight him for your love in a duel with flashing sabers, like vying suitors do in those romance novels you read. However, since he's twenty-five million kilometers away at Mission Control, we'll have to take a rain check. Besides, you know who'd win the fight. As I recall, he's about a head shorter than me, twice my age, and lacks my manly physique and bronzed rippling muscles."

He lowered his voice to a piratical bass as he reached for her. "So, my buxom wench, you might as well surrender now—"

The Last Temptation of Katerina Savitskaya

Martin winced as Katerina's stiff index finger poked him hard in the abdomen and stopped his advance. She laughed, "No 'surrendering' until our wedding night, after we return to Earth early next year. Besides, today really isn't my birthday."

"Well, the chronometer inside says it's March 7th. Unless you're being technical with me about the International Date Line or something, we're both now thirty-three years old."

Katerina's hazel eyes twinkled. "Remember, we're on Mars. Even in its new orbit so close to Earth, a month here is about a week longer than one back home. I still have several more neomartian weeks to go before it's my birthday."

"No fair! You didn't use those rules when I had my birthday last month!"

"Is it my fault *you* don't consider yourself a Martian yet?"

Martin's eyes wandered over his fiancée's lovely face, curvaceous torso covered by a thin plaid shirt, and lightly tanned legs extending from rose-tinted shorts. "If Wells' Martians had looked like you, they could've conquered every red-blooded Earthman without firing a single Heat-Ray. You can experiment on my body any time—"

Katerina prodded him backwards and giggled, "That's enough, Martin! Our space agencies expect us to earn our pay by exploring, not acting like characters in a soap opera!"

"Okay, I'll go clean up."

As Martin retreated back through the openings in their module's science laboratory and other compartments, his voice faded as he intoned, "Can a simple farm boy from Marshfield, Missouri win the love of an exotic Russian beauty? Find out tomorrow on 'As the Red Planet Revolves'!"

A puff of wind caressed Katerina's Mona Lisa lips as her eyes returned to the world outside the module. The rain had stopped. The Sun, almost as bright and large as it shone in the skies of Earth, melted through thinning clouds and suffused the rusty sands with a golden luster. She prayed that God would let her gaze in innocent wonder at many more mystical Martian dawns.

It was a prayer that wouldn't be answered.

"Hurry up, Katerina! The pickup truck's loaded!"

Katerina's tennis shoes tapped with a ballerina's delicacy on the short ramp that led down from the habitation module, elevated a meter on multiple stubby landing legs, to the paprika-colored ground. As she ran outside, the large heavy three-barred golden cross she wore—a traditional symbol of her devout Russian Orthodox faith—swung across her chest from a gold chain around her neck.

"Sorry, Martin. I had to finish my morning prayers."

She hurried to where her crewmate stood by his "pickup truck." The two-seater rover was a sophisticated descendant of those used on the last three Apollo missions a little over sixty years earlier. The vehicle's skeletal open-frame-with-wheels appearance like a dune buggy's was similar to its forebears.

But this rover used the latest regenerative fuel cells for power and lightweight modern alloys strong enough to endure the rocky Martian landscape. The electronics in its navigation and other onboard systems rivaled the processing power of the entire Mission Control Center in Houston during its original heyday in the 1960s. The vehicle's glossy lime-green paint job was designed to stand out against the planet's predominantly reddish-orange hues.

Martin said, "I tested the radio and packed our supplies."

He grinned and pointed his companion toward the rover's passenger seat. "Remember, it's my turn to drive!"

Katerina sighed as she settled into her black cushioned seat on the right. She secured the safety harness and leaned her head tensely against the seat's headrest. Although the rover's technical specs said its maximum speed was about sixty kilometers per hour, the way Martin drove made it seem faster. And "his turn" also meant he had the choice of music.

She silently prayed for patience. After all, Martin hadn't grumbled *too* much when she'd been the driver on their last trip. Traveling southwest to the base of Olympus Mons, she'd played classical pieces with astronomical themes or nicknames. Holst's panoramic paean to the IAU-approved Solar System. Mozart's massive Symphony No. 41. The pianistic "moonlight" masterpieces of Beethoven and Debussy. Haydn's "Sun" string quartets, his opera *Il mondo della luna*, and fleet-footed Symphony No. 43.

She knew the melodies played today would be in a very different style.

Martin plopped down into the seat on her left and fiddled with his baseball cap. After activating the rover he pulled back and twisted its vertical metal control bar. As they sped away towards the Boreal Ocean he poked at their portable media player.

A country music tune replete with twanging guitars and thumping bass erupted from the small-but-mighty speakers he'd duct taped around the vehicle. Katerina squirmed as a female vocalist lugubriously enumerated the heartaches of rural American life.

Martin mercifully turned off the player after stopping the rover a kilometer from the habitation module to check what he'd dubbed "the north forty." It was a rectangular field ninety meters by sixty meters, used to test whether terrestrial food crops could grow in the sandy mineral-rich soil of Mars. Shortly after they landed early in the northern hemisphere's spring he'd used the rover like a tractor, pulling a long thin metal scraper blade attached to its back to level and clear the ground here. Then they'd carefully planted a variety of vegetables and grains.

Despite Katerina's disapproval Martin had placed a plastic pole and placard reading "Garden of Eden" at one end of the field. Earth's media, who'd already dubbed them the Adam and Eve of a newly recreated Mars, loved it.

They'd harvested a crop of radishes last week. Although those red-and-white roots looked edible, the space medicine experts back home denied Martin's request for a taste. Tests in the module's science lab hadn't shown any toxic chemicals in the radishes. But even the tiniest risk he might get sick was considered unacceptable.

Both had been chosen for this mission over older, more experienced space veterans on the assumption that their youth gave them a relative advantage in resisting illness or recuperating from injuries. The limited supply of medical equipment and medications in the module was adequate to treat minor maladies. But with the nearest Emergency Room many millions of kilometers away, calling 911 for a serious ailment or accident wasn't an option.

The biology experts' fears that mice or other lab animals might escape into the Martian wilderness meant there were none in the module to use as taste testers. And so, despite Martin's pleas with the physicians back home, the radishes remained uneaten.

Martin examined the delicate yellow blossoms on his green bean bushes. "Looks like we'll have our first batch soon."

Katerina stood at the perimeter of their garden, looking out over the stubby cornstalks and verdant wheat low against the ground. "It's amazing how well everything's growing."

Her crewmate kicked a patch of powdery pumpkin-tinted soil with his boot and replied, "I wonder what the ground was like before the aliens started working on it. The hematite and other minerals on the surface aren't good for growing crops, but the clay we found digging deeper with our shovels obviously is."

Katerina sighed, "I suppose we'll never really know what the planet was like before the aliens changed the ecosystem so radically. Even with too little atmosphere and too much radiation, the 'old' Mars was still worth going to. But I think this new one is better."

Martin grinned. "Nice speech, but you're preaching to the choir."

The young Russian frowned. "I've never heard that expression."

"It means I agree with you. But I'd feel better if the aliens told us *why* they changed Mars."

As they settled back into the rover Katerina said, "When do you think the aliens will tell us?"

Martin shrugged. "The sooner the better. I appreciate what they've done to Mars, but I hate how sneaky they've been."

Katerina smiled slyly. "You're still mad about that trick they played on us with their artifact the day we landed."

Her companion started the vehicle accelerating toward the northeast. "Yes, I am. The fact that metal slab was gone the next day, with nothing but a shallow one hundred-meter square hole in the ground where it used to be, tells me that it was just a colossal red herring. And I hated the way that alien—or aliens, I'm still not sure which—snuck into the habitation module with us and acted more evasive than your typical politician at a news conference.

"Heck, I can't even describe what the alien looked like! I heard it breathing and almost smelled it hovering over me, like it was a Kodiak bear stretched upright and ready to have us for supper. But all I saw was a vague shimmering shape—like something you'd see in a nightmare."

Katerina nodded, grateful that Martin hadn't turned the music player back on. "At least we had similar impressions about it."

Her driver scowled. "It still irks me that all the alien did was make a deal that the two of us could stay on Mars *if* no other humans come here. Our 'landlords' spent ten years moving Mars closer to the Sun, giving it a breathable atmosphere, and increasing its gravity to nearly one g. So why couldn't our visitor spare us a few more minutes to answer your questions about where they come from and what we have to do to 'buy' the planet from them?

"Instead all we got from 'ALF' before it disappeared was that oh-so-mysterious 'All will be clear.'"

The Last Temptation of Katerina Savitskaya

Katerina gasped as Martin angrily gunned the rover over rocks undisturbed for millennia, crushing them into a spray of gravel behind them. When he started running over the delicate lichen-like plants dotting the plain and turning them into shredded road kill she shouted, "Martin, slow down! If you keep driving like this we'll never find out about the aliens! You'll just get us killed and show them how stupid we humans are!"

The rover slowed. "Sorry. I'm from Missouri. It's called the 'Show Me' state because we natives aren't impressed by fancy words and tricks. We want people—even extraterrestrial ones—to be honest and straightforward with us."

Katerina replied softly, "I'm from Russia. There's some truth to the stereotype that we're a patient people, able to quietly endure many things—including the machinations of the powerful."

The Sun peeked from behind a cloud and cast an aureate glow over them. It reflected off the deeper gold of the cross suspended from her neck. Katerina said, "Keep praying that perhaps today we'll learn the answers to our questions. And if it doesn't happen today—then tomorrow, pray for it again."

Martin murmured, "I wish I had your faith."

Katerina sighed. "I wish my faith was as strong as you think it is."

"Look, Katerina! Surf's up!"

The rover sat atop a low saffron sand dune. Katerina shaded her eyes, enthralled at their panoramic view of the Boreal Ocean. Martin's grin made her even happier.

They'd said little during the last kilometers of their journey. It was rare for the darker side of their situation to surface like that. Though they had each other, they were still strangers in a strange land, far from home or help—their lives at the mercy of powerful aliens whose intentions were still unknown.

But those worries dissipated when they reached their destination. The shallow ocean before them paled compared to the roiling, majestic Pacific or Atlantic. But, until only a decade ago when the aliens began their massive renovation of Mars, its waters had been imprisoned for billions of years in the planet's north polar ice cap.

Now covering the vast lowlands of the north polar region, the Boreal Ocean swayed gently under the influence of a Sun only seven million kilometers farther than Earth's average distance from it. The fourth planet's two midget moons would never produce the powerful tides that the Moon created on Earth. But the presence of any liquid water and waves on Mars was miraculous.

Martin parked the rover near the shoreline. Carrying small packs of collection containers, they walked close to murmuring waves tinged red by rusty sediment from the ocean floor. After obtaining soil samples, they ventured to the ocean's edge and collected milliliters of its water into capped plastic vials for later analysis.

Their task done, they returned to the rover and freshened up. Martin removed a large mylar blanket from the back of the rover and laid it flat on the ground. He extracted two foil-wrapped trays from their thermal-controlled container and grinned, "Ready for lunch? I know you love reconstituted chicken and noodles, so I packed some especially for you."

Katerina removed a bottle of water from the rover and sat on the blanket. "Martin, I told you this is the first week of the Great Lent. That's why I fasted and only drank water for two days beginning on Monday. Besides, this is Friday and I wouldn't eat meat today anyway."

Martin grimaced. "Sorry, I forgot. Wait, does this mean you're following Earth's calendar again and today really is your birthday?"

Her fiancé's smile looked forced. Katerina said, "I didn't mean to offend you. I know you were trying to do something nice for me."

Martin shrugged. "That's okay. We'll work out these culture clashes eventually."

He put her tray back into the rover. After pausing pensively, he re-placed his tray too and sat down beside Katerina. "If *you* aren't a Martian anymore, maybe I should be one instead. After all, even if it doesn't last a million years, we're having a picnic on Mars. I can change my name to 'Martin the Martian'—isn't that lovely, hmm?"

He laughed. "Hey, I just realized my big brother and sister-in-law did me a favor by naming their firstborn 'Timothy.' Remember when we visited my hometown last September? After we gave that talk to his kindergarten class Tim said that 'Uncle Martin' was his favorite spaceman."

Katerina sipped her water. "What you said is probably very clever, but I don't seem to understand it."

"Never mind. I guess I wasted too much of my youth reading science fiction and watching ancient movies and TV shows."

Katerina shook her head. Though she was fluent in English and sever-al other languages, her knowledge of Martin's American "culture" had yawning gaps. She'd fallen victim a number of times to her fiancé's impish exploitation of that ignorance—especially during that brief visit they'd made to see his family late last summer. Sitting together on the couch in his parents' living room, he'd turned on the television and shown her what he said were old black-and-white "home movies" about his mid-twentieth-century ancestors.

She was shocked at how her future husband's relatives seemed more ignorant and uncouth than any Americans she'd ever met. Unlike the elderly woman on the television, her own sweet grandmother in Russia would never have made illegal vodka. And she didn't understand how, if his family was so wealthy, Martin himself had grown up in this com-fortable but modest farmhouse.

The expression on her face after her future father-in-law walked in on them and scolded his son for "pulling her leg" made Martin laugh uncontrollably. His father informed her that, while the family on the television was indeed supposed to have originally come from this part of the Ozarks, the Slaytons weren't related to the Clampetts.

But after Martin shared his genuine family photos and movies with her, she'd forgiven him. Well, not at first—especially when he showed her the ones with him playing with the childhood friend and companion who, he said, she'd replaced as the one he loved most in the world. It was when Martin took her to a far corner of the family farm that she realized he really wasn't joking this time. As they visited the small stone that marked where his erstwhile greatest friend lay buried for twenty years, she felt the heartfelt joy and tears in his memories.

And when they'd driven by the replica of the Hubble Space Telescope in Marshfield, Missouri's town square—a monument to the great astronomer Edwin Hubble from the small town where he was born—she understood the man she loved even more. Before he explained how seeing that model so often as a boy had inspired and led him to the planet they now shared, she saw the dream in his face. It was the same look she'd seen in the mirror as a child after reading about her own country's achievements in space.

Martin got up and grabbed the microphone attached to the transceiver inside the rover. "Breaker, breaker, Mission Control. We're having fun at the beach and collected some souvenirs for you. We'll be moving in the monster lane to our next stop after we cut the coax. By the way, is Dr. Stone on duty? I'd like to talk to him about some radishes. Over."

The transponder at the habitation module received the signal he'd just transmitted. It swiftly relayed his message to an orbiter overhead, which then sent it back to Houston. As they waited the several minutes it would take for the signal to reach Earth and receive an answer, Martin laughed, "Don't look at me like that. I don't criticize you when you talk to your bosses at the Russian Space Agency."

"That's because we act more serious. And don't pester Dr. Stone about the radishes. It's his responsibility to keep us healthy, not please your taste buds."

"Well, as head of space medicine at NASA he's also responsible for our mental health. He'll come around eventually."

"I don't know. I respect him as a physician, but he's always seemed rather cold."

"Nah, he's a Midwesterner like me, and I recognize his type. Hard and professional on the outside—soft and sentimental on the inside."

As Katerina folded the blanket a voice squawked from the rover's transceiver, "That's a big ten-four. Dr. Stone will be here soon. I'll tell him you want to ragchew about the radishes again. I'm on the side for you."

Martin handled the microphone. "Copied, Harv. I'm pulling the plug at this end."

He chuckled, "Harvey's a good guy. We may be romantic rivals over you, but he and I speak the same language.

Katerina sighed. "I wish I spoke it too."

As they drove parallel to the beach, Martin reached for the music player. Katerina quickly said, "Did you listen to the newsfeed from Mission Control before we left this morning?"

She smiled in relief as his fingers returned to the control bar. Martin said, "Yes. Nothing much new. More suicide bombers in Iran. Your country and China are rattling sabers along their border. Drug resistance to AIDS is up again. The famine in Africa is getting worse."

He shrugged. "The usual stuff."

The noonday Sun faded behind a cloud. Now Katerina regretted her ploy to keep the player off.

Martin continued, "I also heard that the Chinese won't postpone their own mission here any longer. Unless our governments convince them otherwise, they're planning to send their people here at the next launch window."

"But they mustn't do that! The alien told us specifically that no one else should come here!"

"The alien told *us* that, and *we* relayed what it said back home. But Beijing thinks NASA and the RSA made up our message so they could keep Mars to themselves."

Martin frowned. "Of course, it's totally unreasonable for the Chinese to believe that. Everybody knows the American and Russian governments would never ever tell a fib."

Katerina leaned away from him. She rarely saw this cynical side of her fiancé without it being softened by childish humor. She whispered, "Let's pray the Chinese have more faith in us before something terrible happens."

"Don't count on it. And it's not just the aliens who could do something terrible. Your country and China have been getting on each other's nerves for years. If my government is too ham-handed, we could get back on China's hate list too. I doubt anybody's stupid enough to start World War III. But as tense as things are back home, it might take just a little spark to start something that could kill lots of people."

Martin glanced at the golden cross around her neck. "*You* may have faith that things will work out okay, but most people and governments don't."

"Are you one of those people, Martin?"

"Once upon a time, when I was an altar boy, I wasn't. Now—I don't know. But I'd rather rely on what *I* can do rather than trust anybody else to do the right thing. Or hope that anyone more powerful than me will save the day."

He grunted. "Another thing about these aliens bothers me. It's wonderful that they've made Mars habitable for us and given the human race a chance for a fresh start. But why haven't they offered to sell us high-tech items humanity could use right away? Like a cure for cancer, a cheap nonpolluting source of unlimited energy, or a warp engine?"

"I don't know. Perhaps they think we'd misuse them."

"Maybe. If we did get a hand-sized fusion reactor, some idiot or government would probably use it to terrorize and murder innocent people."

Katerina's brow furrowed. "Our own science and technology already help us lead healthier, more comfortable lives. Yet all those ideas and innovations, from fire to nuclear energy, can be perverted to cause pain and suffering. That's not because science is bad, but because we humans can be selfish, misguided, or heartless in the way we use it. We could destroy ourselves with the technology we already have, much less what the aliens might give us.

"When enough of us learn to love God and each other, perhaps we'll be ready to use any scientific miracles the aliens give us to make our world a better place. But for now, maybe it's better if we're not tempted to misuse their technology."

Martin sneered, "More likely God would be used to *justify* killing people with that alien technology. The religion I was raised in once used Grand Inquisitors and burned heretics. There are still plenty of people willing to kill for Him or whatever secular cause they've substituted for religion."

"Don't blame God for that. Just as technology can be used well or misused, so can religion. When I was a little girl, my grandmother told me that my teacher at the state school was wrong when he said we humans are merely 'hyperactive dirt with illusions of importance.' She said we should let science tell us what Nature is and how to use it—but let religion and philosophy show us what Creation means and our place in it."

Martin glanced darkly at her cross. "And you think *you* have all the right answers?"

Katerina's eyes moistened at the schism growing between them. "Of course not. I *think* and hope my religious beliefs are true, but I can't prove that to you or even myself. Perhaps—God forbid—my teacher was right and what I believe is just a collection of myths, superstition, and wishful thinking. But if my beliefs have made me a kinder, more loving person than I otherwise would have been, is merely being foolish or wrong such a terrible thing? If my belief in a caring, compassionate God inspires me to love you and help our fellow humans find our destiny in the stars, is my faith really in vain?"

The expression on her crewmate's face held no humor. "Sorry, Katerina. This time the choir isn't listening."

The rover suddenly halted atop a gently sloping sand dune. Martin's eyes focused past her into the distance. He said, "What's that?"

Katerina turned her head away from the undulating ocean, following his gaze. "What are you looking at?"

"I thought I saw a flash of light—or something reflecting sunlight."

Martin pulled a pair of high-powered image-stabilizing binoculars from the small box between their seats. He stood up, peered through the binoculars—and groaned.

"Oh, no!"

Katerina cried, "What is it?"

"Those jerks!"

"Who?"

"The aliens! They must be rolling on the ground laughing at us!"

Katerina snatched the binoculars from him and focused them on the distant speck of light.

Suddenly she smiled and said, "It's a new artifact!"

"Yup."

"That's wonderful! Maybe the aliens are waiting for us there!"

"Maybe. But what's that artifact shaped like?"

She raised the binoculars again. "It's a giant pyramid."

"Right. A *pyramid*."

Katerina frowned. "What's wrong with that? A pyramid is a structurally sound shape. I've visited the largest ones in Egypt. They've lasted for thousands of years."

"You're missing the point, Katerina. After we tell Mission Control about it, they'll have to tell the public. I can just see all the high-fives those 'aliens-gave-their-technology-to-primitive-humans' wackos are going to give each other!"

"What are you talking about?"

Martin grunted. "My poor innocent Katerina, you have so much to learn about the silly pseudoscientific side of American culture!"

He slumped into his seat. "Could've been worse. They could've made it look like a giant human face."

Martin took the microphone. "Houston, we've got a problem. And you're not going to believe what it is."

After several unsuccessful attempts to contact Mission Control, Martin disgustedly dropped the microphone and said, "I should've known. It's just like it was with that first artifact. Déjà vu all over again.

"The aliens are probably intentionally blocking our transmissions to Earth and giving us the same choice we had then. We can return to the module and try contacting our bosses from there about what to do—or plunge ahead into whatever game E.T. is playing this time."

Katerina nodded. "I think we should do what we did before—go there now and find out what they want. Doing that worked out well with their first artifact."

"True—but just because you win one game of Russian roulette doesn't mean it's a good idea to play another."

Martin snorted. "That artifact is so big the orbiters should've spotted it long ago. Either the aliens somehow shielded it from the orbiters' cameras—or they built it this morning after we started on our trip. Either way, they're rubbing our noses in how scientifically advanced they are over us. "

He shrugged fatalistically. "If they're that eager to attract our attention, let's find out why."

As they drove toward the alien pyramid, Katerina was impressed by how different it was from the largest one she'd seen at Giza. The Great Pyramid's two million stone blocks were weathered and ancient, but the steel-gray structure before them looked like it had lanced up from the Martian soil that morning. While the one in Egypt had lost the smooth limestone casing stones framing its high irregular outer walls long ago, this monstrous pyramid's four triangular walls were flat and shiny. The metal that formed its sides looked solid, with no seams or plates riveted together.

Driving alongside this towering alien artifact, their rover resembled the small green plastic car with miniature passengers she'd watched five-year-old Tim Slayton play with before Martin accidentally stepped on it. Young Tim's tears disappeared when his uncle replaced that crushed plaything with a model of the Ares VII rocket, crewed by a pair of Lilliputian figures resembling Martin and her, that would soon send the two of them to Mars. Katerina wondered if the technological giants who'd erected this gargantuan artifact would bother to remedy any damage they caused to the tiny creatures they encountered.

Martin cruised slowly around the square base of the pyramid. "Looks about four hundred meters on each side."

Katerina nodded. "The tour guide on my trip to Egypt said the Great Pyramid is about one hundred thirty meters tall. This one looks about twice that height."

Martin rounded a corner of the artifact. "Reminds me of a Mayan pyramid without the terracing. See how its top looks flat, like the pyramid on a one dollar bill?"

He shivered. "Thank goodness there's no freaky giant eye staring down at us from up there."

Katerina shouted, "There's the entrance!"

The rover stopped near a ground-level rectangular opening. It was the size of a conventional doorway and centered in one wall of the pyramid. Martin said, "I *know* that opening wasn't there the last time we drove around this side. Unless it's some kind of automatic door, the aliens must know we're here."

Above the opening, large purple letters from an alien alphabet writhed like snakes.

"I wonder what that says, Martin."

"'Abandon All Hope, Ye Who Enter Here.'"

Martin peered into the opening. "Looks dark in there. Unless the aliens put a light switch inside the doorway, we'd better bring flashlights."

They got out and searched through their equipment and supplies. Katerina smiled, "I bet you wish we'd brought the high voltage probe and multimeter to make sure this artifact isn't electrified, like you thought about the first one we found."

"That's okay. You convinced me last time that if the aliens wanted to exterminate us, they could do it a lot easier than by making an enormous bug zapper or a comfy motel for us roaches to check into."

Martin frowned at the pyramid. "At least I hope that's not what they have in mind."

Katerina said, "We'd better bring the medical bag, in case either of us gets hurt. I'll put some sample containers in it too, since we might find something to collect. You take the video camera and we each get to carry a flashlight."

Martin turned his flashlight on and off. "Too bad this isn't a lightsaber. And I'd rather be holding a phaser than a video camera."

Katerina slung the strap of the large soft-sided crimson medical supply bag over her shoulder. "I don't think toys like that would work against these particular aliens. They're too powerful."

"I know. Still, I'd feel less doomed if I had a plasma rifle or shotgun."

"Don't worry, Martin. You were angry the aliens haven't answered our questions about them yet. Before the day is over, perhaps they will."

Martin snorted. "Let's hope we like what we hear."

He looked up at the towering structure and growled, "A pyramid on Mars. With our luck, we'll find Sutekh waiting for us inside."

"Who?"

Martin smiled mischievously. "That's right."

"What?"

Her fiancé adjusted his baseball cap. "No, What's on second base. Who's on first."

"Why are you talking in riddles at a time like this?"

"Ever hear the expression, 'Whistling as you walk by the graveyard'?"

Katerina frowned. "I think I understand. And that expression might be too appropriate. Ancient Egyptian pyramids were used as tombs."

"And the Mayan ones were used as temples. Just call me 'Missouri Slayton.'"

He walked toward the dark entrance. "Come on, Lara. We've got a tomb to raid."

Katerina's eyebrows arched as she followed him. She was pleasantly surprised that Martin had read *Doctor Zhivago*—and glad he'd finally made an allusion she understood.

There was no light switch inside the doorway. The flaring white beams from their flashlights' LEDs illuminated barely a few meters of the metal floor ahead of them.

Martin waved his flashlight at the low ceiling and featureless walls surrounding them in the rectangular chamber. "Looks like it's all the same dark-gray metal we saw on the outside."

He stepped forward cautiously until a blank wall reflected light back at him. "This place is larger than a college classroom. But it looks empty, and I can't find any other exit."

Katerina stood close to the open entrance, where shadowed sunlight from outside still assisted her own flashlight's survey of the room. She said, "These near walls look completely bare too. And there doesn't seem to be anyone else here besides us."

Martin's flashlight beam swept rapidly around the room. He muttered, "Unless there's something lurking in a dark corner or hanging from the ceiling ready to pounce on us—"

He spun around. The creature he'd sensed creeping up behind him blinked as his flashlight's magnesium-white glare dazzled its hazel eyes—

Katerina winced and scrunched her eyelids down. "Martin, be careful!"

"Sorry! Are you all right?"

"I will be, when I can see again!"

Katerina blinked several more times, then said, "Are you sure there's no exit along this far wall?"

"No, it's a dead end."

"That doesn't make sense. Why would the aliens build only a single empty room in this huge pyramid?"

"I don't know, maybe they—"

He whispered, "Did this room just get darker?"

"I can't tell. My eyes haven't recovered from your searchlight yet."

Martin stared back at the entrance to the pyramid. He groaned, "Oh, no."

"What's wrong?"

The flashlight's beam darted across the floor as he quickly retraced his steps back towards the outer wall of the pyramid. He stopped abruptly as white light swirled against blank unyielding metal.

With her vision nearly back to normal, Katerina peered through the Stygian darkness towards the sounds of his footsteps. Suddenly she realized what was wrong.

"Martin, what happened to the entrance?"

The clacking of his boots coming slowly toward her across the metal floor sounded like the patter of a giant cockroach. Katerina heard him mumble, "…but they don't check out."

Then she saw his face, ghastly pale in the darkness. "The entrance?" he said. "There is no entrance—or exit. No sign it was ever there. That metal wall looks like it's been pinched shut as if it were wet clay."

They stared at each other for several seconds before Katerina said, "There must be a way out of here somewhere."

Martin grumbled, "If this were a World War II-era movie, all we'd have to do is find a secret sliding panel or hidden trapdoor. But I can't picture the aliens taking notes while they watched old Republic serials on TV. And I don't feel any draft to indicate there's a ventilation system in here. The oxygen we're using up with each breath may not be replaced."

Katerina's lips started to form a prayer for deliverance—then she stopped. It wasn't time for that yet—not until she and Martin had done everything *they* could.

She said, "Well, before we suffocate, let's spend our last moments trying to find a way out. I'll look along that wall, and you search the one over there. They may kill us, but at least we'll show these aliens that humans don't give up!"

Katerina played her flashlight slowly and methodically along the wall. The gleaming gray metal showed no sign of dust or any seam to indicate a disguised door. It didn't even show any smears from her fingerprints as she periodically pressed parts of it the way Martin advised her to do. But there was no sign of any small panel she could push to make a hidden door spring open.

Her breaths were getting harder and faster. She shouted, "Any luck, Martin?"

From the far side of the blackened room a faint "No" echoed back at her.

In desperation she stamped her foot against the floor, seeing if any part of it would give way. But all that did was make her sole ache.

After muttering something in Russian that her grandmother would've chided her for saying, Katerina heard deep sonorous breathing behind her. She turned around angrily. "Martin, there's nothing over here, look somewhere—"

The scintillating glowing lights a meter away from her twisted and writhed in a kaleidoscope of unearthly forms, as vague as the spots she'd seen when Martin's flashlight temporarily blinded her. In the span of only several heartbeats they shifted from a single unrecognizable intelligent shape to what seemed a pair of entities, then into three beings that in some mystical way beyond human understanding were still only one. Another instant and the number of supernatural creatures before her became legion, yet still somehow a unity as its numbers seemed to ebb and flow between one and infinity.

From somewhere within that hypnotic swirl a voice at once timeless and without gender formed in her mind like the tiny whisper of conscience.

Explain why you asked your deity to punish us.

She couldn't tell whether she spoke or thought her reply. "You've put Martin and me in danger."

No one has been injured. No harm has been done.

"If you don't mean to hurt us, why did you trap us in here?"

This is not a trap. It is a path.

"What do you mean? There's no way out!"

There is.

She shone her flashlight at the solid wall beside her. "Then tell me how I get through—"

Katerina gasped and nearly let the flashlight slip from her trembling hand. There was now a rectangular opening in the previously solid wall large enough for her to enter comfortably. It opened into a dark corridor that slanted gently upward, its end unseen past the paltry range of her flashlight.

For an instant she forgot the alien presence close to her. "Martin, come here! We have a way out!"

He cannot help you.

A twist of panic and fear knotted her stomach. Katerina ran toward the other side of the room—then stopped. She raced back and forth, swinging her flashlight wildly.

A solid metal wall now cleaved the chamber in two from top to bottom—and she was the only human being on this side of it.

You have a path. He has a path.

Then she was alone except for the groans of her own breathing.

Katerina walked slowly through the pitch-black corridor, carefully tracking how far she'd traveled from the entrance chamber by making each stride about a meter long. Though the floor kept its same gradual upward slope, the corridor angled sharply to the right or the left every several meters like a labyrinth. Its bare metal walls gave no more than a meter's clearance above or on either side as her flashlight struggled to shine a path before her.

After about sixty meters of twisting turns, Katerina rounded another corner and stopped. Points of lights like a swarm of ghostly fireflies flickered five meters ahead of her. As she cautiously crept forward, the lights resolved into tiny tongues of fire that reminded her of votive candles burning in a darkened cathedral.

Another step and she realized the flames did come from a compact set of stubby candles. They were stuck into the top of a brown cylindrical cake, as tall as a chef's hat, that was sitting atop a round waist-high stone pillar. Creamy white icing capped the cake and drizzled down its sides. Edging closer, she squinted through the miniature flames and saw pink frosting streaked across its top to form Cyrillic letters. She gasped at the words they formed.

HAPPY BIRTHDAY KATERINA.

But it wasn't just a birthday cake. Its shape and dark rich scent said it was a kulich. She could almost taste the candied fruit, rum, saffron, and almonds baked within this sugary sweet bread. Her mouth watered as she remembered those happy Easters of her childhood when her beloved grandmother had prepared the holiday feast. Her stomach, flat and empty from fasting, rumbled greedily and pined for this delicacy.

Katerina transferred the flashlight to her left hand and eased closer to the kulich. The first three fingers of her right hand reached forward to scoop out a chunk of its floury flesh and bring it to her lips—

She jerked her hand back, wiping the crumbs and icing from her fingernails onto the side of the medical supply bag she carried. Her stomach protested her decision, but she ignored its laments.

Explain why you do not eat this food. It will not harm you.

Katerina turned around, unsurprised by the scintillating entity's reappearance. "It's a tradition in my religion to fast at this time."

There is no need to fast if you are hungry and food is available. It is not intelligent to blindly obey rules that inflict unnecessary pain.

Reflexively she clutched the cross hanging from the gold chain around her neck. "My obedience isn't blind. Fasting helps me practice self-control. We humans can be tempted to indulge desires that could cause unnecessary suffering later for ourselves and others. Eating this food now wouldn't directly injure me. But by not eating it I make it easier to resist temptation when it really could cause harm."

That explains why you do not mate with your companion though you strongly desire him.

Katerina wondered if the aliens understood what a blush meant. "Yes, I want us to share our love in that way. But doing that now could put the new life we might create in danger. And if our unborn child or me were to die from a medical problem beyond our ability to deal with on this world, I know Martin would feel terrible pain too. As difficult as it's been to abstain, it might be far worse if we didn't."

Delayed gratification. An interesting concept.

Katerina frowned. "I didn't say those words, I only thought them!"

She gestured at the cake. "That tells me you must've heard Martin's joke this morning. You must be able to eavesdrop on us and read our minds!"

We can hear your words at any time. We can decipher the electrical impulses generated by your brain.

"If you can tell what we're thinking, why are you even asking me these questions? Why are you playing these games with us?"

Your thoughts do not necessarily tell us what you are. They only tell us what you think you are. We must know what you are.

"Why?"

We have a gift for you. It is easy to manipulate matter. We will give you control over matter far beyond your current power.

"What do you mean?"

With this power there need be no harm if you indulge your desires. You can create food and eat without fear of sickness. You can mate without injury to offspring. You will no longer need self-control.

Katerina didn't answer for a long time. "No. That sounds like too much power for any human being to have. It could be corrupted so easily, even with the best intentions."

You are hungry. If you eat the food we offer, you will receive this power and may pass.

"What do you mean, 'pass'? Is this some kind of test?"

There was no answer. The lights and voice were gone.

Katerina turned around and gazed at the delicious festive cake beckoning to her. She shook herself free of its hypnotic flickering lights and tried walking past it—

Suddenly the flames from the candles flared up in a curtain of fire that blocked her path. She stumbled backwards from heat as searing as a dragon's breath.

The prickling on her face gradually subsided. There was no mirror handy to show whether her eyebrows were singed. The wall of flames that held her back burned firm and steady. She suspected that a shout to the aliens that she'd eat their cake would make the fire disappear.

But she wasn't going to find out. More than thinking it, she *felt* that accepting their gift of power was wrong. Even if the fire was consuming a limited supply of oxygen here in the pyramid, even if it meant she was trapped here forever, bowing to the aliens' offer might be even worse.

Still—despite all the danger they'd seemed to place Martin and her in, the aliens had never actually hurt them. Or at least she hoped so, praying fervently for a moment that somewhere else in the pyramid her beloved was still safe. But if there was any chance of seeing him again, she had to pass through those flames without yielding to the aliens.

Then she remembered. *We can decipher the electrical impulses generated by your brain.* If they could do that and read her mind, maybe they could also stimulate her brain to make her see and feel things that weren't there. They could be playing the role of Descartes' evil genie—deceiving her senses for their own purposes.

But if she couldn't trust her own senses, how could she tell if the flames were real or not?

Katerina fingered the cross hanging from her neck, meditating on that question. Then, as if by divine inspiration, an idea came to her. She set the medical bag on the floor and opened it. Extracting several wooden tongue depressors from their paper wrappings, she tied them tightly together end-to-end using a roll of cloth tape to form a wand-like extension. Then she unfastened the braided gold chain around her neck and pulled it through the eyelet that secured it to her heavy golden cross. Finally she used more tape to bind the shorter end of her cross to the tip of one of the tongue depressors.

Her impromptu testing device now resembled a child's short toy sword. Katerina held it at the end opposite where her cross formed the sword's point, hefting it carefully to make sure all the taped connections were secure. Extending her right arm, she positioned the device as far in front of her as possible and walked slowly toward the sheet of fire blocking her way. She winced as the fire tried to bake the flesh off her fingers while she held the far end of her cross in the flames. A nervous laugh escaped her lips as she imagined that Martin was here, telling her he'd get a marshmallow for the end of her stick.

After a minute Katerina retreated to the cooler end of the corridor and carefully examined the cross with her flashlight. The relic seemed unchanged—neither glowing from the heat it'd been exposed to nor melted. She knelt down and placed the flashlight on the floor so that its beam shone in front of her. Then she lowered the cross enough to keep it illuminated and cautiously brought her free hand closer and closer to its golden surface. Finally she grasped the cross itself with her fingertips.

"It must be a trick," she whispered. "Gold is too good a conductor of heat for the cross not to have become hot no matter what temperature those flames are, even if they weren't hot enough to make the tongue depressor burn."

She disassembled her device, placed the tongue depressors back into the medical bag, then fastened her gold chain and cross around her neck. "If the cross had been hot, I would have to assume the flames are real. The fact it was cool implies the fire is really an illusion. Unless the aliens made me only *think* the cross wasn't hot or that I even put it in the flames—"

Katerina sighed. Relying on her reason and senses alone might not be enough to outsmart the evil genie. Then, perhaps remembering how her device had resembled a sword, she thought of Joan of Arc. The teenage heroine said one of the voices that spoke to her was Katerina's own namesake, St. Catherine of Alexandria. Whether madness or miracle, the young French peasant girl's beliefs had led to the triumph of her cause, a flaming death as a heretic—and apotheosis as a saint.

Six centuries later, another young woman wondered if her faith could be as strong.

Katerina knelt another moment, her lips moving reverently in prayer. Then, standing erect with the strap of her medical bag slung over her shoulder and flashlight in hand—she ran through the flames.

Martin coughed as he trotted up the twisting upsloping corridor, his flashlight's beam bouncing carelessly in front of him. His throat was still raspy from shouting Katerina's name and yelling imaginative invectives at the aliens after he'd discovered the impenetrable metal barrier that separated the two of them in the entrance chamber. The new opening that mysteriously appeared in the far wall had only inspired him to ever more creative pejoratives about the aliens' anatomy and personal hygiene.

Stomping through the darkness, he didn't know or care how far he'd walked. Right now he was so worried about Katerina and angry at the aliens that he didn't care what happened to him. If any sneaky extraterrestrials jumped out at him from the shadows he'd demand that she be restored to him immediately. And if they didn't like the tone of his voice, at least he'd leave them scratching their heads—if they had heads—about the meaning of the hand gesture he gave them before they zapped him.

After turning yet another corner he halted, groaning at the flaming apparition in front of him at the far end of the short corridor. "Is that supposed to impress me? If you have something to tell me, say it without the special effects! They had a better one in *The Ten Commandments*!"

Even if the burning bush in front of him had replied, he wouldn't have believed it was the voice of God. Those stories had thrilled him during his grade school religion classes, but as an adult he recognized them as simple myths. He snickered, remembering that incredibly bad Red Scare-era movie, *Red Planet Mars*, he'd shown Katerina during their space flight here, with God broadcasting pious messages from Mars.

Still—as he approached the burning but unconsumed bush blocking his upward advance, he felt its heat against his skin. Maybe it wasn't an illusion. He stepped back, frowning as he tried to figure out how to tell if it were real.

Finally Martin pointed his video camera at the burning bush for a minute. He reviewed the recording—and laughed. As he walked toward the flames he muttered sarcastically, "If this were real, it would have shown up on the recording. So, no matter what I think I'm seeing or feeling, the aliens are just messing with my mind."

But as the blazing flames leapt toward him he hoped his lack of faith in this "miracle" was right.

Katerina kept her measured pace as the zigzagging corridors led her steadily upward. The hand holding her flashlight had finally stopped trembling from her excursion through the kulich's flames. At least she knew a bit more about the aliens' power and their willingness to try deceiving her with illusions. But if they tested her again, she wondered how she'd be able to tell what was real and what wasn't.

She didn't have long to wait. For the last hundred meters she'd noticed the walls around her were becoming dimly visible, illuminated by a soft glow emanating from them. They were now almost bright enough for her to stop using her flashlight.

Fortunately the device was still on and shining downward just in time to prevent her from falling into a trap. In the middle of the corridor she'd just entered, the floor was replaced by a pool filled to the top with clear liquid. It stretched across the entire width of the floor and was longer than a half dozen bathtubs laid end to end—far too large for her to jump across. While the liquid reflecting her flashlight's beam looked like water, she couldn't tell by its appearance exactly what it was or how deep down it went.

"Well, what do they want me to do now?"

There is a way to cross it. Watch.

Before she could turn to see if the aliens were behind her again, Katerina's attention was caught by the change in the fluid before her. In seconds it turned opaque and solid—as if it had suddenly frozen hard enough for her to walk across.

We can change the amount and location of energy as easily as we can manipulate matter. It is easy to manipulate matter and energy. These powers can be yours if you accept them.

"Why do you want me to have them?"

These powers will let you guide or rule your species as you wish. You will be able to control all natural forces on your world and render it safe and secure for every one of your kind. By altering the electrical impulses of their brains you could make them think and act the way you believe is right.

"Are you suggesting that I make the whole human race my slaves?"

You would have that choice. If you do not desire their service or worship, you could help your fellow creatures by eliminating their willingness to harm each other. You could make them act in ways you deem most beneficial to them.

"Any good that did would be at the expense of their free will. That would be too great a price to pay!"

You could choose what you did with the power we offer you. You would still have what you call free will.

"I don't want your power. I'm not wise or good enough to be a god. All I can do is try to be the best human being I can!"

You could do great good.

"I could also do great harm, even without meaning to!"

You only wish to be what you are.

"Yes!"

Then you must be shown what you are.

"What do you mean?"

There was no answer and nothing behind her. Katerina cautiously reached out with her foot to try walking on the frozen liquid. But as her tennis shoe neared its surface the fluid suddenly bubbled and melted, once again blocking her path.

Katerina scowled, wondering what to do next and why the aliens were treating her this way. Were they were trying to help humanity through her—or destroy it? And as powerful as they were, why didn't they just assist or exterminate the human race themselves without all these tricks?

She sighed. There was more going on than she could figure out for now. Best to deal with one problem at a time.

The liquid in the pool was placid again. Though it looked like water, it could be acid or something equally dangerous. Perhaps the aliens were conducting an intelligence test, with her in the role of white mouse in a maze. If so, there must be some way she could safely cross this barrier—if she could figure out what it was. This liquid might be an illusion like the fire she'd confronted earlier. On the other hand, the aliens could be testing her to see if she was smart enough to realize that this time it was a real threat.

Katerina squatted down and searched through her bag of medical supplies, thinking aloud, "There's nothing I could use to create a makeshift bridge. Even if the fluid itself isn't dangerous, it'd have to be buoyant enough for me to swim or float across it if the pool is deep."

The young cosmonaut frowned at the medkit and pile of bandages, splints, tape, and other first-aid supplies she'd placed on the floor. The only items that seemed promising were a glass pipette and the empty plastic vials identical to the ones she'd used to collect ocean water samples earlier today.

Careful not to let any touch her skin or clothes, Katerina drew up several milliliters of fluid from the pool into the pipette, then she emptied it into a vial. In the dim light the clear odorless liquid looked like water. It didn't feel too hot or cold through the vial's walls. The fact that it hadn't melted the glass pipette or plastic vial was an encouraging but inconclusive indication it wasn't too corrosive. Tiny drops of the fluid placed sequentially on small strips of paper tape, gauze, an alcohol pad, a wooden tongue depressor, and the back of one of her fingernails produced no noticeable reaction.

After rubbing a small drop of the fluid harmlessly between her thumb and index finger, Katerina knelt and unclasped the gold chain around her neck. She placed the chain on the floor, refastened it, and tied one end of a roll of five centimeter-wide white gauze to the loop formed by the closed chain. After walking to the edge of the pool, she held the heavy golden cross, still attached to her chain like the hook on an ice fisher's line, over the liquid. Then she slowly played out the length of gauze attached to the chain, lowering the cross at the far end of the chain's loop into the pool.

The cross and chain had barely disappeared into the fluid when she felt the gauze strip slacken in her hand. She bobbed her line up and down a little to satisfy herself the cross was striking the bottom of the pool about half a meter below the surface.

Katerina retrieved her chain and cross from the liquid and examined them carefully. Satisfied they were undamaged, she dried them with the gauze and reattached the chain and cross around her neck. As she put her supplies back into the medical bag, she chuckled. Her grandmother in Russia had sent the three-barred golden cross to Katerina to help protect her on this alien world. The cross really had helped keep her safe during these trials by fire and water the aliens had set for her.

Then it dawned on her that perhaps the aliens had plucked some Mozart from her mind. They might have been testing her character by offering her unlimited power, to see if she had the moral strength to refuse it. Her golden cross had protected her just as well as a magic flute would have done.

Katerina slowly lowered her legs into the knee-deep liquid, wading carefully through it in case part of the pool was deeper. As she stepped onto the floor at the far end of the corridor she wondered if there were more trials ahead—and more importantly, where her dear Tamino was.

Martin frowned at the long pool of fluid in front of him. He didn't expect and didn't receive an answer to his questions, "Are you going to part it for me? Or am I supposed to walk on it?"

He shone his flashlight around the dimly lit area. For an instant, from the corner of his eye he thought he saw a second entrance into this corridor near the one where he'd just emerged. But when he looked at the area on the metal wall directly, it appeared as solid as everywhere else.

Martin turned his attention back to the pool blocking his path. He grunted, "If Katerina were here, she'd figure out a way to test if this liquid is dangerous and how deep it is. I bet she'd do something so ingenuous with whatever's in her medical bag that it would've impressed MacGyver. Let's see what I can do."

He hefted the video camera in his hand. "This thing has ultrasonic and infrared autofocus systems. Maybe I can measure the distance to the bottom of the pool using the camera like an active sonar device. I could put it right above the surface of the fluid and let the camera autofocus on the bottom of the pool. When I switch to manual focus the distance the camera is focusing on should appear on the display screen. Might work—"

But as he stepped to the edge of the pool his flashlight beam caught something on the other side that stopped his experiment. Martin stuck one boot cautiously into the pool, then the second. Stepping carefully through the water, he reached the other side and looked down at the wet footprints leading upwards along this length of the corridor.

Unless the aliens wore tennis shoes, Katerina must be up ahead! His wet boots squeaked excitedly as he rushed to find her.

Martin poked his head through the meter-wide square opening in the top of the pyramid. The late afternoon sunlight hurt his eyes as he reemerged into the open air. He clutched the video camera with his left hand while his right grasped one of the metal bars lining a side of the long vertical shaft he'd just climbed. The bars were as thick as a prison cell's and as long as his forearm. They extended ten centimeters out from the wall of the shaft and were spaced like the rungs of a ladder.

Pulling himself higher through the opening, Martin laid the video camera on the smooth gray metal that stretched horizontally like a floor across the top of the pyramid. Reaching inside a pocket on his shorts, he extracted his flashlight and laid it beside the camera. Then, still squinting in the sunlight, Martin noticed a shadow dancing gracefully along the surrounding shiny flat surface.

"Katerina!"

As he finished hoisting himself from the opening and stood atop the pyramid she ran back and flung herself into his arms. Time stood still as they pressed their lips and bodies together in a passionate reunion whose description would've filled pages of purple prose in a romance novel.

Weaving gently together in a tight lingering embrace, Martin whispered in her ear, "I was afraid I'd lost you. I'd go crazy if that happened."

Katerina brushed her tears across his cheek. "You'll never lose me, Martin. Even if I died I'd wait for you in heaven."

Martin scowled. "Don't talk about dying! You're not going to die!"

Katerina stepped back from him. "Don't be angry."

Her crewmate spat, "Darn right I'm angry! When we got separated I thought something terrible happened to you. All those stories about aliens abducting humans didn't seem so ridiculous anymore. I kept imagining you lying on a table unable to move while some slobbering bug-eyed monster from a pulp magazine's cover did weird medical experiments on your scantily clad body.

"I don't know why the aliens are messing with our minds and playing games with us, and right now I don't care. All I want is to get you down from here and make sure you stay safe!"

Martin trod cautiously to the nearby edge of the pyramid. His gaze absorbed a vast vista of rolling mounds and shallow valleys spreading out like a painted desert around them. A nauseating wave of vertigo rocked him as he peered toward the hard unyielding ground far below.

A strong gust of wind against his back shoved him closer to the beckoning metal precipice at his feet. He twisted dizzily away and stumbled back several meters to where Katerina watched him with growing alarm. Wiping sweat from his face and forcing himself to breathe slower, he surveyed his surroundings again.

The top of the pyramid was a square about one hundred meters on each side. Its level surface seemed solid except for the solitary opening, centered about five meters from the pyramid's nearest edge, where they'd both emerged.

Martin frowned. "Why are those things there?"

He pointed toward the evenly spaced metal rungs jutting up in a straight row along the platform they stood on.

Katerina peered down through the opening, back into the depths of the vertical shaft below. She said, "Those bars look identical to the ones we used to climb up here. See how they line the side of the shaft farthest from the edge of the pyramid, then continue across the surface here out towards the other side?"

"I can see that, but what are they for?"

"Maybe the aliens put them there for us to grab hold to if the wind gets too strong, so we won't be blown off the pyramid."

Martin shivered. "We definitely don't want to go over the edge. It's a long way to the ground, and the sides of the pyramid are way too steep to slide down safely. Looks like the only way to get off this thing is to retrace our steps and hope the aliens have reopened the entrance. Or we could look for another opening up here that leads down to a different exit."

Katerina stepped slowly away from him, following the line of metal rungs until it ended abruptly at the center of the plateau that held them prisoners. She continued walking straight ahead towards the other side of the square, looking down intensely at its featureless sheen. "The aliens must have led us up here for a reason, Martin. Maybe they've written a message somewhere on the surface here, like they did on that artifact we explored the day we landed."

Martin started to trot toward her, but stumbled as his boot slipped. He moved toward her more carefully, shouting, "Don't get too close to the edge, this metal is as slick as a playground slide."

Katerina stopped about four meters from the rim and called back to him, "You look over there. Let me know if you find any writing."

"Okay. But I don't see why, if the aliens want to tell us something, they just don't come and say it in person."

Katerina looked up. "Didn't the aliens speak to you when we were inside the pyramid?"

"Of course not."

Martin turned around and stared at her. "Are you implying they did talk to you?"

"Yes. They said—"

Suddenly the metal beneath their feet began to tremble. The whole pyramid shuddered with a low rumble that grew steadily louder like a speeding train bearing down on them. Martin felt the same sickening dread as when the New Madrid fault triggered its worst earthquake in over two centuries while he was at college in St. Louis.

His body wobbled and fought to stay upright as the spot he stood on began tilting gradually downward like the lowering end of a seesaw. The edge of the pyramid farthest from him arced slowly skyward as its whole top surface slanted ever steeper, like someone raising the bed of an enormous dump truck. It was as if gigantic hands had dug their fingers beneath the base of the pyramid on the side nearest the sole opening in its top. Little by little they were lifting and tipping the whole structure—making the pyramid lean more and more as if they meant to topple it over and crush the tiny scampering creatures on top of it.

Martin watched spellbound as the opening in the pyramid's top rose into view far away across a slippery "floor" that grew ever steeper. His brain finally registered that if the surface slanted much more he'd go sliding and tumbling down to and over the lower edge of the pyramid.

As his eyes darted desperately around for a way out of danger, Martin glimpsed the metal rungs embedded into the rising surface. Instantly he began sprinting straight ahead up an ever-increasing slope toward the closest rung some twenty-five meters away. It was like trying to run up the hill behind the family farmhouse after a winter ice storm. His boots fought for traction as he leaned forward, trying to keep his balance—

Halfway to his goal Martin stopped—paralyzed by a horrifying realization. He turned around and screamed, "Katerina!"

She was closing fast on him, her tennis shoes glancing off the slippery gray metal like an ice skater's blades. As she bounded toward him Katerina yelled, "Keep going, Martin, don't stop!"

He hesitated—then obeyed. The surface was canting so much now he had to crouch, his fingers brushing against its cold metal for a handhold that wasn't there. He barely dodged the flashlight and video camera that skittered past him like miniature boulders before they zoomed over the edge of the pyramid. Despite straining every muscle he was slowing down, his forward acceleration checked and feet slipping.

With a last desperate lunge before the rumbling surface became too steep to stand on, his right hand stretched forward and grasped the bottommost rung of the row of metal rungs that now extended like a ladder toward the opening high above him. As his left hand joined it the top of the pyramid gave one last shudder—and stopped rising, sloping at an angle about twenty degrees from vertical.

Martin's body stretched belly down against the silent metal surface, his arms extended and grasping the rung in its center as if it were a trapeze bar. He struggled to twist his head to look downward, afraid of what he'd see—

Suddenly he felt a heavy weight tugging on his right ankle, and then another hand grabbed his left foot. As he tried to ease the terrible tension in his straining shoulders Martin winced as fingernails dug into his right calf and clawed away its coarse hairs. Reflexively he reached down and shouted, "Grab my hand!"

"I can't reach it!"

He waited as many agonizing seconds as he could to feel Katerina's grasp, then his left hand's loosening grip forced him to bring his right arm back to the rung. He yelled, "Try pulling yourself up again!"

The pain was even worse this time as he felt her palms squeezing then slipping off the bare sweating skin of his legs. If only he were wearing pants instead of shorts—

"I can't do it, Martin!"

His eyes darted up toward the line of metal rungs stretching toward the opening far above them. If he could chin himself up to grab the next couple rungs above him, Katerina could seize the one that now tenuously supported both of them. Freed of her extra weight around his ankles, he could raise his legs and use that lowest rung to support his feet. Then it'd be easy to reach back down and pull her up.

Martin's arm muscles contracted in rippling spasms as his body jerked centimeters upwards toward safety—then slid back down to its original outstretched position along the precariously inclined surface. His mind and heart tried to will more strength into cramped weakening hands that barely managed to maintain their grip, fighting to keep Katerina and him from sliding down and over the edge of the pyramid. At the other end of his tortured body Martin felt a pair of outstretched arms gripping his ankles. He heard a surprisingly calm voice just below his feet murmur,

"This won't work, Martin. I'm dragging you down."

He shouted back, "I've got to do it! I've got to save you!"

Martin grit his teeth and forced his body upward with his last reserves of strength. Suddenly the metal bar he clung to jerked past his chin and upper chest. His right hand whipped up and grasped the next higher rung. Another heartbeat and his left hand held it too, then he swiftly repeated the process for the rung just above it. As he raised his left knee to the lowest rung for support he started to shout to Katerina to grab hold of that rung—and then realized with sickening horror why he'd succeeded in raising himself.

He looked down in time to see her tumbling body fly over the edge of the pyramid.

Katerina's arms and legs skidded across the slick metal surface, leaving scrapes and bruises there wasn't time to feel as she felt herself propelled ever faster toward the precipice below. Suddenly she was in free fall, rocketing away from the side of the tilted pyramid toward the stony ground far beneath her.

Time seemed to slow as she imagined herself on one of the jumps she'd made from high-flying aircraft during her cosmonaut training. She willed the sudden cramping in her stomach away, wheeled into a prone position with limbs spread outward to increase air resistance, and extended her neck away from the onrushing Martian surface. Her hand reflexively reached for the ripcord of a nonexistent parachute.

There wasn't time for her mind to comprehend the pain and probable death only seconds away. Her brain defensibly pretended that this was a textbook problem on how to survive a fall. She remembered that relaxing her muscles and exhaling just before impact might reduce injury. *Try not to hit your head or back, turn so you hit on your side. Cracked ribs and a broken arm aren't as bad as a skull fracture or spinal injury.*

Maybe the medical bag still dangling from its strap around her left shoulder could cushion her fall. And because the aliens had raised Mars' gravity to only 91% of Earth's, perhaps a fall from this height might be survivable—

The Martian wind whistling by her ears stopped. Time slowed nearly to a standstill around her as she hung suspended in space, like a fly in amber.

Explain why you deliberately let go of your companion.

Katerina sensed rather than saw the hazy lights nearby trailing her descent.

"I had to. My weight was pulling him down. If I hadn't let go, in another moment we both would've fallen."

Explain how you benefit by preventing his injury while hastening yours.

"I love him. Even if I don't survive, he will."

You will not survive this fall on your own.

Katerina closed her eyes. "I know."

You will survive if you accept our gift. It is easy to manipulate matter, energy, and gravity. We can show you how.

"Why are you doing this? You deliberately made the top of the pyramid tilt and put us in danger—just so you could offer me power I don't want and no human being should have! This must be some kind of test. But what are you testing?"

If you knew what we were testing, it would no longer be a test.

"Then I'll have to guess. You want to find out if we humans want to become as powerful as God, though we don't and never will completely know the difference between good and evil. You're trying to tempt me to receive more knowledge all at once than I could possibly handle. I can't take the chance that even with the best intentions I might misuse that power and do wrong. I'm hoping that what you're really testing is my character—my strength to *refuse* your gift, even at the cost of my own life.

"And I'm praying that you really don't wish me harm and won't let Martin or me die."

There was no answer. Suddenly the wind was shrieking against her face again and the ground was rocketing up toward her...

Martin stared downward where Katerina had disappeared, frozen like Lot's wife looking back at a scene of unimaginable horror. He didn't feel the pain from his knees digging into the lowermost metal rung as he strained to hear the distant wet thud of a body striking the ground. From the stillness and solitude of his shadowed perch atop the pyramid, he felt that whatever future and purpose his life had were dead.

Another instant and he was climbing frantically up the metal rungs to the faraway opening in the pyramid's top. Perhaps she'd merely slid down the side of the pyramid and was sitting on the ground nursing only scrapes and bruises that'd heal soon. Maybe the aliens only meant to scare both of them, like a *Mercury Theatre on the Air* Halloween prank, and had rescued her before she was harmed. Whatever happened, she needed him and he had to find her!

As Martin scrambled into the opening the vast alien structure rumbled again and gradually lowered itself back toward its original upright position. The shaft beyond the opening, not far from horizontal when he'd reached it, now slowly resumed its original vertical orientation as the top of the pyramid became level once more. He didn't wait for the pyramid's base to settle firmly back on the ground again before twisting and scurrying down the shaft and into the interior. As he retraced his steps downward through the pyramid's once-gloomy jagged corridors, the walls around him now shone with a soft luminescence that guided his path.

This time there were no alien-contrived distractions of fire or water to restrain his flight. When he reached the chamber they'd first entered Martin shouted in relief when his lingering fear that it was still sealed from the outside world proved wrong. As he raced out through the reopened entrance his boots kicked up tiny dust storms in the Martian soil, his eyes scanning frantically for Katerina. The rover still sat where they'd parked it an eternity ago—but there was no sign of her.

She *had* to be by one of the pyramid's other sides. He dashed to his right, imagining Katerina turning the corner before he reached it and running laughing into his arms—

A small bundle of flesh and torn clothing lay still within its own shallow impact crater near one side of the pyramid. As he neared the silent broken mass of limbs and tissue Martin flashed back to when he was twelve years old and found another body sprawled by the side of a busy road. He'd stupidly thought Fred, the copper-colored dachshund who'd been his best friend and companion for most of his childhood, was asleep—until he'd seen the flies and blood.

Katerina lay motionless on her back with her eyes closed, as if she too were only sleeping. Strands of long auburn hair draped her chest like a shroud. Her face and head showed no sign of injury. But her swollen upper left arm was bent at an unnatural angle and there was blood on her thin plaid shirt.

Trembling with terror as he knelt beside her, Martin heard words from old CPR training bubbling back into his brain. *Check responsiveness. She may have injured her neck so open her airway with a jaw thrust. Check breathing and circulation.*

Martin quickly placed his ear near her mouth. Yes, he could feel and hear her breathing! Her breaths were shallow and the carotid pulse he palpated was weak, but she was still alive!

Katerina moaned and moved all her arms and legs weakly. He yelled, "Lay still! I'm going to help you!"

Those feeble motions of her limbs told him that she might not have broken her neck or back. But she should still have a cervical collar and backboard to keep her spine protected—and he had neither of them. All he could do was hope that they weren't really needed.

The mandatory medical training he'd received from physicians and paramedics kicked in again. He checked Katerina visually from head to foot. Her pupils were equal and there wasn't any blood oozing from ears, nose, or mouth. Besides the obvious fracture of her left arm, all he could see were scattered scrapes and bruises. Even the area on her lower left chest where blood had seeped onto her shirt showed only nasty-looking abrasions, although he suspected several ribs were fractured. He didn't have a stethoscope, but pressing his ear to both sides of her chest convinced him her breath sounds were normal, without an obvious pneumothorax.

The bag she'd been carrying lay nearby. It had burst open and the medical supplies it once contained lay scattered on the ground. Martin scooped up packs of sterile sponges and rolls of gauze, iodine swabs and alcohol pads, and material for a moldable splint. He rapidly applied them to Katerina's worst injuries, immobilizing her injured left arm with the splint and speaking soothingly to her as she writhed weakly. For a moment he considered bending the flexible splint material into a loose cervical collar, but decided not to. If he didn't do it right, his impromptu device might choke her.

There was a prepackaged syringe of meperidine in the small medkit. Katerina only moaned when he asked how much she was hurting, but what he had to do next would cause her unavoidable pain. He injected the painkiller into her upper right arm, then ran to the rover and swiftly returned with it. There was no room in the rear of the vehicle to lay her flat. As gently as possible he lifted her up, cradled in his arms like a baby, and set her in the passenger seat.

Martin grabbed the mylar blanket from the back of the rover and draped it over her torso and lower body, trying to keep her warm. Then he quickly fastened her harness, using it to press her left forearm against her chest to keep the broken upper limb from moving. Finally he wrapped and tied a roll of gauze around her forehead and the headrest of her seat to keep her neck stabilized as best he could for the long ride back to the habitation module.

He ignored the portable blood pressure machine in the back of the rover. Even if she was bleeding internally and her blood pressure was low, the IV fluids and other items he needed to treat her were all back at the module.

Martin winced every time the rover dipped and bounced over the uneven ground, glancing at Katerina to see if it made her pain worse. She still answered all his questions with silence or moans as he raced towards the module. And there was no point checking to see if the radio was working again. Even if he could contact Mission Control, there wasn't anything the doctors there could tell him to do right now that he hadn't done already.

That nightmarish drive ended in the twilight of a reddish sunset. Martin carefully extricated Katerina from the vehicle and carried her to the module's science lab. He gently placed her on their diagnostic table and unpacked the most sophisticated medical equipment in twenty-five million kilometers. The pulse oximeter he clipped to her finger showed her heart rate was fast, but oxygen saturation was normal.

Katerina groaned as he inserted an IV near her right wrist. He started a liter bag of normal saline flowing and then wrapped the cuff of an automatic blood pressure monitor around her upper right arm. The first reading on its digital display was 93/60 mmHg—low, but not dangerously so. The fluid entering her vein should raise it.

It was time to try getting more advice. He operated a nearby transceiver and gave the quickest summary he could of how Katerina was injured. During the minutes he waited for a reply, Martin unclasped the gold chain and cross from around her neck. If she'd been more conscious she would have protested his violating her modesty by removing her clothes. He certainly didn't *want* to glimpse her nakedness for the first time under these circumstances—but he had to do it to check for any more injuries.

With her body now covered only by two white sheets too thin to interfere with the tests she needed, Martin placed EKG patches on her chest and did a quick series of digital x-rays. As the blood pressure cuff inflated and deflated periodically, he watched anxiously as the readings on the monitor drifted gradually downward.

While he worked Martin wiped moisture from his eyes. He glanced at the flat colorful icons Katerina had fastened to the door of the small locker where she stored her books and personal items. One icon depicted a smiling young woman who resembled Katerina dressed in ancient garb, her head framed by a golden nimbus. He remembered what she'd said the Cyrillic letters on the icon spelled.

St. Catherine of Alexandria. Virgin and Martyr.

As he prepared the portable ultrasound system, a voice from Earth resounded in the lab.

"Stone here. We received your report. Send us a continuous telemetry feed of all of Katerina's readings, especially her blood pressure and heart rate. Then transmit any x-rays you've done. If you haven't performed one yet, do a FAST scan. When you can, give us video on her, measure her hematocrit, and insert a Foley catheter."

Martin's hands shook as he obeyed those orders. It was hard to keep the blunt transducer steady as he scanned Katerina's heart, abdomen, and pelvis. The fears flooding his mind made it difficult to perform the Focused Abdominal Sonography for Trauma study, much less interpret the shifting images on the ultrasound system's screen. But the experts back home receiving the images would know what they meant.

The blood pressure monitor read a dangerous 80/50 mmHg as he got another liter of normal saline ready to give her. He dropped the plastic bag of fluid as Dr. Stone's voice returned. "Our radiologists and trauma surgeons reviewed the tests you did. The x-rays show fractures of several lower left ribs and the shaft of her left humerus. Those injuries aren't life-threatening.

"We can't tell for sure if she has intracranial bleeding since you don't have a CT scanner. Unfortunately, the ultrasound showed a large amount of free fluid in both upper quadrants of her abdomen. That indicates she's seriously injured her spleen and possibly her liver, and she's bleeding into the abdomen."

Martin screamed, "What can I do about that?"

Dr. Stone seemed to answer that question, although the physician wouldn't hear it for over another minute. "Normally under these circumstances a surgeon would do a laparotomy—an operation you aren't trained to do. For now make sure her legs are elevated and start giving her the stock of artificial blood you have. Since you both have the same blood type, as a last resort you could transfuse her with a liter of your own blood."

Martin shouted, "What if that doesn't work? I love her! We have our whole lives ahead of us, children to have and raise, a future to build! There must be something I can do to save her!"

Long before he could answer those latest words, Stone said softly, "But everything you do may not be enough. You must prepare for the worst."

Martin tenderly touched the pale cool cheek of the most important person to him on this or any world. Only her closed eyelids flickered in response to his caress. He placed Katerina's cross back on her chest, then rushed to pierce her left wrist with another IV and give her every last drop of blood he could.

When the reply to Martin's last words to Earth finally arrived, no one heard the heartfelt agony cracking through Stone's calm professional voice as the cardiologist whispered, "I'm sorry. We're all sorry it happened."

Martin frantically squeezed the IV bags to pump more blood and fluids into Katerina, put an oxygen mask over her face, and rehearsed the CPR protocol again in his mind. But as the blood pressure, heart rate, and oxygen saturation readings drifted ever lower, a numbing realization clamped around his heart like a fist. Whatever he did wouldn't change one simple fact.

Katerina was dying.

You are dying.

The alien voice came from a great distance, muffled by what seemed like pillows pressed over her face. It was getting harder to breathe in her nightmare, but the pain in her left arm and side was fading away.

You do not have to die. It is easy to manipulate matter, energy, gravity, and time. We can show you how. You can use this knowledge to heal yourself.

Katerina tried to ignore the voice. In front of her she saw a great light at the end of a long corridor. It was like, or perhaps because of, what she'd read about in other people's descriptions of near-death experiences. Soon she'd know whether it was a portal to heaven—or merely the last tiny sparks generated by brain cells starved for oxygen before oblivion enfolded her.

The light beckoned her. Her faith should have prepared her for this moment and given her peace. But other thoughts mocked and tempted her. Perhaps it was ignorance or obstinacy that that made her reject a real and tangible good—her very life—for an abstract principle. Was she really unworthy to wield the power the aliens offered? Or did her "humility" mask a sinful pride in her own boastful "goodness"? What if no person or deity *cared* if she became a martyr?

If she resisted this last temptation, she would never make love with Martin and bear their children, never explore the mysteries of Creation again, never feel any of the simple human pleasures each day brought. Was the tiny risk she might misuse a godlike power really worth losing all that?

There were no certain answers to those questions. In these last moments remaining to her, she could only decide what seemed right based on everything she'd ever seen, thought, and felt over her entire life. Without knowing whether it was right or wrong, she had to make one last act of faith. And it had to be based on a love that transcended only her own good.

Though you are dying, you still will not accept our gift.

Katerina's last words were the hardest she ever thought or spoke in her life.

"No, I won't accept it."

Then we must find another way.

The science lab was empty now except for the body lying on the diagnostic table. The room's smothering darkness was illuminated only by tiny multicolored lights glowing softly from the equipment lining its walls. Nothing stirred in the sepulchral silence.

The sheets covering the body fluttered, as if they were disturbed by a faint breeze. A hand reached up and weakly grasped the golden cross hanging from a chain around its owner's neck and lying on its chest. Then the figure slowly sat up and dangled slim legs over the side of the table. An outstretched fingertip touched a switch, and soft fluorescent light bathed the surroundings in a pale radiance.

Reflexively wrapping the white sheets around itself for modesty, the room's sole occupant studied the ragged bloody clothes, tennis shoes, and arm splint on the floor. Slender fingers brushed aside the IV tubing dangling from empty plastic bags hung on short silvery poles. Two bare feet padded softly on the metal floor, slowly wending their way out through the openings inside the dimly lit habitation module.

There was someone wearing a blood-red baseball cap standing in the module's open entrance. His face and back were turned away from her, and he seemed to be staring out into the black night. As she approached, without turning around he whispered, "How does it feel to rise from the dead?"

"The aliens. They healed me."

The man said nothing.

"I remember hitting the ground, and the terrible pain in my arm and side. It was like I dreamed you brought me back here, put IVs in me, and did those tests. I thought I heard Dr. Stone's voice—and then the aliens spoke to me."

Katerina let the sheet covering her upper body fall to the floor. "Look at me, Martin! There's not a scrape or bruise on me! Not even puncture wounds from where you put in the IVs! It's like I have a new body!"

"No. Except for your memories, it's the same body you had yesterday morning, before we went on our trip."

Katerina's grip on her cross tightened. She picked up the sheet from the floor and draped it over her torso again.

Martin turned around and faced her. His expression as he spoke seemed weary. "The aliens can read our thoughts. It's easy for them to manipulate matter, energy, gravity, and time."

Katerina stepped back from him. "When did they tell you that?"

"Just before they showed me how to do it."

Martin snorted. "I knew you'd look at me like that. You don't understand yet that accepting their gift was the only way I could save you. Nothing I could have done on my own, nothing Stone or the others at Mission Control told me would've kept you from dying!"

"You could have prayed for me, Martin."

His sarcastic laughter ricocheted through the darkness. "Dropping to my knees and saying 'Our Fathers' and 'Hail Marys' wouldn't have brought you back to life. I tried that once twenty years ago, and I'll never do it again!"

"No, praying wouldn't have saved my life. But praying I had the strength to die well, without sinning, might have helped me—and you."

Martin's lips curled. "Unlike you, I don't know what happens after we die. But I do know *this* life is worth living—and I don't need that pitiless God you believe in to perform a miracle for me anymore! I can make my own miracles now!"

He moved toward her—then stopped as she shrank farther away from him. "Don't be afraid. I'm not a megalomaniac. I don't want to rule the Earth. The only miracle I really want to do is the one I've already done—to 'resurrect' you."

His face tried twisting into a goofy grin. "I'm still the same simple farm boy who loves you."

Tears trickled down Katerina's cheeks like holy water, anointing the cross she held close to her lips. "No, Martin, you aren't. And unless God grants *me* a miracle, you never will be again."

The dark figure in the module's open entrance turned and walked out into the night. Katerina slumped to her knees, her hands clutching the cross tighter as she tried to pray through her sobs.

Martin trod through the murky blackness, his path illuminated only by starlight filtering through tattered wispy clouds. The night was too dark for human eyes to see the ground he strode on. But it was easy to adjust his visual spectrum deeper into the infrared and let the heat from the rocks and soil, glowing like hellfire, guide his footsteps.

He didn't bother to read Katerina's thoughts. There was no point invading her privacy, especially when he could guess what she was thinking. Eventually she'd get over her silly streak of superstition and be grateful to him for saving her life. He could use his new knowledge and power to do nice things for her. She couldn't object to him performing *little* miracles—could she?

As he walked deeper into the ebony landscape, he sneered. Heck, if anybody knew how to handle what he could do now, he was the one. He'd read all his life about characters who weren't corrupted by having superhuman powers. Superman, Green Lantern, and Dr. Manhattan never did that—unless they were victims of bad writing. Slans, Baldies—they didn't misuse their special talents.

And, unlike the idiotic "hero" in that story by Wells, he was smart enough to avoid stupid mistakes when working miracles. Besides, even if Katerina was too upset to realize it, he was still the same down-to-earth Midwesterner he'd always been. *He* wasn't going to become a Missouri Mule—even if he did have the power now to rule the Galaxy.

Immersed in his thoughts, he suddenly realized he'd wandered into the field they'd visited yesterday morning. His enhanced vision saw corn, wheat, and green bean bushes swaying gently in colors no human being had ever experienced. Careful not to disturb those plants in their slumber, he walked over to where a few late-growing radish leaves still poked up from the ground.

Martin pulled up one of the radish plants, scraped mud away from it, and examined its scarlet-and-alabaster root. His gaze penetrated into its very atoms, analyzing it far more thoroughly than the crude equipment back at the habitation module could.

He snorted. It was a plain radish, with the normal amount of water, cellulose, and other ingredients in its cells. Stone and all those other "experts" back home meant well, but they'd been stupid to tell him he shouldn't eat his own crops.

Martin reached down with his free hand and scooped up some Martian soil. As he stared at it nearly all the dirt flew from his palm, leaving a small pinch of sodium chloride behind. He sprinkled the salt on the radish and took a bite. Its flesh was crunchy and tangy—a delicious taste of home.

Suddenly he smirked, realizing what he'd done. He was standing in the "Garden of Eden" and he'd just taken a bite of the "forbidden root"!

Something moved behind him. He turned around, holding the half-eaten radish by its leaves, like a century-old Hollywood jungle movie's stereotype of a headhunter holding his victim's shrunken head by its hair.

"Want a bite, Katerina?"

She'd put on the blue jumpsuit she'd worn when they landed on Mars.

Her hazel eyes glowed softly like distant stars as she looked silently back at him.

Martin said, "If you're not fasting anymore, maybe you'd like something different to eat."

Nearby, several stubby cornstalks shot upward like a movie made with time-lapse photography. Their sides swiftly bulged with green tawny-tasseled ears.

He continued, "It's easy to change the amount and location of energy. I can heat up the ears if you'd like some corn on the cob. Or, since it's nearly time for breakfast, I could turn them into cornflakes for you."

Her wordless gaze made him uneasy. "I could listen to what you're thinking, but I won't. I won't misuse my power, I'll only use it to do good things! Say you believe in me!"

For a moment a brilliant blue dot peeked through the clouds, shining like a shard of lapis lazuli. Martin pointed at it and said, "Think of all the people there who are suffering because of violence and natural disasters. Millions more are sick or dying. I can protect the innocent, end disease and death, even make the old young again!

"Yes, I know we'll have to think through the consequences of doing that first. There'd be all sorts of social, economic, and political repercussions if I did it right away. But we're both clever enough and care enough about what happens to humanity to solve every problem that comes up."

Katerina replied, "No, Martin. Neither of us, not even the whole human race is smart enough or good enough to handle that much power all at once. Even with the best intentions you could cause more tragedy on Earth than we already have. I gave my life rather than accept the aliens' 'gift,' because I wasn't sure I could resist the temptation to remake the world in my own image. I'll do whatever I must to prevent you from remaking it in yours.

"You're a good man, Martin. But not even the best man is good enough to be a god."

His finger stabbed at the golden cross hanging from her neck. "I thought you believed someone could save the human race by being both man and god."

"He was God and became man. Not the other way around. That makes all the difference."

Martin scowled. "There's no point arguing. Let's both cool off for now. We can decide what to do later."

"I'm sorry, Martin. I'm afraid I can't do that."

He snickered. At least one of the classic SF movies he'd shown Katerina during their flight to Mars had made an impression on her. "And how are you going to keep the pod bay doors closed from *me*?"

When she didn't answer, he turned away and looked out over the barren plain. He pictured it lush and viridescent with vast fields of crops—dwarfing the tiny garden they'd slowly and laboriously planted themselves. Perhaps Mars could be the breadbasket for a new, immortal human race—

Then he sensed it—an alien presence nearby. He looked around for the hazy scintillating lights—listening for the aliens to speak to him a third time.

He saw and heard nothing. Then he realized where his impression of an alien presence was coming from.

It came from Katerina.

Martin stared open-mouthed as the cornstalks whose growth he'd accelerated shrunk back to their original size. An alien voice that sounded like Katerina's murmured, "The only way to stop you was to become as powerful as you. And God forgive me if I've made the wrong choice!"

As the horizon slowly brightened, a cold misty rain began to fall. It splattered against two lonely figures standing far apart on a rusty plain no longer home to anything merely human. Both had survived to gaze at another wondrous, mystical Martian dawn.

But the eyes that looked out over this dawn were no longer innocent.

Wilderness Were Paradise Enow

Ah Love! could thou and I with Fate conspire
To grasp this sorry Scheme of Things entire,
Would not we shatter it to bits—and then
Re-mould it nearer to the Heart's Desire!

Edward FitzGerald, *The Rubaiyat of Omar Khayyam*

"Do you think the aliens killed them?"

Dr. Alexander Stone, NASA's head of space medicine, didn't look at the woman questioning him. The former astronaut stared instead at the three huge screens in front of them at the Mission Control Center in Houston. He focused on the screens' words, numbers, and computer graphics showing the data feed from Zubrin Base—as if trying to use those displays like a telescope to see what was happening on Mars.

Finally the physician turned toward her and replied, "We don't know if Slayton is still alive. It's been over fourteen hours since his last message, but he didn't seem to be in immediate danger then. However, based on the last vital signs and other telemetry information he transmitted on Savitskaya's condition, my medical staff and our counterparts at the Russian Space Agency agree she must be dead by now. The injuries she sustained when the two of them explored the aliens' artifact were too severe for her to survive much longer."

Nancy Kelley, flight director for the project, sighed. "That means it's time to notify Washington and the next of kin, then face the media. Challenger, Columbia, the ISS incident—this is the type of press conference I hoped I'd never have to give. It's been nearly sixteen years since anyone's died from being in space. I know our luck had to run out sometime. But it still hurts."

The flight director briefly removed her wire frame glasses and wiped moisture from her eyes. Although she was only a decade younger than Stone, her face seemed to sag to his age and beyond as she continued, "Everybody, especially Martin and Katerina, knew this first flight to Mars was the most dangerous space mission ever attempted. The biggest wild card was what the aliens would do. After all the good they've done by terraforming Mars and moving the planet closer to the Earth, we gambled they wouldn't turn hostile once our two people landed.

"Looks like we lost our gamble."

Kelley gazed sadly at the cardiologist. "This must be hard on you too. How are you holding up?"

Stone shrugged.

Kelley left to speak with several flight controllers seated at nearby consoles. Stone rubbed his palm over the back of his bristly gray hair and peered again at the silent screens. These last tense hours made him feel every second of his sixty years.

After his great failure on the International Space Station back in late 2020, he'd managed to keep all the astronauts under his care safe and healthy—until now. Crews on the last missions to the ISS, later ones to its successors, and flights to the growing lunar base had experienced only minor medical problems. There'd been no serious injuries or fatalities caused by human carelessness in space—a track record he hoped was at least partly due to lessons learned from his last, tragic journey into orbit nearly sixteen years ago.

And now the person whose success his well-concealed soft sentimental side cared about most was dead—killed on her thirty-third birthday. Katerina was several months younger than Martin and only five years older than his own daughter. Stone remembered that sweet, talented cosmonaut sitting beside her fiancé in the health classes he'd given them before their trip to Mars. He'd intentionally projected himself as a stern father figure to those two young people—trying to teach them right from wrong based on his own mistakes and keep them safe.

When the Russians discovered Katerina and Martin had become engaged and wanted to remove her from the mission, he'd talked them into keeping her. Yes, he'd honestly believed she was the best choice for this project and deserved to go to Mars. But no one else had to know that he was trying to help not just Katerina but himself too. She was his secret surrogate for another young woman he'd once known—a cosmonaut and colleague whose career and *life* he'd destroyed without wanting or meaning to. He'd been forced to choose between his responsibility as a physician to everyone who would ever travel in space and shattering only a single person's dream.

Did it hurt anyone besides him if he hoped Katerina's success might make up a little for what he'd done?

Now the cardiologist knew the answer to that question. History had repeated itself and he was responsible for destroying another life—

Stone noticed a growing commotion among the other personnel crowding the spacious control room. One screen in the front of the room showed an interference pattern that resolved into a picture transmitted from the sole human dwelling on Mars.

A video camera within the habitation module centered on a sight his training and experience as a physician refused to believe. If what he saw wasn't an antemortem recording, it was a medical miracle.

The slim attractive woman on the screen transmitting from over twenty-five million kilometers away had long auburn hair and hazel eyes. "Zubrin Base here. Katerina Savitskaya speaking. Martin and I are both alive. I cannot provide you now with more details about our situation. Do not, I repeat, do *not* try to contact us. I will send you an update when and if I can. End of transmission."

Stone stared at the screen where Katerina's image had just disappeared. The relief he'd felt momentarily was replaced by fear. She was alive—but based on her injuries and the limited medical care

Martin could give her on Mars, she *shouldn't* be alive. Only something more than human could've healed her—and the price it demanded for doing that might be so high she'd be better off dead.

Something was very wrong on Mars—and he hoped Katerina and Martin could make it right.

Katerina stabbed a button on the communications console and ended the transmission. Her chair inside the habitation module's cramped compartment creaked as she rocked and prayed—struggling against the terrifying thoughts that tormented her. Her blue jumpsuit and black boots were caked and filthy with red Martian mud. Her whole body felt unclean.

The young cosmonaut's right hand clutched the three-barred golden cross hanging from a gold chain around her neck. She tried in vain to use this sacred symbol of her devout Russian Orthodox faith to exorcise the evil that now possessed her. Attempting to free herself from the fears looping in her mind, she grabbed her music player from atop the console and fingered its touch screen. Finally she found a piece that matched her self-flagellating mood of anguished despair.

Hidden wireless speakers shook the tomb-like cabin with the Kyrie from Haydn's *Missa in angustiis*. Katerina felt herself engulfed by shadows of D minor darkness too deep for the brightest light from heaven to dispel. The orchestra's slashing strings and solo organ's clashing chords mocked the pleas for divine mercy screamed by the chorus and soloists that echoed the ones in her own mind. Brutal fanfares by three piercing trumpets and a pair of pounding kettledrums sounded like steel-gray spikes being hammered through the outstretched limbs of the crucified Savior.

The music ended in a thundering repetition of its savage opening notes with no hint of hope or healing. Exhausted in mind and body, for now at least Katerina felt able to resist the "gift" the aliens had forced her to accept—the unwanted knowledge of how to manipulate matter, energy, gravity, and time that tempted her to be more than human. And while she possessed that hard-won self-control, she had to confront a challenge even greater than her own death had been.

Katerina walked stiffly through the habitation module's compartments to its open exit. Her boots thudded onto the short ramp leading down from the module to the surrounding plain. She trudged out onto reddish-orange soil still damp from a recent shower and took deep breaths of the warm oxygen-nitrogen atmosphere the aliens had bestowed on Mars over the past ten years.

The morning Sun brightened a clear azure sky tinged with a roseate blush. Katerina fingered her golden cross and braced herself for what she had to do. She had to find the man she loved and redeem him.

And if he couldn't be saved, she had to destroy him.

Martin Slayton stood floating a meter above the ground and laughed. The aliens were right about the gift they'd given him. It *was* easy to manipulate gravity.

He rocketed up another forty meters into the air—chuckling at the feathery tickle that ascension made in his stomach. Curling himself up as though he were about to do a cannonball dive, Martin did several slow head-first rotations in place—just as he'd done in microgravity four months ago on the Ares VII rocket traveling to Mars. Still suspended in mid-air, he eased himself into a prone position with arms extending straight out in front of him.

Of course, flying took more than just changing how his body was affected by the ambient 0.91 g gravity the aliens had given Mars. But they'd also shown him how to manipulate matter and energy in any way he desired. He just had to provide all the molecules in his body with the right amount of energy and correct vectors to move at the same time in the direction he wanted.

As he flew in lazy circles above the Martian plain, Martin didn't care if he seemed to be violating the conservation of energy and several other laws of physics. It didn't matter that the aliens hadn't explained why he could do all these things now. The fact they had shown him how to do them was enough. After all, he'd learned to walk as a toddler without knowing he had bones and muscles in his legs—much less how they worked. His new abilities required no more effort than moving his arm. They were as natural as speaking—as easy as thinking.

Martin zoomed farther up into the sky—arms spread outward to embrace a Sun only slightly smaller and dimmer than it shone on Earth. But he stopped before rising too high—content to be Daedalus instead of Icarus. There he relaxed and enjoyed his bird's-eye view of the scenery far below.

He soared over the garden that Katerina and he had planted a kilometer from the habitation module. The green bean bushes, cornstalks, and wheat growing there seemed to look up in awe at the Missouri farm boy-turned-astronaut sailing high above them. He imagined the denizens of that garden cheering him as their protector—a super scarecrow.

Martin smiled—pretending he was one of the four-color superheroes whose classic adventures he'd enjoyed reading as a boy. He pictured the maroon pullover shirt, white shorts, and ebony boots he wore and the scarlet St. Louis Cardinals baseball cap covering his close-cropped black hair replaced by more colorful garb. In his mind a red cape with stylized yellow "S" fluttered behind him in the Martian breeze.

Next he imagined himself donning instead a darker uniform of green, white, and black, then slipping a power ring onto the middle finger of his gloved right hand. The aliens had given him a gift that made him the most powerful man alive. All he had to do to save the world was to be honest and without fear—

His alien-enhanced vision spotted movement on the ground beneath him. Martin stopped in mid-flight—scowling as the blue-clad figure walked to the edge of their garden and stood looking up at him. He glided feet first to a soft landing five meters from where Katerina gazed at him with an undecipherable expression. His subtle attempt to pry into her mind and read her thoughts was instantly blocked by her own alien-augmented will power.

Locked in a silent stare with her inscrutable hazel eyes, Martin didn't feel fearless anymore.

Katerina masked her thoughts and feelings from the stranger frowning at her. The stone face she showed this parody of the man she loved hid her fear that the Martin she knew was lost forever.

The alien body that looked like Martin sneered, "You don't have to just walk anymore."

"You said the only miracle you really wanted to do was to 'resurrect' me."

"Yes."

"But that's not all you want to do now."

"No."

Martin shook his head. "Don't you see, Katerina? We've been given an opportunity no one's ever had before. The aliens gave us the power to manipulate matter, energy, gravity, and time. I'm still experimenting to see what exactly that power lets us do—especially how we can manipulate time—but I know *how* their gift should be used. There's so much suffering, violence, disease, and death on Earth. We can use our powers to end all that misery and turn the world into a paradise!"

"Is that why you think the aliens forced us to accept their gift, Martin?"

"Heck, they're aliens! Who knows what they think or why they did it! Maybe they're trying to save humanity but have some variation of the Prime Directive that forbids them to do it directly. Maybe they believe it's okay to delegate their powers to natives like us to do the job for them. After all, we're the 'insiders.' We're in a better position than the aliens to know what's best for the human race and have the strongest motivation to help it!"

"Maybe the aliens are using us as their instruments, Martin—but not to help us. Perhaps their 'code' prohibits them from destroying us themselves. Instead, by giving us enough power they expect *we* will destroy Earth or conquer it for them!"

Martin waved his hands dismissively. Then he concentrated on a patch of ochre Martian soil several meters from where they stood. The dirt swirled up in a miniature dust storm that sculpted itself and congealed into the form of a straight back chair. Martin sat down in it, still facing his fiancée.

"That's one of the oldest SF clichés around, Katerina. The first thing every mutant, any member of *Homo superior*, or anyone struck by an Evolvo-Ray does is to try to conquer or crush 'normal' humans. That plot makes for exciting stories—but *I* would never do that!"

"Then why are you sitting on a throne?"

Martin stood up. He glanced back at his creation and made it crumble back into dust. "Sorry. It was supposed to be a club chair, like the one in my parents' living room."

His eyes darkened. "I hope you're not thinking about pulling an Elizabeth Dehner on me."

"You're referring to the second *Star Trek* pilot, 'Where No Man Has Gone Before.' No, I don't want to fight you, Martin."

"I'm surprised you've seen that episode. I didn't think you knew or cared much about science fiction. I usually have to sweet-talk you into watching my collection of old SF movies and TV shows with me."

"I haven't seen it—but you have. I saw your memories of it in your mind."

"So you're against me using my powers and won't let me read your thoughts—but you're perfectly willing to do it yourself! Well, do whatever you want inside my mind! Keep watching and listening to what I'm thinking! Maybe that'll convince you I won't let this power corrupt me!"

"I know you'd never intentionally hurt anyone, Martin. But although we've been given superhuman powers, our minds are still human—all too human. Even with the best intentions we could cause terrible pain and suffering because we don't know the best way to use these powers."

"But if we don't use the aliens' gift to help humanity because we're afraid we'll do the wrong thing, we'll be shirking our responsibility to help others. Better to try and fail than to not try at all!"

"The stakes are too high, Martin. Instead of saving the world we could unwittingly doom it. The powers we've been given are so great we might not be able to undo our mistakes. 'The Moving Finger writes; and, having writ, Moves on: nor—'"

Martin cut her off. "I know some quotations too—like 'With great power comes great responsibility.' It's too late, Katerina. The genie's out of the bottle. I'm ready now to let Mission Control know what's happened—unless you've already done it."

"I've only told them we're alive. Nothing more."

"I presume you used our communications console. No need for that anymore."

Martin stared up at the sky. His mind probed out from the Martian wilderness into the void—searching through space until familiar images in Houston entered his consciousness. "You should try this, Katerina. It's like watching 3-D TV. Don't ask me how, but I can even hear what they're saying—and thinking."

He smiled. "Nope. They don't have a clue at Mission Control. Hey, Dr. Stone's there too. I bet he's wondering how I cured you. Let's see what he's thinking."

Seconds later Martin's grin collapsed in embarrassment. "Who would have thought…so much guilt over what he did…"

"So now you're using your powers to invade other people's private thoughts. How long will it be before you're telling them *what* to think?"

"Okay, I made a mistake. Now I know better. There are other ways to test my powers that I'm sure will help people."

Martin stroked his chin. "Maybe I should start close to home. Look in my mind and see what I do…"

The isolated farmhouse shuddered as rain and golf ball-sized hail pelted its walls in front of an approaching tornado. From the gray night sky the thunderstorm ripped peeling paint from the dwelling's weathered wooden siding and tore shingles from its roof. Howling winds whipped the heavy limbs of the ancient oak tree in the front yard—splitting off a large branch that crashed through the home's picture window.

Amy Gale screamed as glass shattered and sprayed across the family room above her head. She sat hunched on the basement's cold concrete floor, surrounded by a thick darkness broken only by the small fading flashlight beside her. Three-year-old Dottie scrunched closer and desperately clutched her mother's blouse. The child whimpered as lightning flashed again outside the tiny basement window nearby— followed almost immediately by a thunderclap that shook the house like a miniature earthquake.

After the electricity went off thirty minutes ago their only link to the outside world was the ancient battery-powered weather radio nearby. Its computer-synthesized male voice blandly informed them that a severe thunderstorm watch was in effect for Webster County, Missouri until 9:30 p.m. and suggested they take shelter immediately. The voice added that conditions were right for the creation of a tornado.

Amy hugged her daughter and whispered that everything would be all right. But as the storm's fury grew she couldn't calm her own fears. She was only twenty-five—too young for the Lord to call her home. Little dark-haired, blue-eyed Dottie hadn't even begun to live. And there was no way to know whether her husband was safe. After their latest argument several hours ago, Nick had stormed out of the house and driven off in his pickup truck. Instead of being with his family he could be anywhere on the road between here and Marshfield—perhaps lying dead in a ditch...

Close to her ear Amy heard her daughter murmur through the thunder, "Please, God, make the storm go away. Keep Mommy, Daddy, and me safe."

Neither knew that in spite of Dottie's prayer the tornado would reach them in four minutes. Winds swirling at over three hundred kilometers per hour would blast away the roof, then crumple and splinter their house into a massive pile of debris. Seconds later the floor over their heads would be ripped away and expose the pair's sheltered hiding place in the basement. Mercifully they would feel only an instant of terror before their bodies were crushed and impaled by an avalanche of wood and metal collapsing on top of them—

Suddenly a miraculous stillness settled over their home. No more flashes of lightning illumined the basement's window. Amy listened in vain for thunder, rain, or shrieking winds. Then she heard a tiny voice snuggled near her smile three words.

"Thank you, God."

The man who'd once been merely Martin Slayton chuckled. "See how easy it is to manipulate matter and energy, Katerina? A little change in temperature and barometric pressure, and the rain and lightning go away. Bleed off some energy from overexcited molecules in air, and no more tornado. Hurricanes, tropical storms, earthquakes, tsunamis—we could stop them all with our powers. Think of all the people we could save—the destruction we could prevent!"

"'He arose and rebuked the wind and the raging of the water; and they ceased, and there came a calm.' I heard people praying to you, Martin. Do you enjoy being worshipped?"

"Nobody knows *I* saved them! It was an anonymous good deed! I'm not interested in getting thanks or glory. I don't care if they think it was a miracle!"

"Even if you don't call yourself a god or want to be one, you're still acting like a god. What are you going to do now, Martin? Are you going to continuously monitor weather throughout the world or check for every tectonic plate shift that could produce an earthquake for the rest of your life? And when do you decide to make a change? The same mild shower that gives farmers the rain they need for crops could also produce a rain-slicked highway that causes a fatal car accident!"

Katerina frowned at him. "I heard what you just thought about the 'butterfly effect.' You were remembering an old-time science fiction story and a later analogy based on chaos theory—that the flapping of a butterfly's wings in Brazil could produce tiny changes in atmospheric conditions in a ripple effect that eventually causes a tornado in Texas. You saved lives *now* by stopping that particular tornado, Martin. But how do you know you haven't inadvertently doomed many more people in the future?"

"Next you'll be telling me that one little girl I saved will grow up to be a ruthless dictator—and that by keeping her from dying today more people will die years from now. No, Katerina, the aliens didn't give us the ability to predict the future. But by that same logic no one would be able to do *anything* for fear it might have unintended bad consequences.

"According to you, no doctor should cure a dying child because she doesn't know what kind of adult that child will become. Nobody should have children at all because none of us knows how they'll turn out! Police, firefighters, and paramedics shouldn't save anybody who's in danger because they don't know what kind of life the victim they help will lead afterwards! At least I'm *trying* to help people. *You* want to be the Angel of Death!"

"When you make changes this great, Martin—far beyond what the person you *used* to be could do—the consequences of your actions are equally great for good *or* bad. The aliens' 'gift' has brought you closer to being omnipotent than any human being has ever been. You may rival God now in that one attribute—but not others. You're not all-wise, you're not all-knowing, you're not eternal, you're not—"

Marvin interrupted his companion contemptuously. "You want us to be like cattle and sheep—passive playthings in the hands of God, Fate, or whatever—afraid to do anything because we *might* make a mistake! I believe we should do what seems right today and deal with the future when it comes. I wonder how many people have died while we've been arguing about this—people we could've saved! If you won't help me, I'll do it myself—"

The hospital room where Manuel Cruz lay dying had smiling teddy bears and rainbow-striped dinosaurs painted on its walls. Dolores Cruz sat beside her nine-year-old son's bed, holding his feverish hand. The boy seemed to be sleeping, his breaths coming in gasps through the clear plastic oxygen mask covering his lower face. The beeping from the heart monitor above his head and hiss of the blood pressure cuff periodically inflating and deflating around his wasted arm were the only other sounds she heard.

The nurses who wafted in and out of the room glanced at her sympathetically. Like her, each one was swathed in a yellow paper gown—hands encased in latex gloves, hair hidden beneath an azure surgical cap, mouth and nose covered by a mask. Dolores knew these "reverse isolation" measures wouldn't help her son anymore. But they made it easier for the professionals caring for Manuel in his final illness to fuss over his IV fluids and do their other work without lingering with her any longer than necessary. They didn't want to give her false hope or admit the truth any more than she wanted to hear it.

Dolores's glove wiped away tears. She and Carlos knew this day might come when they adopted Manuel at six months old. Both were in their late thirties and successful lawyers when they'd married. The fertility clinic they'd visited after failing to start a family had done everything medically possible to help. But after yet another miscarriage, she and her husband had decided on another option.

They could've adopted a "perfect" baby—not one innocently suffering from the sins of his drug-addicted, HIV-positive biological mother. But here was a baby who needed even more love than usual—and she and her husband had more than the usual to give. The doctors said the latest medications could suppress development of AIDS for years—and despite all those decades of setbacks there was hope that a cure might be discovered soon.

But time had run out for Manuel. His immune system had collapsed with that elusive cure no closer than when he'd been born. For the last two years he'd spent more days inside than out of the hospital—suffering from vomiting, diarrhea, and infections. Nutritional supplements, then a thin feeding tube passed through his nose and down into his stomach, and finally "central hyperalimentation" IV fluids hadn't prevented her son from wasting away to a skeleton covered by a layer of dry skin.

Manuel had been too sick in the hospital to even go to the funeral when his father died of a heart attack two months ago. Still reeling from that loss, Dolores knew that soon she would lose the other person she loved most. Her son no longer responded to the best treatments the doctors had for this latest recurrence of *Pneumocystis jirovecii* pneumonia. Their medicines kept him from suffering too much. But there was nothing they could do to ease the ache in her heart.

Her vision blurred—imagining what her son would look like if he were well. She saw his sunken cheeks plump with health—his arms strong enough to give her a loving hug. Exhausted from grief and worry as evening turned into night, her head nodded for a few moments of soothing sleep...

Dolores jerked awake when a gentle hand touched her cheek. A startled cry escaped her throat as she saw a stranger sitting in her son's sickbed. She blinked and tried telling herself she was dreaming—but she wasn't.

The boy's hospital gown was too small for his filled-out healthy frame. He removed the oxygen mask with strong muscular fingers, a puzzled expression on his robust face. Then he spoke in a voice she couldn't mistake for anyone else's.

"Mom, why are you crying?"

Stone sat in Mission Control and watched a small television screen near his elbow. CNN showed Kelley giving a press conference updating what they knew—or rather, *didn't* know was happening on Mars.

He glanced at his wristwatch. 11:38 p.m. That meant he'd been here for eighteen hours—a typical work shift for a cardiologist. More importantly it meant relatively few people—at least in the U.S.—were awake and watching Kelley evade questions about what the media dubbed the "Great Martian Mystery."

As reporters grilled the flight director for answers neither she nor anyone else on Earth had, Stone focused on the news items scrolling across the bottom of the TV screen. Some of them read like headlines on a checkout line tabloid. Eyewitness accounts of tornadoes and hurricanes being snuffed out could be attributed to overwrought imaginations or freak meteorological conditions.

But those reports coming from a growing list of reputable hospitals and clinics worldwide couldn't be dismissed. According to the TV, people on the brink of death were being inexplicably cured. Those with end-stage AIDS, cancer, heart disease, and other serious diseases were now completely healthy. Nursing home residents with Alzheimer's or old strokes were suddenly as mentally sharp and neurologically sound as they'd ever been. Amputees grew back new limbs and paraplegics walked.

The blind now saw and the deaf could hear.

The physician grunted. If those stories were true, he might have to retrain in another profession—hopefully one with better hours…

Suddenly he realized there might be a connection between what Kelley was saying and these other events. If the aliens had healed Katerina they must also be responsible for those other cures. He wondered when someone else would think of that too.

Stone hoped that wouldn't happen soon. For it wouldn't take the public long to realize that a world in which miracles were routine might also be ripe for an apocalypse.

"Not bad for somebody who barely passed college biology."

Martin's voice had a taunting edge. "I didn't even have to know any fine details about human anatomy or physiology to do it. All I did was will all those cures and healings in general terms—and they happened!"

"'Young man, I say to thee, arise.' Are you enjoying playing God, Martin?"

"I keep telling you, this isn't about me! It's about correcting the mistake the God *you* believe in made by allowing all this pain and suffering!"

Martin folded his arms. "Of course, the aliens gave you the same power over matter, energy, gravity, and time that I have. You could reverse everything I just did. But if you make those children sick again or let people die, don't tell me it's for their own good!"

"I don't deny that what you did is good—today. But what about tomorrow? You didn't cure every person in the world. How do you think those you *didn't* help will feel? Even as we're talking more people are getting sick and being injured. Are you going to prevent or treat *every* illness and accident from now on?"

Martin scowled. "Even if I can't help everybody, helping *some* people is better than helping none at all! I intentionally didn't do some things I could've done, like making the elderly young again. I'm not sure yet that would be a good thing in the long run because of all the social and economic disruptions it could produce. So—responsible person that I am—I'll wait to do it until I figure out how to minimize any problems it might cause."

"You may already have done more damage than you realize, Martin. Besides being grateful for them, how *else* do you think people will react to these 'miracles' you performed? Will they live more carelessly—expecting that any damage they do to themselves or to others will be healed by another of your miracles? Will it discourage researchers and doctors to find new treatments that, though not as perfect as yours, rely on what's possible by human effort and don't depend on your godlike whim? Are you ready to let all of Earth's people transfer responsibility for their welfare from themselves and place it on *your* shoulders?"

"No, I can't do everything. I won't be like the robots in 'With Folded Hands.' I'm going to leave people who can help themselves alone and let them succeed or fail on their own. But there are many others who through no fault of their own don't have the ability to help themselves. And I know how to start…"

It was already hot as the Sun crept above the horizon. Far too little rain had fallen on this region of sub-Saharan Africa for months. Parched grasslands and cracked powdery soil baked beneath a cloudless sky as the inhabitants of the village stirred. In one of those mud huts thirty-three-year-old Nehanda was already awake and dressed. Though she didn't know why, she felt stronger than ever.

In the dim sunshine filtering through the shack's sole doorless entrance, even her four surviving children, ages two through seven, looked better than they had for days. Last night Nehanda feared the youngest child, her bloated belly and wasted limbs a stark reflection of how severe the drought and famine were, would be ready to be buried this morning next to her father and two siblings. But now the little girl looked healthy—as if the tiny daily ration of food she shared with the rest of her family really was enough to keep her alive.

But it was useless to be thankful for even the rare good things in their lives. Maybe the soldiers would come back today and leave more death and tears behind. Perhaps the village's only well would run dry and add the pangs of thirst to the rumbling in their empty stomachs. The small plots of maize, wheat, and other crops worked and shared by her neighbors and her, now coming to final ripening, might've been picked clean by birds during the night.

As Nehanda walked outside her hut several other women nodded to her. They all trod silently toward where they hoped their next meal still lay. Nehanda's face fell as she saw how little there was to gather. The shriveled stalks of grain lay flat and lifeless. Her family's share of this meager harvest, ground and baked into coarse bread, would be enough for only several mouthfuls apiece. But it would be enough to keep them alive one more day—and that was all she could hope for.

As Nehanda bent over within one of those plots, a shadow fell across the land. She looked up—and the few dry stalks in her hands fluttered to the ground. Her voice joined the cries of amazement shouted by the other women.

Enormous dark clouds gathered above their heads at a speed so fast they seemed like racing animals. Seconds later a gentle sheet of rain bathed the village in a soothing shower. For the first time in ages Nehanda laughed. She let the cool droplets dance on her tongue, then cupped her hands and rubbed the tiny pools of moisture across her chest.

Something tickled her bare legs. She peered down—and gasped. All around her and throughout the other small fields, wheat and other crops were springing up from the ground at an impossible pace. What normally took months of slow germination and growth was happening in a moment. Soon she was surrounded by a lush harvest that would keep her children and everyone else fed for months.

There was no explanation for this miracle. There was no need for one. It was enough that it *was*.

"If I heal the sick, I also need to keep them healthy."

Martin walked under a noontime Sun into the nearby garden. He fingered a cornstalk's leaf approvingly. "I grew up on a farm and know what crops need. And it sure helps to be able now to accelerate their growth by a factor of thousands. No one needs to go hungry anymore!"

Katerina said nothing. Inside Martin's mind she saw millions of people—suffering through no fault of their own—rescued from the brink of starvation and death. They laughed and rejoiced—grateful to be spared the agony of watching their loved ones sicken and perish, then dying themselves.

For the first time since she and Martin had been transformed into something more than human, she doubted herself. She wondered if the role she'd assumed as devil's advocate to Martin's plans might be literally true. Perhaps great power didn't corrupt *all* the time. Katerina thought of the kings and queens, emperors and czars, dictators and presidents she'd read about. Some were sadistic butchers. Many were mixtures of good and evil. Others had honestly tried to help people but lacked the wisdom to do lasting good.

But she wondered if even the rare paragons of self-control and service to their citizens like Marcus Aurelius or George Washington would have been corrupted too if they'd acquired as much power as she and Martin now possessed. There was probably a good reason no actual *saints* she could think of had possessed any personal power except their own words and example. Even Tomás de Torquemada was said to be honest and pious in his private life. Yet when given absolute power, he saw no contradiction to defending the Gospel's message of love and forgiveness with torture and murder as fifteenth-century Spain's first Grand Inquisitor.

Katerina scanned her memories of all the great works of philosophy, religion, and literature she'd read—seeking guidance on what she should do. As ideas percolated through her brain, passages in Plato's *Republic* converged with plots from science fiction movies Martin showed her on the flight here. There *was* a way to persuade him to stop using his power—but it meant she had to use hers.

She wrestled with her conscience before deciding there was no other choice. Besides, Martin told her she could do whatever she wanted inside his mind...

"Remember, Martin—'Man does not live by bread alone.' Those people you fed today will be hungry again tomorrow. What will you do then?"

Martin exited the garden and walked close to her. "I don't need to help people who can already help themselves. I'll confine my miracles to areas where they can't grow enough food to live."

"What if the problem isn't caused by Nature? What will you do if someone comes to steal that food you gave them—or uses violence against them?"

"That's a job for governments and police. And yes, I know those systems sometimes fail or can be part of the problem. But if no one else can stop violence, I'll help the innocent."

"And are you willing to use force, Martin—even kill—to prevent killing? With your power you could be judge, jury, and executioner for every criminal or anyone you deem 'evil'—and no one could stop you. They wouldn't even know *you* were the one who did it!"

"You know me better than that! I'd never use my power to deliberately hurt anyone!"

"But you could do it unintentionally. What if you lost your temper—or even just *dreamed* about hurting people?"

Martin grinned. "I've seen and read enough science fiction to anticipate anything that could go wrong. I'll be a well-behaved Star Child—and I've watched *Forbidden Planet* umpteen times. I'll will my power to not work while I'm asleep. That way there'll be no Monster from the Id—and I won't inadvertently change someone who wants to fly into a seagull like in an old Green Lantern story!"

"You're still underestimating the danger. Even if you control yourself, you'll still be like one of Plato's guardians—the ultimate arbiter of what people can do or not do. But who will guard *you*?"

Martin frowned. "I'll guard myself. And I don't have to stop force with greater force. You've made me think of a better way to stop violence. Let me show you…"

Rustam Shahidi's sweaty palms clutched the steering wheel of his pickup truck. Sitting alone in its cab, he tried to look inconspicuous as his vehicle moved cautiously through the streets of Tehran.

Along the avenue vendors offered their wares to hundreds of shoppers in this large outdoor market on a sunny Sunday morning. Rustam's dilapidated truck, stuffed with lettuce and other produce along its metal bed and wooden sides, blended in well with similarly laden ones. But none of them carried the deadly cargo hidden within his vehicle.

The young man tried not to think about what would happen to him in several minutes when he arrived at his target. There'd be a dozen soldiers around the checkpoint his truck was approaching. A simple calculation of the number of enemy lives lost compared to his meant his martyrdom would be worthwhile.

He eased the truck behind a small green car that formed the end of a short queue of vehicles stopped at the checkpoint. As the line in front of him gradually shortened he jerked—startled by the face staring back at him from just outside the open driver side window.

The boy smiling at him was about ten years old. Rustam nodded back—squelching an urge to whisper to the youngster to run away. The bomb in his vehicle would produce a blast radius of around a hundred meters. He prayed that the boy and other innocents would be far enough away to survive. But if they didn't, they would join him in paradise.

At least he hoped there was such a place for all of them. As these last seconds of his life ticked away, doubts about the supernatural significance of what he was about to do crept back into his mind. But even if the sum of his sacrifice was only a blow against those who repressed his country's people, it was enough to justify his death.

Rustam lost sight of the boy as his truck crept forward. There were only three more vehicles in front of where the soldiers checked a frightened driver's papers. He was close enough now that a press of the button near his hand would make his mission a success. Before any more doubts or regrets entered his brain he reached for the detonator—

The uniformed man walked cautiously toward the stalled produce truck, slipping his rifle off his shoulder into a ready position. Instead of advancing when the vehicles in front of it had moved past the checkpoint, this one sat in the street frozen in place. In the tense atmosphere that now blanketed Tehran, anything that looked even remotely suspicious could be the harbinger of sudden explosive death.

His heart pounding—terrified the next instant could be his last—the soldier crept close enough to the open window beside the driver to hear what the young man behind the wheel was muttering.

"It's wrong to kill. I shouldn't detonate the bomb. It's wrong to kill. I shouldn't det—"

That mantra was silenced by the sharp *crack!* of bullets from the sergeant's rifle tearing through Rustam's head. Gun smoke filled the soldier's nostrils as he lowered the rifle. He called back to the privates who'd started toward him to contact the bomb disposal team. Then—trying to exude nonchalance instead of the nervous relief he felt—he sauntered back to the checkpoint. By the time he reached it, he was already wondering if his deed might earn him a medal.

In this fifth year of the bloody Iranian civil war, Sgt. Bahram Bayat of the Revolutionary Guards had single-handedly stopped a suicide bomber. The government whose nearly sixty-year-old grip on power was weakening from a violent homegrown rebellion needed every hero it could find.

Though it'd been many hours since he'd slept, fear kept Stone alert and focused on the TV screen. Several of his colleagues had wandered from their posts to look over his shoulder or at other small television monitors scattered around Mission Control.

Every screen showed nonplused newscasters and reporters relating a burgeoning series of bizarre events around the world. Police stations were now jammed with people turning themselves in for every violent crime and act they'd committed. Bank robbers laid down the pistols they were aiming at tellers and surrendered. Child molesters, those guilty of domestic violence, and rapists tearfully begged to be put in jail. Criminals ranging from street thugs to the top bosses of organized crime demanded punishment for the injuries and deaths they'd inflicted. Those ranks also included an alarming number of "respectable" citizens confessing to heinous deeds no one had ever suspected them of doing.

Stone shuddered. It was as if millions of people with a sick or nonexistent conscience had suddenly been healed. But his long career as a physician had taught him many uncomfortable truths. One was that a person's basic personality and actions weren't improved without great effort—and only then if the individual cooperated. Another was that no medicine or treatment was risk-free and worked all the time.

He wondered what side effects this particular "cure" might have.

Martin floated upright five meters above the ground and smiled. Waves of contentment rippled through his mind as he sensed images and thoughts from Mission Control and all across Earth.

A voice from below interrupted his reverie. "So that's your solution to violence. You're going to control people like puppets and destroy their free will!'"

"No one has a right to 'freely' hurt another person, Katerina. All I'm doing is implanting feelings and ideas in people's minds that should've been there all along. Things like empathy and remorse."

"And love? Are you going to *make* people care about each other?"

"No. I'm just giving them the chance to love others. Whether they choose to do that is still up to them."

"But it's just as important that they *choose* not to hate or hurt others!" Katerina glared up at him. "You're not treating those people like human beings. To you they're just wild animals that need to be tamed. Even if it isn't the physical type, *you're* using force on them!"

"But I'm just using gentle force—in a good cause. The people I've changed deliberately threatened, injured, or murdered others. The only way police can deal with criminals and killers is with the same weapons the bad guys use.

"What I'm doing is much more benign. It's like a surgeon operating on someone with a brain tumor. My treatment causes less pain to sick patients and heals them better than a doctor could—"

Martin flinched as an unexpected power seized his body and dragged it to the ground. As his boots settled back onto the paprika-colored soil he laughed. "Good. I finally got you riled enough to use your own power. Maybe now you'll understand how easy it is to use."

"No. I just want you to look into my face when I talk to you."

Katerina walked closer to him. "Don't compare yourself to a doctor, Martin. Unless someone is mentally incapable of making a decision, a physician can't treat a patient without that person's consent. *You* didn't ask those people you changed if they wanted to be treated or not. And even if you did and they refused, you would've altered their minds anyway!"

She scowled. "Have you ever read Dostoevsky's *The Brothers Karamazov*?"

182

"Tried to read it. Never finished it. Long meandering novels make me fall asleep. Besides, what does that have to do with—"

"If you'd read it, Martin, you'd know you should really be comparing yourself to Grand Inquisitors. *They* thought they were doing good by protecting their flock from dangerous ideas. *They* thought they were being merciful to heretics and unbelievers by trying to save their victims' immortal souls—even if it meant rending their bodies with the rack and wheel or burning them at the stake!

"The method you're using is more subtle but ultimately just as corrupt. You're imposing your own orthodoxy of action—*making* people be 'good' instead of *choosing* to love and care for others. Yes, I know your intentions are good. But even the most caring, well-intentioned, and wise Grand Inquisitor is still a Grand Inquisitor. And you're infinitely more powerful and dangerous than any of them ever was!"

Martin snapped, "You sound like the Jesuits who taught me at the university. I regurgitated enough of what they said on tests to pass the theology courses I had to take. But they couldn't make me believe what they said."

Katerina took hold of the golden cross hanging from her neck. "Maybe those priests asked you this question. After being taunted, tortured, and crucified, why didn't the Savior come down from the cross and show the whole world who He really was?"

"Well, we both know the obvious answer!"

"Of course, Martin. *If* He were only a human being whose goodness inspired His followers to make Him into God, He didn't do it because He couldn't do it. But just assume for a moment that He really was both human and divine.

"If so, why did He choose to 'only' die and rise again instead of stopping His execution and creating a paradise on Earth? Like you, He could heal the sick, feed the hungry, and inspire sinners to repent. *I* think the reason He didn't stay to miraculously eliminate all evil and suffering is that He wanted *us*—humanity itself—to do it! He became weak to show us how we could become strong!"

Katerina's hazel eyes softened. "None of us will ever be perfect or without pain. Though we delay it for as long as the Old Testament patriarchs are said to have lived, we all eventually die. But whatever measure of paradise we create on Earth, Mars, or other worlds will be one we *earned*—not something given as a 'gift.' If we make life better it'll because *we* used science to make Nature less dangerous and relieve human suffering. If we choose to be kind and care about others, *we* can claim credit for doing it.

"He showed us what we could do with our own human abilities. It's up to us to freely accept His challenge and imitate Him."

Martin grunted. "Are you finished? I was afraid you were going to make a speech longer than John Galt's in *Atlas Shrugged*. I admit you can weave a pretty bouquet of ivory tower ideas together like a Jesuit. But even the nicest words can only accomplish so much. What I'm doing is actually helping people and not just making rhetorical noise!"

"Is it, Martin? Maybe you're right that I should use my own power more. So far I've just been inside your mind seeing what you've done to Earth. Let's both go there to see *everything* you've done."

"Challenge accepted!"

Katerina closed her eyes and extended her consciousness outward. She sensed Martin's mind accompanying her as she seemed to float up through the inverted bowl above them and move sunward through space.

Then a cacophony of sights and sounds on faraway Earth flooded Katerina's brain. With a neurosurgeon's finesse she separated images and sounds, thoughts and emotions like threads in the intricate tapestry of humanity's entire experience. Instantly she absorbed countless stories of terror turned to joy, suffering changed to health, and hunger relieved. Based on what she sensed and felt across the continents, Martin's actions had indeed brought justice to the innocent and guilty.

But like sunspots scattered across Sol's face, the young cosmonaut also found instances of pain and savagery caused by the changes he'd thrust on unwilling hearts. Some of those whose sinful deeds he'd laid bare or stopped were now battered and bleeding—others killed by those whom they'd threatened or hurt. Whether those people had truly received justice or greater punishment than they deserved was now moot.

Katerina's attention returned to her fellow watcher standing nearby. The stunned look on his face showed he too had seen the horrors he'd caused.

"Are you proud of *everything* you've done, Martin?"

"What I did wasn't enough to prevent violence. I thought it was enough to begin by stopping people who'd committed or were about to commit the worst kinds of crimes. I should've known those I affected weren't the only ones capable of hatred and murder."

"That's because it's easier to hate than to love—to seek revenge than to forgive. Do you think you can change human nature, Martin?"

"I can try!"

Lieutenant Sergei Kijé shivered as his boots trudged across the frigid ground. He stopped and placed both hands in the pockets of his brown army jacket, then glanced up at a slate-colored afternoon sky promising snow soon. Behind him voices murmured from the two parked open-backed troop transport trucks where the twenty men he commanded sat bunched together. His soldiers, rifles slung carelessly over their shoulders, were trying to keep warm by bragging about their latest exploits on leave. Those inflated accounts of how much vodka they'd drunk and how many women they'd satisfied helped relieve their boredom.

The young lieutenant raised the high-powered image-stabilizing bino-culars suspended from his neck and peered at the border three kilometers away. After studying the empty landscape he lowered the binoculars and sighed. Fortunately, it was rare for anything to actually happen on one of these routine patrols. He hoped the negotiations between his government and the Chinese were going well today. But if they didn't, Moscow might send orders for another token incident. Perhaps a quick incursion of his soldiers across the border, or a barrage of artillery to make some craters on the foreign land to the south—just enough to let the other side know that their northern neighbor was displeased.

A faint whistling crescendoed into a terrifying shriek. Three hundred meters to his right a geyser of soil erupted as the mortar shell hit. His men leapt out of the trucks, scattering and stretching prone along the ground. The lieutenant unsnapped a transceiver from his belt and tried to contact field headquarters for orders. Hopefully they'd be told to re-treat instead of retaliate—

He winced as another blast rocked the earth two hundred meters to his left. The fact only one mortar seemed to be firing instead of multiple weapons blanketing them implied the Chinese weren't very motivated to wipe them out. They might not even know his troops were here and were just creating a token political incident of their own. But an un-intentionally lucky shot would be just as deadly to him and his men as a deliberate one.

A deafening third explosion close behind him drowned out the reply spluttering from the transceiver. He sent a signal back to repeat that mes-sage and groaned when he heard it. His men cursed when they heard their orders. They rapidly removed their long-range mortars from the back of the trucks and started setting up to return fire.

As he supervised their work Sergei prayed that today wouldn't be the start of a real war—and that he and his contingent wouldn't be its first casualties. In the lull following that third explosion the lieutenant listened for the screaming descent of a final shell aimed directly at him. But his men's weapons were ready before it came. Though they'd be firing blind, at least they'd let the other side know he and his troops weren't defenseless. Unfortunately it'd also let the Chinese know they had a living target—

But as he started to give the order to return fire, Sergei stopped. He and his men stood frozen—their minds seized by an overpowering force. Thoughts not their own repeated in their brains like the incessant rumble of a distant drum. The same command pressed down on each man's consciousness—trying to crush his will.

Violence is wrong. War is wrong. You must not hurt others.

A great silence engulfed the whole Earth. On every continent each human being ceased moving and heard that command in his or her own language. Every heart and soul reverberated with that same overwhelming decree. For a brief moment over eight billion people lived without hatred or brutality in a world where only peace reigned.

And then humanity began to destroy itself.

Two minutes before the global apocalypse started Stone woke from a catnap and refocused on the TV screen. A news commentator was describing the public's muted reaction to the day's "miraculous" events. Comparing it to the panic that raged when Mars and Venus began inexplicably moving closer to Earth a decade ago, she suggested people might still be too emotionally exhausted from that previous crisis and the reported existence of aliens to react as violently this time.

Stone groaned. It was more likely people were in denial and suppressing their fears than that they'd been desensitized to this new uncertainty. At least the newswoman didn't make a direct connection between the aliens and what was happening now. That idea might still be the spark to make the public's pent-up terrors explode once again—

The physician's mouth froze in the middle of a yawn. Suddenly his thoughts, feelings, and consciousness were seized by a power and will not his own. It felt like his brain had been plunged into an ice-cold ocean and strong unseen hands were holding his head beneath the surface.

Sweat leached from his forehead and he gasped through the terrified pounding of his heart.

A sense of impending doom seized Stone as he struggled to thrust off the vise squeezing his mind. He barely sensed the words about violence being wrong thundering within his head as he fought to retain his own identity. Something *alien* was stripping and peeling his very reason away like a flaying knife. The sickening dread of what madness might be left behind after that unknown force finished its work made him fight ever more fiercely for the release of freedom—or death.

Stone dimly heard the muffled whimpers and shrieks of everyone around him at Mission Control. Suddenly, as if a ticking bomb planted in his head exploded, an exhilarating howl burst from his lips. For an instant he felt only relief—freed at last from whatever parasite had invaded his brain. Then the shredded debris of what had been his personality and self-control scattered like dust in a tornado—never to return again.

With an agony beyond human endurance Stone's mind caved in—crushing his finely structured ego. Defenseless now against his own inner demons, he plummeted screaming into the hell he'd created for himself...

For the first few of the handful of seconds Martin thought it would take to rid humanity of its own evil, everything went well. Then the smugness on his face faded. The corners of his lips drooped as he felt the inexorably growing reaction to the mental ultimatum he'd delivered to the whole human race. The stunned surprise he'd sensed in all those individual brains when he'd first linked with them unraveled into countless threads of fear, anger, and hatred. He'd seized the minds of over eight billion people and pulled them in the direction he wanted—but now they were pulling away from him—fighting back and attacking him!

Martin's face tensed from an agonizing effort that consumed every bit of his energy and power. His body stiffened as his mental tug-of-war with his fellow humans settled into an unstable stalemate. Standing dumbstruck on the Martian plain, he was assaulted by a combined consciousness far stronger than its individual members. Though each mind was only a spark compared to the stellar radiance of his own, focused together with laser precision at the source of their pain they formed a raging conflagration.

He clenched his fists and tried desperately to end the titanic struggle he'd started. For a moment the tiny corner of his mind still reserved for thought considered giving up. If humanity was too afraid or perverse to be changed—if all those people couldn't understand that eliminating their capacity for violence was for their own good—then they deserved the world they lived in!

But then Martin remembered all the crimes, wars, and other injustices that claimed so many innocent victims in the past and present. If he didn't use the aliens' gift—if he didn't stop that sordid history from perpetually repeating itself or ending in humanity's self-inflicted extinction—who would?

As his mind wrestled with the unwilling ones of an entire world Martin sensed another presence standing silently nearby. He felt that other enhanced consciousness inside his brain passively observing—like someone watching a movie—the life-and-death conflict being played out on two planets. *She* held the balance of power to end this war—and surely the woman he loved wouldn't desert him when he and the entire human race needed her most!

He barely had enough strength to speak. "Help me, Katerina! I can't control them on my own! If you add your power to mine we'll beat them and make them give up violence forever!"

Martin saw her nod.

"Yes, Martin. I'll help you."

He started to smile—and then a blinding light like a supernova seared through his brain. For an instant the rage of an entire world flooded his defenseless mind. A jet-black emptiness swallowed him as his body fell limply to the ground...

Millions of people died during those moments Martin waged a one-man war against human nature. Airplane pilots in flight, drivers racing on busy highways, firefighters rescuing people in burning buildings, surgeons performing operations all found their minds ripped away from their surroundings. Those whose bodies were suddenly crushed in coffins of speeding metal never felt the impact. Others standing paralyzed while individuals they'd been trying to help died didn't notice their loss.

Then the great force clamping humanity in its unwanted grasp suddenly disappeared. Released from its chains, the human race found itself free again. But that freedom came at a terrible price.

Some, mainly babies and children, lay quiet and catatonic—their minds emptied of any volition or will. The power they'd experienced had rendered them incapable of hurting others. It also destroyed their fragile developing personalities and rendered their minds forever *tabula rasa*. Only their most primitive neurological functions remained.

Others weren't as fortunate. The struggle against the power gripping their minds demolished the well-constructed psychological defense mechanisms they'd constructed to protect their sanity. Now all the fears, anxieties, and regrets buried within their psyches and memories erupted like molten lava—searing away every other thought and feeling. Immersed in guilt, self-pity, terror, and grief, some sat perpetually weeping and screaming—trapped forever in a cocoon of pain.

The stronger-willed chose more directly self-destructive paths. Across the world, people jumped from bridges and tall buildings. Some used knives and guns to end their lives. Fire and water snuffed out the existence of still more.

But for others that abrupt removal of inhibitions shielding them from their true nature or curbing their worst instincts led to destruction and death on a global scale.

Sgt. Bahram Bayat shuddered as his mind broke free of the power trying to bind it. He focused again on the crowded Tehran street and found new targets for the rage boiling within him incited by that nearly successful attempt to enslave his very being. The fear and disgust he felt toward the civilians standing nearby waking from their own mental struggles swelled to a murderous level.

Several young men near him suddenly went berserk. They ran toward him screaming curses and threats. But just before their fists reached him a burst from his AK-47 left the men bleeding and writhing on the ground. Bahram laughed as he emptied his rifle into them until their punctured corpses stopped jerking.

As he reloaded he ordered his fellow soldiers at the checkpoint to join him. More rifles sprayed bullets into the mostly unresisting crowd. As the sergeant and his men concentrated on mowing down women, children, and any other civilians in range they didn't notice one man slip into the parked truck close to them. The man searched beside the driver slumped dead at the wheel, found the detonator button, and pushed it—

The explosion shattered windows over a block away. A blasted smoking crater, masses of debris, and shredded body parts marked where the truck had been. Sgt. Bahram Bayat, his soldiers, and more than a hundred other people no longer existed. Most of the wounded farther from ground zero soon joined them in death.

But the casualties on that single street were trivial compared to the millions injured and dying elsewhere.

In eastern Russia the force enslaving the minds of Lt. Kijé and his men disappeared. They staggered—shaken out of the stupor that had suddenly seized them. Then a savage hatred devoid of thought erupted within them. The men quickly obeyed their commanding officer's order to launch the mortar barrage they'd prepared.

As the projectiles whistled toward their distant targets, the soldiers gleefully followed their next order to pile back into the trucks and drive south. As they crossed the border into China, each man readied his rifle and hoped that the enemy was near. The vision of their bullets ripping through the bodies of those who'd attacked them drove them wild with pleasure. There was no fear within them—only a white-hot obsession to kill without mercy.

Bouncing along the scrubby terrain toward their destiny, they would've rejoiced over what their superiors in Moscow were doing at that moment. The nation's top political and military leaders felt the same berserk blood-lust possessing the occupants of the two trucks now invading the enemy's homeland. Top-secret orders and codes spread quickly throughout Russia's military network. Bombers scrambled into the air and missile silos opened.

Unaware of the massive attack being readied, the lieutenant sat in the cab of one of the two trucks and scanned the horizon for movement. He barely noticed when the other truck, driving several hundred meters in front of him, hit a land mine. By the time his truck reached the site his driver managed to swerve around most of the wreckage and ruptured corpses scattered across the plain.

By luck their remaining truck avoided running over a mine. The lieutenant gritted his teeth as he saw several heads bob above a trench half a kilometer ahead. He unholstered his automatic and prepared to bark an order to halt—

He never gave that order. Two rocket-propelled grenades hit the front of the truck and turned it into a fireball of shrapnel and flying chunks of uniformed bodies. But the half-dozen Chinese troops who'd repelled this initial enemy thrust into their country had little time to celebrate. An hour later the first of hundreds of nuclear bombs and missiles rained down on China's population centers and military installations.

Even as Beijing, Shanghai, and other cities with their millions of inhabitants vanished beneath mushroom clouds, an equally massive retaliatory strike was on its way toward Russia. Within several hours Moscow, St. Petersburg, and other former names on the map were graveyards of radioactive rubble.

Smaller nuclear exchanges across the Indian-Pakistani border and in the Middle East killed more millions. Other millions farther away from those firestorms were now sentenced to die in hours, days, or weeks from injuries or radiation exposure. Over the next months billions were destined to perish from disease and starvation as the Northern Hemisphere's late calendar winter changed into a nuclear one covering the entire globe.

In areas yet untouched by atomic catastrophe, millions used fists and whatever weapons they could find against family, neighbors, and strangers. Wherever there had been suppressed resentment and anger against individuals, races, or religions, people divided into passive or unwilling victims and into murderers. Explosions, gunfire, and screams deafened the world.

Meanwhile, a great stillness reigned on Mars.

The Sun was settling toward the western horizon when Katerina awoke after what seemed hours later. Her head pounded and eyes throbbed as she sat up. She flicked dusty auburn hair back over her shoulders and squinted up at the empty sky.

As her vision cleared Katerina struggled to retrieve her last memory. She'd been waiting for the right time to use the full power the aliens had forced on her, and when it came she—

The young cosmonaut rose awkwardly to her feet. A crumpled figure dressed in red, white, and black lay motionless on its back several meters away. Her heart raced as she stumbled toward the spot where Martin's body sprawled in the orange dirt. His glassy gaze seemed to be looking up at circling Martian buzzards beginning their descent.

"Martin! Are you all right?"

There was no reply as she knelt by his left side. The wide-eyed stare and open mouth he directed at the heavens terrified her. Martin looked as if the last thing he'd seen was Satan's laughing face coming toward him. Katerina did a jaw thrust to open his airway. Her right ear hovered above his lips as she peered down at his chest—hoping to feel his warm breath against her skin. As she waited to see if his life and hers had ended, Katerina prayed for a miracle.

A wisp of air like the fluttering wings of the Holy Spirit caressed her ear. She saw the blood-red shirt Martin wore rise and fall slightly with his shallow breaths. Her fingertips moved to his neck and she gasped with gratitude for the strong pulse there. Katerina reached out to gently touch his mind—

And felt nothing. She sobbed as her miracle was snatched away. Martin's body was still alive—but it was like a dried cocoon left empty by a long-departed butterfly. Katerina stroked the pale forehead of the man she loved—as if her fingers could meld into his flesh and give him the handhold he needed to pull himself up from the abyss he'd stumbled into. Her mind delved deeper into the void within his brain—searching in the darkness for any hint of consciousness that would tell her he was not forever lost.

Her thoughts plunged deeper into him. *Don't leave me, Martin! Come back to me!*

Then Katerina sensed the whisper of another awareness at the boundary of her enhanced senses. *Follow me, Martin! Let me help you!*

From out of the depths his mind touched hers. Together they rose back into the light—

Martin groaned. He looked up at Katerina's tear-streaked face, touched her lips—and then bewilderment twisted his face. "What happened?"

"I don't know, Martin. It was like something grabbed and squeezed my mind so hard the pain made me black out. I just woke up a few minutes ago."

"The last thing that I remember was..." Martin's gaze turned distant and vacant. As he absorbed sights and sounds on distant Earth his face contorted with horror.

He staggered to his feet. "It was like I was asleep all that time having a terrible dream. But my mind must have still been linked to everyone on Earth—*and it's all real!* Everything I saw in my nightmare—the nuclear war, the suicides and murders, Dr. Stone and everybody at Mission Control going crazy—*it really happened!*"

Katerina stood up and tried to kiss his lips. Martin ignored her, walking away and shouting, "Why did it happen? What went wrong?"

Katerina reached out to blend with his mind again. The ghastly visions she saw in it sickened her. Either Martin had gone mad—or the world had.

Then he was walking back toward her—his enraged face almost as ruddy as the soil they stood on. "What did you do, Katerina? I remember now I asked you to help me! *What did you do?*"

"I helped you, Martin. I used my own power to nullify yours."

He stopped ten meters away and stared at her. She wondered if the Savior had looked the same way at Judas in the Garden of Gethsemane.

Martin clenched his fists. "Why did you do that?"

"I couldn't let you enslave everyone on Earth—and I had to prevent them from hurting you! I didn't know there'd be some kind of mental backlash that would make us both lose consciousness when I did it!"

"No, Katerina, you must've done more than that! Just stopping what I was doing wouldn't have caused all that death and destruction! I begged you for help—and you betrayed me! Were you so jealous I was proving you wrong—that despite what you said my power really was helping people—that you *made* me fail?"

"No, Martin! I'd never intentionally hurt you or anyone else! I don't know what caused everyone on Earth to go insane! Maybe if we work together we can stop the killing and heal those who are still alive! Look into my mind and see I'm telling the truth!"

Martin's voice held only hatred and contempt. "No, Katerina, you have the same power as I do. You can make the thoughts you *let* me hear lie to me. I need to know what you did so I can prevent you from doing it again and killing more people! And the only way I can be sure you're really telling me the truth is if I *force* it out of you!"

Martin strode toward her like an executioner. His mind whipped out and squeezed hers in a mailed fist. Katerina screamed with skull-splitting agony at his brutal psychic assault. She reflexively raised her mental barriers again—barely able to defend herself from Martin's relentless telepathic attempt to rip through her brain searching for an admission of guilt that didn't exist.

Last night she'd faced death and expired with quiet dignity, with only fleeting doubts and fears clouding final resignation to her fate. Today she saw Death walking toward her wearing the face of the man she loved—and this time she was very afraid.

On Earth, Nature responded to the rage in Martin's mind and joined humanity in going mad.

Calm winds suddenly whipped up into hurricanes and tornadoes. In the Missouri Ozarks a three-year-old girl whimpered in her bed. In the next room her reunited parents screamed at and attacked each other—obsessed with revenge for every disagreement in their marriage.

Then a revived tornado slammed into their house and passed on, searching for more victims. In its wake the tornado left a crumpled pile of wood and metal with nothing alive inside.

In a city on the West Coast a mother and her newly healed young son vacantly hugged each other and wept over all the pain and loss they'd endured. The hospital they sat in trembled as tectonic plates kilometers away shifted. As the earthquake rocketed up the Richter scale their building and hundreds of others crumbled, leaving only mangled bodies inside the wreckage.

In southern Africa the gentle raindrops nourishing accelerated crops suddenly grew and froze into deadly baseball-sized hail. Rampaging flash floods washed away plants, animals, and whole villages. Elsewhere ocean waves churned to skyscraper heights, capsizing ships and ferries. Tsunamis innundated costal regions, leveling towns and cities. Lightning flashed and struck, turning forests and jungles into infernos. Every minute air, water, fire, and earth slaughtered thousands more people.

On Mars, Nature also joined Martin's side in a deadly personal battle. The peaceful garden beside its two combatants tore itself apart. Green bean bushes, cornstalks, and wheat uprooted themselves and rocketed toward Katerina's face like shrapnel. They were too light to hurt her directly—but the distraction of deflecting them with arms and mind weakened her defenses against Martin's continuous telepathic attack.

She stumbled backwards—battered by mental blasts like a tornado's winds. All around her Martian dirt swirled up and enveloped Katerina in a miniature dust storm. A barrage of pebbles stung her face like a swarm of hornets. She winced as small rocks flew up and pummeled her blue jumpsuit.

Coughing and choking from the dust infiltrating her nose and throat, with a desperate burst of telekinetic power Katerina repelled the soil and winds around her. For seconds she stood in the clear eye of a hurricane. As the frustrated Martian dirt and air raged furiously in an opaque fog a meter away from her, their attack barely held back by the force of her mind, she concentrated the remainder of her mental energy on repelling Martin's unceasing attempts to seize and viciously probe her brain.

Suddenly Katerina saw a pair of bare hairy arms reach out toward her from that dense reddish-orange cloud. She didn't notice the maniacally swirling dust nearby collapse back onto the ground as Martin grabbed hold of her shoulders. Katerina cringed at the savage face staring back at her from centimeters away. Her mind reverberated with deafening words.

"It's your fault everything went wrong, Katerina! What did you do? Confess! Tell me what you did to sabotage me!"

Katerina jerked back from Martin's brutal grip and struggled to break free. He shook her until she tripped over her feet and tumbled backwards. She gasped as her back struck the hard Martian soil and Martin fell down on top of her. He pinned her arms against the dirt before she could try pushing him away. Katerina writhed helplessly beneath his heavy body as he tore away the last thin layers of fading will power she had protecting her from his assault.

With his attack on the verge of consummation there was only one way to stop him and heal the sickness inside his mind. There wasn't enough time to convince him of her innocence or even to pray. Through the maelstrom of fury assaulting her consciousness she hoped he'd hear her last words to him and understand.

"I love you, Martin. Goodbye."

Martin grunted triumphantly when he felt the fallen woman crushed beneath him go physically and mentally limp. All resistance to him collapsed and he began to penetrate her innermost depths—

Suddenly he stopped and raised himself to a kneeling position. His mind delved deeper into a blackening void whose final glimmer of light faded and disappeared.

Katerina lay motionless on her back with her eyes closed—as if she were sleeping. Her face was powdered with dust except for scattered lines like a spider's web on her cheeks, where tears had cleaned away the filth he'd flung at her. The blue jumpsuit she wore was ripped where he'd manhandled her, exposing the pale imprints of his fingers on her bare flesh. Her auburn hair was matted and tangled beneath her lolling neck.

"Katerina! Are you all right? I didn't mean to hurt you!"

There was no response. His heart raced as he moved rapidly to her left side and reflexively began the CPR protocol he'd used on her only yesterday. Yes, she was still breathing and the carotid pulse he checked was strong. Her body was still warm and alive.

But her mind was gone—wiped clean as her last act in life. Martin wailed in grief as his consciousness found nothing within her brain but the lowest autonomic activity. Her personality and intelligence, her ability to think and love had all vanished—and not even the great power the aliens had given him could bring those things, could bring *her* back to him. She'd prevented him from becoming her murderer or worse…by destroying herself first.

Shocked back into a semblance of sanity by her self-sacrifice, Martin bent down over the empty body of the woman he loved and kissed her forehead. His heartbroken sobs slowly subsided. He wanted to die now, he *deserved* to die—but not yet.

No, first he had to help whoever was still alive on Earth. There might be enough survivors even after this day of Armageddon to eventually rebuild civilization.

Kneeling beside Katerina, Martin raised his lost bride-to-be's upper body enough to embrace her. Then his mind reached out toward a wounded world. He saw the raging winds and other destructive forces of Nature stirred up by his anger and calmed them. Next he directed his power to manipulate matter, energy, and gravity at the radioactive ruins and clouds of dust, soot, and smoke that covered huge swaths of post-World War III Earth. Those death-dealing isotopes and molecules were gripped and flung out into space on high-speed trajectories toward final resting places in the Sun.

Then Martin turned his attention to the physical injuries inflicted by war and smaller-scale violence. Across the world burns, broken bones, and radiation-induced damage to vital organs were all healed.

Finally a command inspired by a favorite TV episode spanned the distance between him and every other living human being. What remained of humanity was too weak and distracted to resist his order.

Sleep.

Across Earth bodies slumped to the ground and found respite from the torment within their minds. Now there'd be time for him to heal their damaged psyches. Martin's consciousness flitted through the minds of billions of his comatose fellow beings, searching for the means to restore their mental health—

But it was too late. His thoughts touched an emptiness within the remnants of humankind only slightly less than that within Katerina. Whatever personalities they had possessed—whatever had made them unique individuals—was gone forever. All that remained were crude neurological reflexes or the rage and remorse they'd accumulated over their lives. No hint of rationality remained behind to curb their unfettered emotions or help them become human again.

A terrible pressure grew in Martin's chest. *He* was the only sane human being left alive.

Then he laughed—realizing his mistake. There were *no* sane human beings left.

"You were right," Martin whispered to Katerina's empty body—unable to muster the faith to believe her soul was somewhere she could hear his words. He remembered a line from Byron's *Manfred* he'd read in a college English Literature class.

I loved her, and destroy'd her!

And not only her—the whole human race too. The fictional Krell destroyed themselves by unwittingly releasing their own inner monsters. His guilt was much greater. *He* had known the risk. And only *he* was responsible for using his power to strip his fellow beings of everything that made them human—leaving only their lowest animal impulses and instincts.

Martin's arms were too weary and unwilling to release Katerina to shake his fist at the heavens—and at the aliens who'd tempted him to know more than he should. His bleary eyes watched the setting Sun reach the horizon. Twilight shadows draped the barren plain and the two "gods"—one already dead, the other soon to be—alone on it. He and his lost love would share this final sunset—then they and every human being would go gently into their last good night.

His mind reached out through space one last time. With no hope for recovery, no way to relieve all that endless suffering, Martin willed the heart of every surviving person on Earth to stop. As humanity died peacefully in its sleep, it was time for Katerina and him to do the same.

The late Dr. Stone said during CPR classes that it took only about five seconds for a person to become unconscious after his heart stopped—not long enough for the last man alive to have any second thoughts. Such a simple final action for someone who'd been granted such great power over matter, energy, gravity, and...

The noontime Sun was slowly descending from its zenith as two figures confronted each other on the ochre plain.

Martin frowned. "I'll guard myself. And I don't have to stop force with greater force. You've made me think of a better way to stop violence. Let me show you..."

His face froze. For long moments he stood petrified—as if staring at the hissing serpents writhing on Medusa's scalp.

Finally Martin snapped out of his trance and whispered, "Look into my mind, Katerina."

She did—and saw him replay a hellish nightmare. Her alien-enhanced consciousness absorbed horrifying events occurring over what seemed hours compressed into a rapid montage lasting only moments. While devils delighted at the destruction of billions the world ended in a nuclear inferno and madness untouched by any heavenly intervention.

In that hypnotic vision of humankind's terrible last day Katerina saw herself and Martin standing here locked in a titanic struggle ending in her own self-inflicted death. As the final act of that tragedy played out he told her what happened next.

Martin said, "Just as I was about to kill myself I remembered what else the aliens gave us the ability to manipulate—time. I used that power to restore your health last night when you were about to die. But I wasn't sure how else I could manipulate time—or if I could use that power to save the world.

"So I experimented. I found the aliens' gift didn't let me physically travel back in time. Then I recalled a story I read in an old SF magazine. It was about a musicologist who inadvertently causes a nuclear war that destroys humanity on a parallel Earth. His 'future' self goes back in time long enough to tell the 'earlier' version of him how to avoid that disaster."

He grinned weakly. "Just a silly story by some obscure writer—but remembering it saved us and the world. I discovered that the aliens *had* given me the power to send *information* into the past. So I sent my memories of that future I created—one that *won't* happen now—back into my mind moments ago. And now I *won't* make the mistake of trying to change human nature too much or too soon!"

Katerina said, "Why didn't you send your memories farther back into the past, to before you started changing the weather or healing people?"

"I couldn't bring myself to do that. Maybe you were right about that too and something bad will eventually come out of what I did to help them. But I couldn't let those people suffer and die!"

Martin stepped closer to her. "I learned a humiliating lesson, Katerina. I was so eager to stamp out stupidity, hatred, and evil in others that I forgot they're part of me too. Before I can control others I have to control myself first.

"I made a terrible mistake—but I've learned from it. The next time I try to improve the way people think I'll be more subtle and test it on only a few of them first—"

"*What?*"

Katerina looked furious. "I just saw how you and your good intentions exterminated the whole human race! Are you going to risk doing that again?"

"I have to do *something* to make the world better, Katerina! It's so full of greed, ignorance, and violence that it'll eventually wreck itself if I don't change things. I have a responsibility to use my powers to save the Earth!"

"And do you think that's what the aliens want you to do—or will even *let* you do? We don't know why the aliens forced their 'gift' on us, Martin. We don't know why they chose *us* to receive it.

"Maybe we're just a sick, depraved form of entertainment to them. Right now they could be waiting to see what you'll do next—hoping that foolish insignificant ant I'm talking to will think up some new way to inadvertently torment and destroy his entire anthill. And when it *does* happen again—when you've amused them once more with your antics—they'll watch you use the power they gave you to undo all that damage for yet another fruitless try!"

Katerina sneered, "'As flies to wanton boys, are we to the gods; They kill us for their sport.' But once you've annihilated and recreated humanity enough times, maybe the aliens will get bored. Perhaps, after you've left the Earth once more in flaming ruins and massacred billions, as a parting joke they'll remove your ability to make it right again.

"Imagine how they'll giggle as you realize that *this* time you've destroyed the world permanently. As the final curtain falls on the human race, maybe they'll let you hear their applause for a fine performance before they head for another inhabited planet searching for someone else as gullible as you!"

Martin shifted his feet and tried hiding the doubt bubbling up in his brain. The confident look on his face sagged. "I don't know what to do, Katerina. I want to do the right thing—but I'm not sure what the right thing is!"

"Then follow the rule that Dr. Stone mentioned in one of his classes. He told us physicians always want to give their patients the best treatment—but they don't always know what the best treatment is. So they follow the precept 'First, do no harm.' If you're not sure how to use your power—and I pray you aren't—then *don't* use it.

"I don't believe you, I, or any human being is wise enough yet to know how to use this much power. If I could, I'd pluck the aliens' 'gift' out of me and fling it back at them! Better to be 'only' human and do whatever limited good we can than to be a 'god' and commit terrible sins, even with the best intentions!"

Katerina's mind touched his. "If you could, Martin, would you become human again with me?"

Martin felt his surroundings melt into a mystical vision. The beautiful woman standing nearby seemed transfigured into a heaven-sent saint glowing with otherworldly radiance, calling him to repentance. The golden cross hanging from her neck swayed like a hypnotist's watch—drawing him into a trance.

His desire to regain this celestial being's love and approval tempted him to submit to her will. The deadlocked struggle raging inside his soul tilted slightly—just long enough for him to reluctantly murmur, "Maybe I would…"

The smile emanating from Katerina's angelic face almost convinced him he'd said the right thing. Then a sense of intense dread snapped him back to reality.

Martin's skin tingled with prickling fear. His gaze whipped around the landscape searching for his terror's source but already knowing what it was. He felt its ponderous presence like the bottom of a giant's foot rushing down to crush him into a Martian grave.

An impossible living mass of sparkling pinpoint lights writhed and undulated several meters away. Their countless numbers scintillated in all the colors of the spectrum, like the manic motion of every star and galaxy in the cosmos seen by some eternal being peering in from outside the Universe itself.

Then he and Katerina waited while the aliens decided their fate.

Sweat trickled down Martin's sides as the aliens focused their attention on him. A passionless voice rippled at him from infinity.

You wish to renounce our gift.

Martin glanced at Katerina. The sad plea in her puppy-like eyes melted whatever resistance he could mount. He whispered, "Yes."

Then it was Katerina's turn for attention.

You wish to renounce our gift.

"Yes!"

The shimmering lights expanded toward the two of them—twisting menacingly in psychedelic hues.

You both wish to renounce our gift.

Martin nodded slightly.

Katerina screamed, "YES!"

There is nothing to renounce. You never had the power you thought you had. Your ability to understand and manipulate what you call Nature is limited by your own nature.

We do not have your limitations. Each time you believed you were manipulating matter, energy, gravity, and time we responded to your thoughts. We created and did what you wished. Everything you saw, heard, thought, and felt beyond the range of your own minds and senses you did through us.

Katerina murmured, "So you really are like Descartes' evil genie."

Martin frowned. "Who? Oh, you mean the—"

Katerina interrupted, "I think what you did was a test. You wanted to see what we would do with godlike powers. Well, we don't want them! Yes, we have great limitations—but despite those limitations we're still capable of great things.

"We don't *need* to be as powerful as you to love, to feel compassion and caring, to fill our world with happiness and joy. Even if our intelligence is nothing compared to yours, it's enough to let us marvel at Creation and use whatever science we can develop to explore its mysteries. We may never be able to travel to other planets and stars as easily as you—but when we do we'll have earned that destiny!"

Martin began, "I'm not sure they're really interested in what you're saying—"

Katerina continued, "It's that curiosity, our need and struggle to explore, to learn all we can, that makes us what we are and gives our lives meaning! I feel sorry for you if you already know all there is to know. What gives meaning to *your* lives?"

Martin cringed—expecting the aliens to be so annoyed after Katerina finished pontificating that they'd zap the two of them into quarks. But as the seconds passed he relaxed slightly. Maybe his overzealous fiancée had managed to beard the lion—

You are a curious species. Your "Earth" is one of many worlds we tend and nurture. When your planet was young we made it possible for life to one day arise on it. We moved and settled it into an orbit ideal for life based on water and carbon chemistry to develop over time.

We made a body similar in size to this one collide with your world to create a moon large enough to produce higher tides, slow its rotation, and reduce its winds to accelerate the development of complex life. We adjusted your planet's axial tilt to make seasons that would moderate its temperatures and directed small bodies rich in organic chemicals to strike it.

After we prepared your world and sowed those seeds on its fertile surface, we waited to see what forms life would take. When a path proved sterile, with no hope of developing a suitable level of sentience, we altered your planet's biosphere by directing more bodies to strike its surface and by other simple methods. This let other types of life come to dominance and follow new paths.

Martin shuddered. It was one thing to read a science fiction story—quite another to be living one. If the aliens were telling the truth, those mass extinctions in Earth's past weren't random accidents—

Your species is the most promising your world has developed. We have given you every opportunity to show us you are suitable. We moved the two planets closest to yours deeper into your sun's habitable zone. We altered them to make it easier for you to travel to and live on them. Then we waited to see if you would send the best your species has to offer to discover why we did it.

Martin suppressed his chuckle at being described as "humanity's best." The aliens could read his thoughts—and they might not value humility or self-deprecation.

As you approached this planet we created an artifact to evaluate your curiosity and encourage you to stay here. We made a second artifact to motivate you as strongly as possible to accept our gift. We have watched how you used that gift.

All this has been done so you could show us what you are. You have been tested to see if you are suitable.

Katerina said, "We've shown you both our best and our worst—our weaknesses and our strengths. We make mistakes—but we *learn* from them. We can be foolish—but we're also wise enough to realize that we shouldn't keep your gift. With all our faults, we can still feel love and compassion great enough to even give up our lives to save others. Based on *everything* you've seen, I hope you do find us 'suitable'."

You have indeed shown us what you are.

Martin glanced at Katerina. The serene expression on her face was the same an ancient Roman martyr displayed before a mighty emperor—

confident he could only break her body and never shake her faith.

Then the aliens spoke again. *You have failed our test. You are like the animals you call cattle and sheep. Your kind has no future.*

We grant you enough time to prepare for your end.

The shimmering lights lingered for a moment before disappearing. A cold breeze ruffled the clothes of the two human beings standing alone on the silent plain. Each of them pondered the parting words of the vanished aliens.

Both of them were afraid—and one of them seethed with a growing anger.

Stone's attention seesawed between the TV monitor showing reports of medical and meteorological miracles and the mammoth screens in the front of the room. He kept hoping for another transmission from Mars to explain why so many inexplicable good things were happening and to ease his fears that they were the prelude to some catastrophe.

Then he noticed Nancy Kelley, newly returned from her press conference, huddling at the other side of the room with several of the project's other senior people. The worried expressions they shared indicated that whatever they were discussing wasn't good.

Kelley separated herself from the group and walked toward Stone. He met her halfway and said, "What's going on?"

The flight director murmured, "I'm not sure—but if the aliens really have turned hostile, it may mean the end of the world!"

Martin was the first to move after the aliens left. He ignored Katerina and trudged past her, heading back toward the habitation module.

She caught up with him. "What do you think they meant, Martin?"

He scowled wordlessly at her and kept walking.

After Martin mutely rebuffed that same question again, Katerina resigned herself to patiently accompanying him back home. The tension between them was so strong and distracting she nearly slipped several times—as if the ground were shifting beneath her feet.

When they reached the module she followed Martin into its communications center. Still waiting for him to speak, she watched him sit down and activate their primary transceiver.

"Mission Control, this is Slayton speaking, audio only. I'll send a detailed description of the situation here after you acknowledge reception. Over."

As they waited the several minutes it would take that message to reach Houston and receive a reply, Martin acted as if he didn't see his fiancée sitting beside him. Katerina tried reassuring herself that he couldn't stay angry forever.

Then he looked at her and hissed, "Is there anything you want to tell me, Katerina?"

"I don't know what you're talking about, Martin!"

"No? Just before they disappeared the aliens gave me a private telepathic message. They informed me you really *did* sabotage my effort to save humanity! You used your 'power' to pull a stunt on me from one of those grade-Z 1950s science fiction movies I showed you during our flight here, *Invasion U.S.A.*

"I let you have free access to my mind to show you I had nothing to hide—and you took advantage of my trust! You used your power to put those ideas in my head about how to change human nature—and then you hypnotized me! And while I was in that trance you told me what the aliens said you called a 'noble lie.' All those terrible things I thought I did—everything that seemed to happen to you, me, the people at Mission Control and throughout the world—*none of it really happened!* I thought I'd saved the world by using one bad SF cliché. Instead you made me fall for the biggest cliché of all—'It was all a dream!'"

Martin shouted, "I only *thought* I tried to change human nature! I only *imagined* I destroyed you and the whole human race! Those 'memories' I seemed to oh-so-cleverly send back through time were just a noontime nightmare *you* created inside my mind using my own thoughts, doubts, and fears—a nightmare that seemed to go on for hours but really lasted only moments! It was all just a mental melodrama you deliberately directed—even acting out the role of my 'innocent' victim— to convince me I was wrong about how we could help humanity!

"*That's* why we failed the aliens' test to see if we could improve human nature—*because you never let me try!*"

A voice at Mission Control crackled from the transceiver's speaker. "Stone here. Please describe your current medical condition and Savitskaya's. Let us know if either of you is in any immediate danger."

Unintelligible voices murmured excitedly in the background before Stone continued, "I've been asked to tell you that the orbiters at your location and ground-based observations indicate Mars is experiencing a significant new decay in its orbit. The planet's rate of movement towards the Sun is more rapid than when the aliens moved it previously.

"There's insufficient data yet to determine where or if Mars will resume a stable orbit. If you have any information about this new anomaly, please send it immediately! "

Martin glared at Katerina contemptuously. "Well? Should I tell them what happened? You were afraid that I might accidentally destroy the human race if I tried to help it. Now, because of *you* it will be destroyed!"

"What do you mean, Martin?"

"You were so sure the aliens were surrogates of Satan, tempting us to accept and use power we shouldn't have, that you didn't think how things might look from *their* point of view. Instead of improving humanity like they wanted us to do, you tricked and pressured me into joining you in throwing their gift back in their faces. No wonder they decided we were a couple of cowardly obnoxious ingrates and that our entire species wasn't 'suitable' for their help!"

Martin sneered. "Don't look at me like you don't know what happens next. You heard what Stone said about Mars moving toward the Sun again. The aliens practically confessed to redirecting an asteroid to wipe out the dinosaurs and causing other mass extinctions. They also claimed to have created the Moon by slamming a Mars-sized planet into Earth billions of years ago.

"*I* think they're planning to do it again with the *real* Mars—and when those two worlds collide it'll be the last thing the whole human race ever sees!"

Katerina stammered, "I can't believe—" But the heavy hands that this time grabbed and shook her shoulders for real cut her off.

Martin glared at the deceitful woman he'd loved and screamed, "*What have you done?*"

Thus Spake the Aliens

Man is a rope stretched between the animal and the
superman—a rope stretched across an abyss.

Friedrich Wilhelm Nietzsche

E arth was doomed.

Katerina Savitkaya, the woman responsible for her world's impending destruction, knelt alone and miserable on the metal floor of the sole dwelling on Mars. The filthy blue jumpsuit shrouding her shapely thirty-three-year-old figure like sackcloth reeked with sweat and fear. Tears stung her ashen cheeks as she prayed before the colorful religious icons attached to a closed locker door in the habitation module's science lab.

The young cosmonaut's trembling hands clutched the heavy golden three-barred cross hanging from her neck on a gold chain. Her hazel eyes gazed penitently upward—begging for humanity to be spared and for her to be forgiven.

But the devout grandmother who'd inspired Katerina's fervent Russian Orthodox faith had never taught her orisons for a sin this great. Greasy lifeless strands of long auburn hair draped Katerina's shoulders like a cloistered nun's veil as she waited for some heaven-sent sign that her prayers were heard. But no soothing miraculous whisper murmured from the mouths of the sacred icons before her. The painted pinpoint eyes of the Savior and her patron saint, St. Catherine of Alexandria, stared blindly back at her.

Katerina rose to her feet. Her black boots tapped the muffled rhythm of a funeral march as she passed through the openings in the habitation module's compartments. She paused at the module's open exit and viewed a spectacle only two humans had ever beheld. Though it was afternoon twenty-five million kilometers away in her native St. Petersburg, here the young Russian watched the rosy light of a Martian dawn gradually brighten the surrounding reddish-orange plain.

But today, on what was March 9, 2036 in the city of her birth, she was oblivious to this scene's beauty. Her throat ached as unbearable grief turned the warm moist oxygen-rich air filling her lungs into sobs.

Katerina trudged down the short ramp that led from the module to the barren ground. Her boots kicked up clumps of paprika-tinted mud.

She stopped—wondering if the mysterious aliens who'd terraformed Mars were listening to her thoughts now. Because of her they'd condemned this world and Earth to mutual annihilation. Perhaps she should pray to the aliens—not to the God who'd abandoned her and might as well be dead.

Over the past ten years those enigmatic beings had used godlike powers to change Mars from a frigid stillborn world to a wet balmy "paradise" where humans could walk its cinnamon-colored surface without protection. With superhuman skills they'd increased the planet's gravity to 0.91 g and moved it to a circular orbit only seven million kilometers farther from the Sun than Earth's average distance. After devoting such enormous energies to those projects, perhaps the aliens might still be persuaded to reconsider their decision to destroy their work by obliterating both Mars and Earth in a titanic collision.

But first she had to plead her case. The aliens appeared and disappeared at will. Yesterday afternoon they'd passed judgment on her and vanished before she realized that she was responsible for their decision to sentence the entire human race to death. Throughout the longest darkest night of her soul she'd tried repeatedly to summon them back by her thoughts and words. She'd even set the main transceiver in the module to transmit a continuously repeating recorded message on the frequency the aliens themselves had suggested to call them on her first day on Mars.

So far her appeals were unanswered. There was one more thing she could try to get the aliens' attention—even if it meant her own death. Before taking that desperate measure, Katerina closed her eyes and extended her arms straight out from her sides like the transverse beam of a cross, in a humble gesture of supplication. She murmured, "Please answer me. Do whatever you want to me—but don't destroy billions of innocent people because of what I've done!"

A low dark voice replied, "Nothing you say or do will change anything. Earth is doomed."

Katerina opened her eyes and turned around to face the only other human on Mars.

Martin Slayton stood several meters away and returned his fiancée's gaze. The expression on his clean-shaven face now showed more disappointment than the anger and contempt it held yesterday when the aliens revealed how she'd deceived him. The boots and blue jumpsuit he wore matched Katerina's, though his uniform was cleaner and filled out a taller, muscular frame. After a troubled night's sleep he'd just finished showering, dressing, and mustering enough courage to track down the woman he'd loved.

The farm boy-turned-astronaut from Marshfield, Missouri ran a hand through his black close-cropped hair. "I heard you praying and moving around in the module every time I woke up last night. After I cleaned up this morning I went to use the transceiver to check in with Mission Control and found that message you're transmitting. It won't work. If the aliens wanted to see us beg for mercy, they would've reappeared by now."

"I agree, Martin. That's why I'm going to them."

"Good luck finding them! Who knows where they come from when they pop out of nowhere or go when they disappear. Even the few times they've talked to us it's like they're barely there. Just a tele-pathic voice in our heads and sparkly psychedelic lights like the cheap special effects in a late 1960s acid trip movie."

"They appeared after we explored the two artifacts we found here. If they created a third artifact, I expect I'll find them there too."

"*If* they decide to make another artifact. Or they might reappear if you tick them off again like you did yesterday!"

The fury in Martin's eyes dissipated as quickly as it appeared. "Sorry, Katerina. I know you were trying to do the right thing when you tricked me. I never disagreed with you that the power the aliens gave us to man-ipulate matter, energy, gravity, and time could be dangerous in the wrong hands.

"But it hurts that you didn't trust me enough to believe *I* wouldn't misuse those powers—that you didn't think I was smart enough to avoid inadvertently using them to destroy the world. Sure, I saved millions of people from dying due to natural disasters, disease, and famine. But what if you'd let me use those powers to change human nature—to elim-inate our capacity for violence and war, to instill a sense of empathy and conscience into every person?"

Martin shook his head. "It's too late now. You renounced your pow-ers because you never wanted them in the first place. I made the worst mistake of my life and gave them up because you made me think I'd used them to temporarily destroy the human race. And because the aliens believe we're cowards or worse for giving up that chance to im-prove humanity, they're going to destroy it and search elsewhere for a better, more 'suitable' species than us."

"I realize what I did was wrong, Martin. I shouldn't have tricked you or lied to you. I know that being sorry and asking forgiveness isn't enough. I'll do everything I can to make things right again—or die trying."

Martin studied the determined look on Katerina's lovely face. "And I'd die trying with you—if there were anything we could do to save the world. But there isn't."

"There is, Martin. The aliens *have* created a third artifact. We can go to it together. And if the aliens are there, they'll have to either listen to us—or kill us."

Martin stiffened. "How do you know there's another artifact?"

"I kept in touch with Mission Control while you were sleeping. Twelve hours ago the Scout orbiter spotted a new anomaly on top of Olympus Mons. Our superiors in Houston said that based on imaging and radar data it looks like a building four hundred meters high."

"And I bet it suddenly appeared when nobody was looking, just like the aliens' other artifacts. But why'd they put it there? Their other two artifacts were designed to attract our attention and lure us to explore them. They were also in locations we could reach easily."

"The top of Olympus Mons definitely does not qualify as easy to reach. If I remember correctly, it's about three thousand kilometers away and almost twenty-seven kilometers above sea level. Even with the atmosphere on Mars being similar to Earth's now, we'll need our spacesuits at that elevation. It also took us several days of fast traveling in the rover the other week to reach just the outskirts of its base—and that was over three hundred kilometers from the caldera complex at its top. Even if we drove to Olympus Mons, there's a steep escarpment six kilometers high surrounding the central plateau on its top. We don't have the skill or equipment for that level of rock climbing!"

Katerina sighed. "Mission Control said the same things to me when I talked with them. Then I told them how we could reach the top of Olympus Mons."

"Unless you found the transporter NASA forgot to tell us they built into our habitation module and plan to beam over to that mountaintop, there's no way—"

Martin's eyebrows arched. "Our ascent vehicle. You told them we could use the only way we have to get off this planet and back to Earth."

"It's perfect for a short suborbital flight. We have plenty of propellant for a round trip and enough reserves to refuel it for whenever we need to reach orbit. I've already moved all the equipment we'll need into the vehicle and programmed the flight path. We can start launch procedures immediately. "

"Silly question, but did Mission Control or your bosses at the Russian Space Agency approve your suicide mission?"

"Of course not. But they can't stop us."

Katerina's hazel eyes bored into her fiancé's darker ones. "And only *you* can stop me."

"Launch systems go. T minus 50 seconds and counting."

Martin listened to Katerina's calm voice over their helmets' communication link and tried convincing himself he wasn't making the second-worst mistake of his life. Katerina, rubbing shoulders besides him on his right, showed no trace of the doubts distracting him from his prelaunch tasks. She calmly checked the ascent vehicle's instrument displays through her clear helmet and continued the countdown.

Though the form-fitting white plastisuits Katerina and he wore were less bulky than a standard-issue spacesuit, they were scrunched together so tightly in their padded seats within the rocket's tiny windowless cabin that it was hard to move. Normally he would have enjoyed sitting so close to his fiancée and the way Katerina's suit accentuated her curves. Instead it felt like they were strapped together in a flying coffin.

"T minus 45 seconds."

Even if they managed to reach the top of Olympus Mons, find the aliens and persuade them to not destroy Earth, then fly the vehicle back to the vicinity of the habitation module—well, in the immortal words of Ricky Ricardo they'd have some 'splainin' to do to Mission Control.

Then again, getting on NASA's naughty list was the least of his worries.

"T minus 40 seconds."

Martin checked the propellant pressure gauges and reflexively pressed a switch with his gloved hand. He wondered if the aliens were peering inside the rocket right now—laughing at the puny humans who thought they could still save their world.

Maybe those omnipresent extraterrestrials were also watching when Katerina talked him into going along with her crazy scheme. She'd said the latest word from Mission Control was that Mars was still spiraling slowly inward toward the Sun. Data from the orbiters overhead and ground-based observations indicated the planet would reach Earth's orbit within a year.

"T minus 30 seconds."

The margin of error in those measurements was too great to determine if the two worlds would collide when that happened in the ultimate Torino 10. But neither the two of them nor anyone on Earth could come up with a more optimistic reason why the aliens had decided to move Mars again. Martin shuddered as he remembered the last words they'd directed at humanity through Katerina and him.

You have failed our test. You are like the animals you call cattle and sheep. Your kind has no future.

We grant you enough time to prepare for your end.

"T minus 20 seconds."

Martin wondered when the aliens would end this quixotic farce. Those beings from beyond could move planets at will. They'd terraformed Mars in a decade and were well on their way to doing the same to Venus. They could read minds, create illusions, control weather, perform miraculous cures, and build gigantic artifacts out of nothing. Surely annihilating a spaceship and its crew was child's play to them.

Still—if this was the end, at least Katerina and he had spent these last few hours together. He remembered her shouting at him, "You can be like the cattle and sheep the aliens called us if you want. I'd rather die trying to save the world than cower here doing nothing like you!"

Common sense crumbled before that kind of argument and determination. And so, freshly encased in their plastisuits, they'd exited the habitation module for probably the last time and trudged the half kilometer north to the ascent vehicle. It was the most advanced single-stage-to-orbit craft ever developed—a distant descendant of the venerable Delta Clipper from the early 1990s.

A recent shower had washed most of the fine coating of reddish Martian dust from the vehicle's white surface. It was shaped like a blunt-nosed cone over fifty meters tall, with its broad base resting firmly on five stubby landing legs. After Katerina and he sealed themselves inside they'd started the same protocol used before a spacewalk—switching the internal atmosphere to pure oxygen for them to prebreathe and then gradually reducing the cabin's pressure to meet the lower pressure requirements for their suits before finally putting on their helmets.

"T minus 10 seconds."

Martin squinted at the OLED screens showing the scene outside caught by the vehicle's external cameras. The rocket began to vibrate as Katerina's countdown reached zero and the engines ignited. He felt himself pressed back into his seat as the two of them headed up face-first into the clear Martian sky. The ground displayed on the screens receded and vanished in a billowing cloud of exhaust and dust as they rose higher and faster.

With the displays still showing all systems nominal, Martin glanced at Katerina. Her lips were moving in prayer behind her helmet. As the rocket arced gracefully toward Olympus Mons, he thought of Alan Shepard's fifteen-minute voyage back in 1961. Their suborbital flight would last only several minutes longer than his. Martin grimly recited the bowdlerized version of the prayer America's first astronaut said when Freedom 7 blasted off.

"Please, dear God, don't let me mess up."

Katerina stopped praying as the vehicle began shaking and warning indicators flashed on the display console. The attitude jets were malfunctioning. They'd been designed to maneuver the rocket primarily in space so it could dock with the return vessel waiting in orbit to take them back to Earth. But until now they'd done well adjusting the craft's orientation for a nose-up landing on the summit of Olympus Mons, now only ten kilometers away and three kilometers below them.

Martin's hands beat hers to the controls. His voice crackled through the transceivers in their helmets, "Switching to manual."

Katerina scanned the display. "Propellant levels still good. Orientation still go for landing—"

Suddenly she was thrown against Martin's shoulder as their craft jerked down toward the left. The rocket threatened to go into an uncontrolled tumble as her crewmate strained to right it. Though the vibrations rattling the craft stayed strong Katerina relaxed slightly as the instruments showed the rocket was back in the base-downward direction needed to fire their main engines.

Then a reading on the display grabbed her attention. She cried, "The attitude jets aren't the problem! Look at the wind speed and atmospheric pressure around us!"

Martin grimaced as he fought to maintain control of the ascent vehicle. "That's impossible! It's like we're in the middle of a windstorm! There's not enough air at this altitude to do that—unless the aliens are—"

His words were cut short as they both stared at the images on the OLED screens. The cameras on their craft's outer hull were pointing down toward the layered caldera complex on top of Olympus Mons. But beneath them a raging dust storm roiled like a dense reddish-orange fog—covering and obscuring over thirty square kilometers of the cratered landscape rushing toward the rocket.

Katerina shouted, "We're heading right toward that storm!"

Martin nodded. "And we don't have enough leeway in our trajectory to avoid it."

He stared at a display—then flicked it futilely with his fingers. "Great! Radar's on the fritz so we can't measure exactly how far above the ground we are! No telling how high the dust is above the surface or what visibility is like inside it. Let's hope we can see the ground well enough to use the jets to maneuver us someplace that's level enough to land!"

"At least we're on target! There's the artifact!"

One screen showed the uppermost end of a gigantic solid shaft poking up out of the swirling opaque cloud of dust. It looked like a gleaming gray metal cube one hundred meters on a side floating on a billowing ocean of fog the color of dried blood.

Katerina said, "The artifact is supposed to be four hundred meters tall. Based on how much of it we're seeing, the dust storm must go up about three hundred meters above the ground!"

"Thanks for the info, but we're still in big trouble!"

They jerked back in their seats as the main engines fired. The vibrations rattling their falling decelerating craft grew stronger as they entered the dust storm and the pictures on the screens showed only a thick gritty red mist.

Martin glanced angrily at the malfunctioning radar altimeter and fought to keep their rocking craft upright as he yelled, "I can't see where we're landing! Hope it's not in a crater or on a slope—"

A deep bass *thump!* rattled the base of the rocket and quickly shot upward to shake its two occupants high in the vessel's nose section. Katerina cried, "Main engines off!" Then she looked at Martin, sitting frozen at the controls.

The craft quivered as gusting winds flung themselves against its outer shell. Silence filled the tiny cabin. Katerina murmured, "Touchdown."

Her smile vanished as she realized that her body was slowly listing forward. The restraining straps confining Katerina to her seat stretched taut to keep her from falling toward the display console. Someone outside the rocket would've seen it tilting like the Leaning Tower of Pisa— and then, like a towering oak felled by the last stroke of a lumberjack's ax, the craft toppled over. Her cry as they fell was choked off as they smashed against the cold hard Martian ground...

As the rocket tumbled over Martin's mind flashed back to when he was thirteen. He was sitting in the log flume ride at an amusement park in nearby Branson for the first time—slowly ascending to a point nearly twenty meters high. Suddenly he was plunging down a steep chute toward the waiting waters below. As the ascent vehicle accelerated downward with him seated at about twice that height Martin felt the same sickening tightness in his stomach he did as a teenager—but this time there was no thrill, only terror—

His teeth rattled and his head whipped forward as the rocket's side struck the ground. For an instant his consciousness faded—then a brief pounding headache made him realize he wasn't dead after all. The lights and glowing displays in the cabin flickered but stayed on—for now. If the craft's batteries failed it would be as dark as a coffin with its lid closed.

Martin winced from scattered bruises—but nothing felt broken. He twisted his body rightward to check on Katerina. Though the blinking face peering out from her clear helmet looked stunned it showed no obvious sign of pain.

Then a terrifying second memory flooded his brain. He remembered reading about the tragic last test flight of the modified Delta Clipper, the DC-XA—their craft's ancestor. A faulty landing strut made the vehicle tip over when it landed. After it fell on its side liquid oxygen from the unmanned rocket's damaged fuel tank fed a fire that destroyed the craft. In a wave of frenzied déjà vu Martin imagined smoke filling their cabin and the flames of a raging inferno engulfing them.

"We've got to get out!"

A calmer voice replied, "Yes, Martin. Help me with my oxygen pack."

Katerina unfastened her restraining straps and leaned forward. Martin released the small square metal oxygen pack attached to the rear of her seat and secured it to the back of her plastisuit. As she returned the favor with his pack he wondered what they could've done to escape if their craft had toppled over with them sitting upside down.

His crewmate stood on her seat and wriggled herself up through the small open hatch in what was now their curved ceiling. Martin followed her into the short narrow crawlway that led to the storage compartment just behind their cabin. As he squirmed through the cramped passage Martin saw Katerina lower herself feet first into another open hatch close to what used to be the floor of the compartment but now, with the vessel lying on its side, formed a wall instead. He looked down through the hatch and saw Katerina using the gear and supplies secured to the compartment's cylindrical side and erstwhile floor as impromptu footholds and handholds to reach its bottom some five meters below.

She opened a storage container and extracted a large coil of rope. Her voice came over his suit's radio. "I'm going to toss you the end of this rope. Then I'll tie the heavier equipment and supplies we need to the other end so you can pull them up to the crawlway."

They worked rapidly, bringing up tool chests, food, water, and spare oxygen packs. Martin yanked each item through the hatch, untied it, then pushed it ahead of him just beyond the sealed access door directly above the crawlway and several meters down toward the rocket's base. He tried not to think about any fire that might be raging about the rocket as they worked—or the threat of an explosion.

Finally Martin used the rope to pull the last and most precious cargo up through the hatch—Katerina herself. She crawled in front of him and then flipped into a supine position to depressurize the crawlway and unseal the access door above her. It opened outward—letting in a fine mist of reddish dust.

Katerina lifted her upper body through the open hatch and twisted around to scan their surroundings. "This dust storm is like a dense fog, Martin. The wind doesn't feel too strong now. But visibility is only about four meters and we're too high to see the ground through this dust. At least I don't see anything that looks like a fire in the direction of our fuel tanks and engines."

"Thanks for the weather report. Now let's get our supplies and us out of here!"

After looping one end of the rope around the base of the open access door Katerina rappelled down the side of the fallen rocket to the ground. Over the next few minutes they repeated cycles of Martin pulling the rope back up, tying equipment and supplies to it, then lowering the rope to where Katerina could untie those items and stack them near her.

Finally Martin used the rope to join her on mars firma. Then he employed a long-unused skill he'd picked up before a rodeo competition during high school—flicking the looped end of the rope off the door until it fell at his feet. After winding the rope into a loose coil he slipped it over his right arm and onto his shoulder.

Martin looked at the fallen ascent vehicle. "So much for our ride home. Hope our bosses don't take this out of our paychecks."

He examined the containers piled nearby. "Good thing we have enough oxygen packs to last each of us over seventy-two hours. There's plenty of water to resupply our suits' reservoirs and power packs for temperature control—but we're going to have to find someplace where we can take off our helmets to use our food rations. You're used to fasting a couple days at a time during Lent, but I'm not. Maybe the atmosphere will be breathable inside the artifact when we—"

Martin glanced around him. "Katerina? Where are you?"

Only static crackled over his helmet's radio. Dust swirled thickly around him like a bloody mist as he stood alone beside the wrecked rocket on a desert-like plain.

A nightmare vision of Katerina falling off the nearby edge of the caldera to shattering death kilometers below overloaded his imagination. Or perhaps she'd fallen prey to bloodthirsty sandsharks from an old *Outer Limits* episode erupting from the Martian soil. Maybe the aliens had returned and snuffed her out of existence with a single thought—

Suddenly he spied a wraith-like figure floating toward him. As he shivered and faced his doom the apparition spoke.

"The damage doesn't look as bad from out here."

Martin's jaw dropped at Katerina's presumably unintentional quotation from Episode IV. Her plastisuit's form-fitting exterior coated with a patina of reddish-brown dust made her resemble a copper-colored version of C-3PO.

For an instant he was six-years-old again on a family vacation to the Smithsonian's National Air and Space Museum. He'd wandered away from his parents and older brother and hightailed back to a favorite exhibit. They'd found him sitting inside the mockup of a Gemini capsule working the controls as he orbited Earth. Now he reflexively repeated his mother's words.

"You scared the daylights out of me! Don't ever wander away like that again!"

He saw Katerina's eyebrows arch through her dusty helmet. She replied, "Two of the landing struts fell into a small crater about a meter deep. If we'd landed a few meters to one side we wouldn't have fallen."

"Unfortunately we did, and there's no way we can get the ascent vehicle upright again. But I think we have enough rope and supplies to climb down the escarpment to an altitude where we won't need our suits or supplemental oxygen anymore."

"First we need to do what we came here for, Martin—find the artifact and talk to the aliens."

"Right. Just one problem, Katerina."

Martin looked out several meters into the opaque dust storm swirling around them. "Where *is* the artifact?"

Katerina frowned. "We were heading toward the artifact when we crashed. I'm not sure how far away it is, but if we follow the direction the nose cone is pointing we'll come to it eventually."

Martin shook his head. "Not necessarily. Those winds we went through on the way down blew us sideways and spun us around. I wouldn't trust using the rocket as part of a game of 'Spin the Bottle' to point where the artifact is."

"Do you have a better idea?"

Martin walked over to a metal case on the ground and opened it. "Maybe. Remember when we explored that first artifact the day we landed? The metal platform the aliens made emitted lots of RF energy, like an analog radio transmitter."

He extracted a rectangular palm-sized transceiver. A short flexible plastic-coated antenna extended from the device's top.

Katerina smiled. "That's right, you used one of those to pick up their signals!"

Martin turned the handheld transceiver on and pressed small buttons on its front. One of the buttons wirelessly linked the transceiver's audio with the radio in his helmet.

He scanned through several bands. "I still remember what frequencies that other artifact used. Good, there's a strong AM signal at 700 kHz with what sounds like a test tone…and some FM carrier waves between 824 MHz and 894 MHz with a weird warbling sound!"

Martin held the transceiver in a fixed horizontal position in front of his chest. He slowly rotated his body back and forth in short arcs— listening to how loud the transmission was and checking the signal strength bars on the device's small display. "The signal's strongest in that direction—right in front of me and about forty-five degrees to the right of where the rocket's nose is pointing. Now to do some triangulation and estimate how far away the artifact is."

Katerina watched Martin walk sideways to his left, measuring off the distance with meter-long strides while he kept the transceiver's antenna oriented toward where the artifact's signal was strongest. Two minutes after he'd disappeared into the dust storm he hadn't returned.

"Martin?"

Only static answered her. She reassured herself that he was simply out of range. The radio frequency energy the artifact produced could be interfering with the signals from the radios in their helmets—reducing the distance they could communicate.

Three minutes later he still hadn't reappeared. "Martin! Are you all right?"

No answer. She began edging away from the ship in the direction he'd vanished. As she lost sight of the rocket Katerina tried to keep her bearings so she could retrace her steps before she became hopelessly lost—

A shadow moved at the very edge of visibility several meters away. It resolved into a spacesuited figure walking toward her with a slight limp.

"Martin!"

The figure stopped. "Thank goodness! I *was* moving in the right direction!"

Martin frowned. "Wait a second. Where's the rocket?"

"Right over there—I think!"

He grabbed Katerina's hand. "Hope you're right!"

She was. Safely back with their ship and supplies, Martin said, "I was coming back after triangulating the artifact's position when I stepped in a crater the size of a gopher hole and took a tumble.

"The transceiver flew out of my hand. Took me a while to find it—

and when I did it wasn't working. Might've hit a rock when it fell. Then I realized I wasn't sure which direction you and the ship were. Fortunately I guessed close enough to find you before we both got lost!"

Martin placed the damaged transceiver back in its metal case. "No way to repair it here. At least I know from my signal strength measurements that the artifact is about three kilometers away."

He oriented himself beside the ship. "This is the approximate direction I was facing before when I got the strongest signal. Guess that's the way we should go. Still—it'd be nice to have the transceiver working to make sure we weren't veering off enough to miss the artifact in this storm.

"But even if we find the artifact, how will we know which way to go to get back to the ship? We can carry several extra oxygen packs and supplies with us when we go meet the aliens—but we'll need some of this other equipment here to climb down the side of Olympus Mons afterwards. Too bad we don't have any breadcrumbs to leave as a trail back here."

Katerina bent down and opened a metal case on the ground. "I went over the ascent vehicle's cargo inventory list last night. This case should contain—yes!"

She handed Martin the spare transceiver and smiled as its display lit up when he pressed the power button. "I hope you like your gift, Martin."

"I'll treasure it always—and keep it away from rocks!"

Katerina opened her other hand and displayed a small circular object. "You'll like this compass too. It wouldn't have worked on the 'old' Mars—but when the aliens terraformed the planet they gave it a magnetic field complete with north and south poles similar to Earth. Now we have everything we need to keep our bearings."

"We make a good team, Katerina. I can't think of anybody I'd rather be marooned on Mars with."

"Let's hope we can impress the aliens too."

The dust storm grew murkier around them as they trudged cautiously across the rock-strewn plain. Martin led the way with his transceiver directing them towards the signal transmitted by the artifact. The coil of rope lay draped around his shoulder. He'd cut off a short piece of the rope and used it to tie two extra oxygen packs together. Then he'd hung the cord across the back of his neck. The metal oxygen packs rattled across his chest as he walked. His free hand clutched a toolbox's handle.

Katerina carried a similar chain of two oxygen packs across her neck. She walked hunched forward slightly, trying to keep the packs from bouncing against parts of her chest more prominent and sensitive than Martin's. Her left hand carried a case containing spare water and supplies. The compass rested in her right palm.

Several meters ahead of her Martin said, "Too bad we didn't bring a pedometer. I think the artifact's close now—what the—!"

Suddenly Katerina couldn't see him anymore. She trotted forward shouting, "Where are you?"

Suddenly she stopped—dazzled by bright glaring light. Her raised right hand cupped the compass and shielded her vision from the awful radiance around her. Then she realized where that blazing brilliance high above her originated.

It was the Sun.

Katerina stared up at a clear blue sky with a pinkish tinge dominated by that golden orb at its noontime zenith. She turned her head and saw the opaque dust storm she'd just exited seething a meter behind her—as if separated from her by an invisible curtain. She was in a column of still air and light like the eye of a hurricane that extended up to the heavens and across a circular plain three hundred meters in diameter. In the center of the plain stood the tall dark structure whose top they'd spotted during their descent—its full form and immediate surroundings now cleared of the dust storm still raging outside this oasis.

Martin cried, "Look at that!"

He stood near her—gazing up at a tower formed of gleaming gray metal. Its height was every centimeter of the four hundred meters that the orbiter had estimated—a rectangular prism with a square base a hundred meters on a side. Halfway up the artifact, beginning two hundred meters above the ground, a pair of solid cubes one hundred meters in all three dimensions jutted out from the main tower. Each of those cubes was attached to one of the tower's two visible sides.

Martin snorted. "Let's hope the aliens didn't get the idea for that artifact from one of the 1950s monster movies in my collection. Don't think I've shown you that one—it's called *Kronos*. I can't see from this angle if that thing has a *really* big rabbit ear antenna on top—but if it starts coming toward us on humongous pillar legs moving up and down like pile drivers we're in big trouble!"

Martin squatted, laid his tool chest and transceiver on the ground, and removed the chain of oxygen packs from around his neck. Then he opened the chest and removed a pair of high-powered image-stabilizing binoculars. He raised them to his helmet and adjusted their focus to compensate for the longer than usual distance between his eyes and the device's eyepieces.

Katerina set her burdens down too. "Do you see any markings on it or an entrance anywhere, Martin?"

"No. Looks all solid—just the same gray metal the aliens used to make the other two artifacts. Except—there's a thin horizontal line indenting it about a quarter of the way up from the ground—then another line halfway up…"

Martin lowered the binoculars. "The main tower isn't one continuous piece. It looks like four cubes stacked on top of each other—like some gigantic child's building blocks. Then Junior put some glue on one side of those two cubes most of the way up the main tower and stuck them on the sides of that third cube from the bottom..."

He groaned. "Oh, no!"

"What's the matter, Martin?"

"Wait here!"

Katerina watched him run toward the artifact and disappear around its right corner. He didn't answer when she called to him over her helmet radio. Just as she decided to go after him he rounded the left corner of the tower and trotted toward her. His panting voice reached her several meters before the rest of him did.

"I was afraid of that."

"What, Martin?"

He pointed toward the artifact. "See those two cubes attached to each side of that third cube from the bottom? There are two more just like them attached to the other two faces of that cube."

Katerina frowned. "Then that structure is really a tesseract—a four-dimensional hypercube—that's been unfolded into eight three-dimensional cubes. I remember Salvador Dali used that form in his painting *Crucifixion*."

"Yeah, I read about that painting in a classic turn-of-the-century SF novel. No telling why the aliens made their artifact in that shape—but I hope they haven't been reading early Heinlein lately!"

They moved their equipment and oxygen packs to the middle of the artifact's nearest wall. Martin grumbled, "No sign of a doorbell or an entrance. Didn't see any obvious door on the other sides either when I ran around this thing."

"Maybe there's some hidden button on it we could push to make a secret panel slide open, like you thought there might be in that pyramid the other day."

"Could be. But I'm not going to touch this thing until I'm sure it's safe to do it. Just because the aliens didn't electrify their other artifacts to zap us like Emperor Ming tried to do to Flash Gordon in the third serial doesn't mean they won't do it this time. And I brought this tool chest with us because it has what I need inside it!"

Martin extracted a multimeter, high voltage probe meter, and a short metal rod. He placed the multimeter near the artifact and pushed the metal rod into the soil close to the tower's side. Then he clipped the high voltage probe's ground lead to the rod, gripped the probe's insulated handle, and said, "When the other end of this thing touches the artifact's side I'll see if there's high voltage running through it. If the reading's low enough, the multimeter will tell us exactly how much voltage and current is present."

The far end of the probe reached toward the artifact—

Martin froze. He said, "Didn't expect that!"

"Let go of it, Martin!"

Instead he retracted the probe, studying its apparently undamaged distal end. Before Katerina could warn him not to repeat his experiment he thrust the probe like a rapier back at the artifact. Its point passed through the unscathed gray metal as if the wall in front of them wasn't there. The end of the probe vanished from view—then partially reappeared as Martin worked it in and out of the artifact, as if he were using a fork to check the doneness of a juicy steak.

Finally he extracted the probe completely and said, "The aliens have used illusions on us before—but not on this scale. Or maybe this wall is real but is permeable to solid objects…as if what I'm saying makes any sense!"

"Let me try something, Martin."

Katerina walked a few paces back and picked up a baseball-sized rock. She lobbed it at the metal wall—and watched the rock disappear through it without a sound. Several more rocks thrown at the wall met the same fate.

Martin said, "Pretty obvious what the next experiment is." Before Katerina's horrified gaze he passed his left arm up to the elbow through the wall, then extracted it.

He wiggled the extremity. "No pain—still five fingers—looks okay."

Katerina shouted, "That was a stupid thing to do! What if that wall turned solid when your arm was inside or sliced it off like a guillotine blade!"

Martin shrugged with nervous relief. "We came here to explore the artifact, Katerina. No point holding back now. And you know what comes next."

"Yes. We go inside and look for the aliens."

"Right—except for the 'we' part. I'm going inside and you're staying here."

"No, Martin. We're in this together. We succeed and live or fail and die as a team."

"Being a team doesn't mean we should jump out of a plane together to see if the parachute we're testing works. Better for one of us to test it—and if the parachute fails only that person gets splattered, not both. *You* jumped solo on that first artifact we found. We went into that second artifact together—and both got trapped. Now it's *my* turn to go first— and if I strike out, there'll still be one last out in the bottom of the ninth for you to try hitting a home run for our team."

Katerina's face turned crimson behind her helmet. She stamped her boot and shouted, "I'm not interested in taking turns or your silly metaphors! If only one of us goes inside it should be me! *I'm* the one who made the aliens angry and put Earth in danger! *I'm* responsible, *I* should be the one who takes the risk first!"

"No, you've just given the best reason why you *shouldn't* go in there. If the aliens are still mad at you, they might zap you before you have a chance to play Portia and use your oratorical skills on them.

"On the other hand, *I* didn't give them any flack when they offered me their gift. *I* didn't want to give up the power they loaned us—and they know I only did it because you tricked me. Even if they bring that up I'll quote Scripture and say, 'The woman made me do it.' *I* know that's not an excuse, *I* take responsibility for what I did—but maybe it'll mollify the aliens long enough for me to pretend I'm Perry Mason and save *H. sapiens.*"

Katerina started to reply—but everything she tried to say tasted wrong. She knew her greatest objection to Martin's plan was really based on her love for him and the fear she'd lose him forever. She was willing to die if it meant saving him and Earth. But if he really did have a better chance than her of saving the world—and she couldn't honestly argue against his point—she'd be putting her own personal good over that of the entire human race.

It'd be less terrible to die than to live without Martin—but even if it meant more pain for her she couldn't let others suffer because of her.

Behind her helmet, tears trickled down her cheeks. Katerina murmured, "Let's get you ready."

"It's time, Martin."

Katerina checked the gauge on the full oxygen pack she'd just helped him replace on his back after he'd helped her replace the one on hers. "You have enough oxygen for eight hours—if you don't exert yourself too much."

"Okay. Now let's set up a backup communications system in case we lose radio contact once I go inside."

Martin unwound one end of the rope coiled around his shoulder. He knotted it tightly around the middle of the short length of rope connecting their two remaining full oxygen packs.

"Remember, Katerina. I'll play out the rope until I enter the tower.

After I'm inside, I'll put some slack in it. If I need you to come in I'll give the rope a tug and you'll see the oxygen packs move toward that wall. Hopefully I'll find the aliens right away, get the answer we want, and leave without needing you to come in after me.

"But if I'm not back or you don't see the rope pulled by seven hours from now, come in with an oxygen pack. That'll mean I'll either need it soon—or I never will and it'll be *your* turn to deal with the aliens."

Martin removed a flashlight from his tool chest and stuck it into the belt around his waist. "It could be dark in there, like it was most of the time we were in that pyramid. You'd think the aliens would put a few cheap fluorescent lights from Galaxy Depot in their artifacts—but I bet *they* don't need them. "

As he turned to go Katerina said, "Wait, Martin."

She opened a small pouch secured to the belt circling her waist and extracted her most precious possessions. "It wasn't practical to wear these on the way here—but I didn't want to leave them behind."

Katerina reached toward Martin and fastened her gold chain around his neck. He looked down at his chest and the two golden objects hanging from the chain—his fiancée's diamond engagement ring and her three-barred cross.

She said, "These will remind you that I'll be thinking of you and praying for you while you're gone. My grandmother in St. Petersburg sent me that cross before we left Earth to protect me here. I hope it'll keep you safe too."

Martin fingered the cross—remembering how Grandma Slayton gave him a scapular for his First Communion back in second grade. She'd told him that if he died while wearing it he'd go straight to heaven.

But though he knew his saintly grandmother gave him those bits of blessed cloth with the best intentions, he wasn't a child anymore. "I don't believe in magic, Katerina."

"I don't either, Martin. But I do believe in love."

The plastisuits made their last hug awkward and a final kiss impossible. They exchanged a last "I love you"—and then Martin Slayton marched toward his fate.

Martin didn't dare turn around to look at Katerina again as he reached the gray gleaming wall and played out more of the diminishing coil of rope in his hands. Seeing her again for what might be the last time would hurt so much he wouldn't be able to concentrate on what he was risking his life to do. He calmed himself by imagining he was the Golden Age superhero Doctor Fate preparing to walk through the wall of his sealed tower in Salem.

Then Martin plunged through the wall into darkness. He reached down to retrieve the flashlight in his belt—but stopped when he realized he wasn't alone.

For an instant Martin thought he'd found the aliens. Then the room exploded with light and the entire universe crumpled and turned inside out around him.

He was surrounded by countless three-dimensional visions writhing and floating in every direction like an infinite cascade of manic macroscopic amoebas. Chaotic images in the form of undulating amorphous blobs and shapeless bubbles of kaleidoscopic colors saturated his sight as if he were trapped inside a monstrous lava lamp. They swelled and contracted like balloons being twisted into distorted animal shapes by an invisible insane clown—shifting with hyperactive energy from pinpoint size to that of Number Six's nemesis Rover and everywhere in-between. Those surrealistic nightmares engulfed his mind—rapidly darting toward and away from him like a swarm of angry bees stinging the deepest recesses of his brain.

To his oversaturated senses existence was distorted into a hallucinogenic reality infinitely more intense than any psychedelic drug could induce. Every sound and noise in the entire cosmos seemed to murmur at once in his ears. He heard the voices of every living creature alive whispering their secrets to him. Martin felt himself drowning at the bottom of a crystal-clear ocean with gigantic polychromatic globules like immiscible oil swirling everywhere around him with superheated Brownian motion. His right arm swept out and frantically tried to bat them away—and then his mind recoiled at a new horror.

He saw the muscles, bones, blood vessels, nerves, and other tissues in his arm simultaneously in a rapidly shifting series—as if an unseen hand were swiftly flipping the pages of an anatomy textbook in front of him. With the slightest effort his eyes could focus on each layer of that limb from the innermost cavities of its bones to the outer fibers of his plastisuit—as if he were wearing overpowered X-Ray Specs from a classic comic book ad. Closing his eyes did nothing to blot out these sights—this unwanted ability extended to seeing through his own eyelids.

Martin lowered his arm and stared once more into the face and fury of infinity—teetering on the brink of madness. But his will power was just strong enough for his consciousness to adjust slightly to the chaos enveloping him. For fleeting instants the blurred hues of several floating scenes bobbing around him resolved into images he could almost under-stand—like the stream-of-consciousness happenings in a vivid dream.

In one ballooning shape he glimpsed a brightly lit room loaded with archaic mainframe computers with jerkily rotating reels of magnetic tape. The next glob of scenery contained a reddish-orange desert re-miniscent of the Martian plain near the habitation module he knew he'd never see again. Another pulsating blob showed a placid beach scene of the planet's new Boreal Ocean that lazily rotated until its gently swaying waters were upside down without spilling. Yet another showed verdant fields of young wheat that reminded him of his boy-hood farm.

That montage of confusing scenes ranging from vaguely familiar to incomprehensibly alien flashed toward and away from him in a never-ending deluge. Then his vision lingered on the image of a great spiral galaxy that might be the Milky Way viewed from far above its plane, like the last scene in Episode V—its hundreds of billions of stars whirling together like God playfully blowing an enormous pinwheel. In an instant his mind raced through its multitudinous jewel-like stars and dust mote planets—penetrating their knobbly surfaces and molten cores like an early twentieth-century watchmaker using his loupe to examine the exposed gears of a pocket watch.

On some of those atom-like worlds he sensed countless tiny mites crawling on their crusts, wriggling in their oceans, and soaring in their skies in endless seething cycles of birth and death. Those planets and the animalcules living on them were all different yet all alike—except for one miniscule splotch of matter and energy dabbed into an unremarkable spiral arm. There a collection of creatures that resembled humanity in thoughts and aspirations though not in form occupied a small cluster of planets and solar systems. Slowly…tentatively…painfully, with enormous and difficult effort they extended their presence, hopes, and dreams from one star to another in a continuing journey of exploration.

But Martin's fascinated study of that extraterrestrial race's history suddenly stopped as a nebulous black shape eclipsed and blotted out those inspiring scenes. Unlike the colorful formless blobs that still writhed randomly around him *this* one sensed his presence—and somehow he knew he was its prey.

The coil of rope in his hands jerked as he tried to sidestep the approaching menace coming to devour him. He dropped the rope and raised both arms to protect himself as the expanding ebony globule reached and engulfed him. Martin fell into an endless blackness that wasn't filled with stars. Instead a bleak cratered landscape like the Moon's rushed toward him head on.

If he'd had several more seconds to think his last thoughts would have been of Katerina. But just before he struck that world's jagged surface only two words formed in his brain.

"The horror."

Martin sprawled face down and motionless on a desolate plain. Wisps of carbon dioxide and nitrogen wafted against his plastisuit beneath an ebony sky whose untwinkling stars gave no warmth. The puff of dust stirred up by his impact settled languidly back onto the surface of the shallow crater where his body lay.

Rumbling tremors sporadically shivered the landscape as the faintest glow of sunlight peeked over the horizon. Here time had no meaning without anyone to measure it—then suddenly an invisible clock started…

A clear helmet rose from the gritty ground and shook itself. Limbs creaked and stretched like an unfolding deck chair until Martin wobbled to his feet. He brushed dirt from his faceplate and studied his surroundings.

The dim pockmarked landscape around him had a ruddy hue. Its low dunes and small scattered rocks suggested he was on some unexplored region of Mars. But the oddly sparse stars shining above him formed no familiar constellations. Still peering up at the heavens, he turned around—and knew he wasn't on Mars anymore.

The gibbous alien planet overhead spanned nearly ten times the Moon's angular diameter as seen from Earth. It was shrouded by sunlit featureless white clouds with a lemon tinge—like a monstrous Venus. That gigantic world seemed to grow gradually larger as he stared at it…

Suddenly Martin realized where he was and how well the aliens could manipulate matter, energy, gravity—and time. He laughed with horrified appreciation at the karmic joke they'd played on him. The aliens had made him the only one of humanity's doomed billions who wouldn't have to wait a year to see what happened when Mars smashed into Earth.

For the world high above him must be the Earth of over four billion years before his birth—and he was on the smaller planet rushing toward a Moon-making collision with it.

From the corner of his eye Martin saw a puff of dust billow up behind a nearby dune. He wondered if a meteorite might've slammed into the ground there—and if one with his name on it might be streaking down through this world's thin atmosphere even now.

He grunted. It was already a race which would kill him first—suffocating when his oxygen supply gave out in around eight hours or ending up as road kill in an interplanetary collision. What did it matter if another lethal danger beat them to the punch?

Still—he wasn't dead yet and wondered what produced that cloud of dissipating dirt. Fortunately this small world was too young and inhospitable to have produced life big enough to create a miniature dust storm that size. But maybe the aliens had transplanted some large predators here to make his last moments of life even more interesting. Hopefully they hadn't plucked a memory about Coeurl from his mind—

Martin stepped warily toward the summit of the nearby dune. As expected, this doomed world's gravity seemed similar to the "old" Mars. He reached his new vantage point—and bounded down the dune's far side toward the plastisuit lying prone at its base.

Just before he reached Katerina she shook herself unsteadily to her feet. Martin cried, "Are you okay? How did you get here?"

"I think I'm all right. But where's here?"

A brief survey of her surroundings and the looming death hanging high in the sky convinced her that Martin's theory was all too plausible. She said, "A few minutes after you entered the artifact I saw the rope and oxygen packs get pulled partway to the wall. I followed you in, just as we agreed."

"It's my fault! I must have accidently yanked the rope just before the aliens shanghaied me here. Now we're both trapped!"

"Perhaps the aliens maneuvered us both here for a reason, like they've done before. We just have to figure out what they expect us to do."

"That's obvious, Katerina. They expect us to die!"

She ignored his pessimism and climbed to the top of the dune. There she surveyed the landscape in every direction. "I wish I'd brought our binoculars—but I wasn't expecting to need them inside the artifact."

Then she pointed excitedly in front of her. "There! I saw a flash of light near the horizon! It looked like sunlight reflecting off metal—just like that pyramid you found the other day. It must be another artifact!"

Katerina rejoined her fiancé on level ground and said, "If this world really is the same size as Mars the horizon should be the same distance on both planets—about three kilometers. We both have around eight hours worth of oxygen—plenty to reach the artifact and explore it! Maybe the aliens are there—or it might even be a way home!"

"Thanks for the realistic mission appraisal, Pollyanna. Still, going exploring is better than waiting here to suffocate or get splattered. I—"

He stared at the oxygen pressure gauge on Katerina's plastisuit, then checked his own. "Oh, no."

"What's the matter, Martin?"

"You know that eight hours of oxygen you said we had? Make that about one hour for each of us."

The infant Earth gradually blotted out more of the sky as they trotted toward the artifact.

Katerina sighed, "It doesn't make sense. You weren't in the artifact more than a few minutes, and it seemed I was transported here almost instantaneously. How did we each lose seven hours worth of oxygen?"

"No logical reason for it. Probably just one more thing we can thank our extraterrestrial 'friends' for."

As Martin trudged ahead of her, Katerina stopped to rest for a moment. "That artifact ahead of us looks like the twin of the one back on

Olympus Mons. If that one could transport us here, maybe this one can get us home!"

"Or it might send us somewhere even more dangerous. What did you see when you entered the artifact back on Mars, Katerina?"

"It was a nightmare—like someone cut out chunks of space from all over the universe and threw them at me. Something like a three-dimensional shadow swallowed me—and then I was here."

"Same thing happened to me. It reminded me of '—And He Built a Crooked House,' only scarier. If we were being manipulated through a fourth spatial dimension inside that unfolded tesseract it would explain a lot. Like why I could see through my arm and, with a big twist in time added to the mix, how we wound up here—"

Martin staggered as the ground around him suddenly rocked and quaked. A terrifying vision of the planet tearing itself apart before they reached the possible safety of the artifact flashed through his brain. He dropped to all fours and pressed his knees and palms against the powdery soil—desperately hanging on to the bucking world.

A scream crackled in his helmet. "*Martin!*"

He twisted around until he saw Katerina—then crawled back toward her as fast as the convulsing landscape around him allowed. Her fingertips were dug into the shallowly ridged edge of a gaping rift where the planet's tortured crust had just cracked. Katerina's helmet bobbed above the surface as the rest of her body dangled over a wide deep chasm.

As he neared her a long thin fissure appeared parallel to and just over a meter from where she desperately clung to the rift's edge. Katerina cried out as the slab of rock and packed dirt where her fingers maintained a tenuous handhold slowly buckled downward until it rested at a shallow angle with the nearby solid ground.

The tremors subsided as Martin reached her. He laid his legs flat against the soil as best he could and stretched his right arm and torso towards her. "Grab my hand, Katerina!"

Her left hand swept upward and he grabbed it with his right. As Martin started to pull her out of the dark deep pit threatening to swallow her the meter-long plane of rock his upper body rested prone on collapsed to a nearly forty-five degree angle. A wave of dizziness rippled through him as his torso jerked downward on the hard shifting slab. His waist teetered precariously on the fulcrum formed by that tilted sheet of rock and the firm level ground his legs rested on.

His free left hand clawed at the ground trying to use it to brace himself so he could pull Katerina up. But his blunt gloved fingers couldn't dig into the tightly packed soil covering the rock. Now her weight was slowly pulling him down toward the bottomless pit too—

Katerina screamed, "Let go of my hand, Martin! We're both going to fall!"

"No! I've got to save you!"

As he felt his body sliding gradually downward toward their mutual doom the fingertips of his left hand clawed again at the dense soil for a firm grip it couldn't find. Then something brushed against that searching hand. Martin glanced over and saw Katerina's cross hanging from the chain he'd forgotten was still around his neck.

Instantly he grabbed the cross and thrust its long end into the hard soil. The golden relic was narrow enough to act as a blunt stiletto yet thick enough that it didn't bend as he used it to stabilize his body and pull Katerina closer to him without sliding down himself. He scooted back a little until his waist was on firmer ground, then rapidly pulled his impromptu spike out and jammed it into the soil again closer to him. Several more cycles of pulling on Katerina and using the cross like a rock climber's wedge finally brought them both back to firm flat ground.

No more tremors rocked the landscape as they lay close together catching their breaths. "You should have let go of me, Martin!"

"Well, excuse me for saving your life! It sure didn't look like you were going to make it back up by yourself!"

"No, I probably wouldn't have made it. But you could've fallen too!"

"Hey, it worked, didn't it? And look, I didn't even bend your cross—I think…"

"Yes, Martin, I'm glad we're still alive—but if we'd *both* fallen into that pit who'd be left to save the Earth?"

"If you died, I'm not sure I'd care if it were saved or not!"

Katerina stared at him. Then she got up and said in a tight voice, "It's time to go."

By the time they reached their goal each had about fifteen minutes of oxygen left. Martin walked up to the towering artifact's closest gray metal wall and said, "No way to tell what we'll find inside. Maybe we'll see the same weird stuff we did at the other artifact. We could meet four billion year-plus younger ancestors of the aliens—or maybe the *same* aliens—working inside. Maybe we should go in one at a time, like we did on Mars."

Katerina tapped her oxygen gauge. "No time for that, Martin."

They walked hand in hand toward the beckoning wall, prepared for anything that might happen—except what did. Their bodies bumped against a hard unyielding wall.

Martin bounced back from that impenetrable barrier and stared at it. He ran his palms over the cold metal surface—then beat his fists against it. "It isn't fair!"

Katerina pressed her fingertips against the wall and examined it closely. "Maybe *this* wall has a hidden button you press to open a secret panel—"

"Even if there were one we don't have enough time to find it! We're each down to about ten minutes of oxygen!"

Katerina frowned. "This bottom cube looks about one hundred meters on a side, like the one on Mars. Maybe there's an opening farther along this wall, or on one of its other three sides. You go left and check this wall and the one around the corner. I'll go right and do the same. We'll meet at the wall on the other side of this one. Hurry!"

Martin nodded. He walked away from Katerina, carefully examining the wall for a door he doubted was there. Then he turned the corner and did the same for the left side of the cube. But its featureless metal sheen gave no hint of any entrance either.

He turned another corner and arrived at the side opposite where he and Katerina had started. She wasn't there—no doubt still scrutinizing the right face of the cube with methodical precision. Martin jogged parallel and close to the wall—still seeing nothing that looked like an entrance. After traveling the wall's entire length he peeked around the far corner to see if Katerina had been more successful.

She wasn't there.

"Katerina! Where are you?"

Only static crackled inside his helmet. Then Martin was racing along the side of the cube Katerina should've been exploring—panting as he turned another corner to view the empty space in front of the side they'd started from. Sweat beaded over his body and he knew he was using up his sparse oxygen supply more rapidly in this frantic search—but he didn't care. The planet's lower gravity helped him accelerate and bound at a dangerous speed along the rocky ground as he skidded around yet another corner to the side where he'd started his own exploring.

Finally he stopped, standing and gasping for breath along the face of the cube where Katerina and he had agreed only minutes ago to meet. Martin gulped mouthfuls of precious diminishing oxygen and croaked out her name over and over. There was no answer.

Katerina was gone. In these last few minutes of life before he suffocated, Martin impulsively grasped the golden cross still hanging from his neck and prayed that she was somewhere safe. For an instant he was tempted to fall to his knees and beg for a miracle for her sake. But instead he stared up to see the approaching Earth mocking him—and he screamed his defiance at the uncaring heavens.

Martin glanced at his oxygen gauge. "Running on fumes now," he muttered to no one on the empty planet. He glared at the blank metal wall in front of him, curled his hands into fists, and flung himself forward to hit the artifact as hard as he could—

Suddenly he plunged through an instant of blackness into an ocean of dazzling white light. He staggered and tried blinking away the pain in his eyes. His forehead throbbed like a pounding heart.

Something he couldn't see grabbed his left arm. He pictured a slimy tentacle attached to a hexadecapod from *War of the Worlds* yanking him towards its slobbering maw. He jerked away, dimly sensing a gray metal floor rushing up towards him as he fell. His head rattled inside his helmet as he struck the cold hard surface. Then a voice from beyond the grave echoed in his stunned mind.

"Martin! Are you all right?"

Two gloved hands helped him back to his feet and a lithe body embraced him. He glimpsed a tear-moistened smile through Katerina's clear helmet.

Martin stumbled a step back from her. "Where did you go? I thought you were dead!"

He blinked his sight back nearly to normal in the brightly lit surroundings. "We *aren't* dead—are we? All this light—if this really is Heaven, I wouldn't mind if you rubbed it in and said 'I told you so!' for eternity."

"No, Martin. The first wall we reached on that other artifact was solid. So was the one on the side I checked. But when I reached the far side of that cube and touched its wall I felt myself pulled through it and back here. You must have reached it and went through too!"

She pointed towards nearby objects on the floor. "We're back in the aliens' artifact on Mars. There's the coil of rope you dropped before being transported to that other planet."

Martin squinted, following the trail of the end of the rope as it snaked across the floor and disappeared through the wall closest to them. Then his gaze swiveled around the chamber they stood within—scanning its walls and peering up into its heights with growing puzzlement. He gasped, "What the heck are those—"

"Never mind that now, Martin! We need to get out of here and get to the two full oxygen packs we left outside!"

Martin glanced at Katerina's oxygen gauge and then at his own. Their ominous readings made his breaths come quicker. "Right. Let's go change our packs and then come back in for some more exploring. All least the aliens turned off those weird home movies they were playing inside here."

He trotted away, following the path of the rope on the floor to the nearby wall—and bounced off it. Once again his fists pounded rigid unyielding metal.

Several meters away on the other side of that barrier, two full oxygen packs lay waiting on the sandy cinnamon soil of Mars. But as one final joke the aliens had contrived the wall to allow passage only *one* way—and Katerina and he were trapped on the wrong side of it.

"*It isn't fair!*"

Martin's fists struck the wall one last futile time. The massive metal didn't even vibrate beneath his blows. He wobbled with the same queasy wooziness he'd experienced during his first microgravity simulation on the latest iteration of the Vomit Comet during astronaut training. There was no point checking his oxygen gauge to see how many seconds of life he had left. If he died first at least he wouldn't have to see Katerina suffer when her oxygen gave out too—

Katerina scanned the floor, then picked up part of the rope halfway between the coil and the wall. "Even if we can't get out, we were able to get in. And when you tugged on the rope before—help me, Martin!"

He stumbled toward her and grabbed another section of the rope. They pulled it together and watched a growing length of the cord appear through the wall—until the two oxygen packs still tied on its other end clunked onto the floor.

A moment later Martin took a deep breath of his replenished oxygen supply and felt his head clear. "Okay, the clock's reset. We're still trapped inside here, but we have eight more hours to figure out what's going on."

Katerina nodded, refreshed by her own new full oxygen pack. She looked up and around, scrutinizing the intricate interior of the huge chamber they stood inside. Fluorescent-white light just bright enough to illumine their surroundings glowed softly around them from no obvious source. There was nothing on the gray metal floor except the rocks she'd thrown into this room ages ago and the few items they'd brought with them.

The wall through which they'd entered the artifact was made of the same smooth metal. But about five meters above the floor, the wall's blank surface merged into what looked like a colossal cat's cradle suspended above them and extending as high up as she could see. It was constructed of close-packed zigzagging gray metal planks that filled most of the huge structure's volume. They formed an irregularly perforated ceiling obscuring what lay at the very top of the artifact.

Each plank in this massive lattice was approximately one meter wide and about twenty centimeters thick. They ranged from five to seven meters long. The planks were joined together at their ends at odd angles—gently rising and falling as they crisscrossed and interlaced with each other like the skeletal beams of a skyscraper designed by M.C. Escher. They wound around an empty central metal shaft with a square opening eight meters on a side extending up into dark unseen heights.

Katerina's first impression was that this intricate framework resembled a gigantic metal version of the Gordian knot. But closer examination showed it was really a fiendishly elaborate spiral stairway. Several isolated planks were welded along one side of their narrowest dimension to each of the chamber's three other walls. They formed shallow ramps leading up from ground level into the innermost recesses of that baffling maze.

Martin shook his head at that colossal spider web of beams above them. "Looks like somebody's been playing with the biggest Erector Set of all time."

He peered up into the blackness of the vast structure's square hollow central core. "That would've made a great shaft for an elevator—but then, the aliens always make us do things the hard way. Hopefully those planks really lead up to the top of this thing and aren't like the recursive stairways in 'Castrovalva.'"

Katerina frowned. "What?"

"No, Who—oh, never mind. We've got lots of climbing to do. Let's go."

There were no handrails on the alien-made stairway. Martin took the lead while Katerina followed him single file. Each of the gently sloping planks they walked on held their combined weight easily. But they quickly reached the point in their steady climb upward when a fall over the side would result in bone-shattering injury or death.

Fortunately the planks had short poles the length and greatest width of a baseball bat set into them that served as handholds. Those metal rods jutted vertically upward a bit off-center every one to two meters apart like the posts for a wire mesh fence.

Each individual plank angled mildly at its end to join with the next one or, more often, branched into two separate paths. Several times Martin and Katerina had to backtrack when the route they'd chosen turned out to be a dead end. One time the last plank in the path terminated in empty space, with only a wide chasm between it and the other planks. Another time the end of the final plank wound up welded into the wall of the artifact itself. But as their climb continued they became more adroit at picking out the path that kept them moving upward.

Martin paused, adjusted the coil of rope circling his right shoulder, and tentatively glanced down. It looked like they'd reached the half-way point in this long climb. He grabbed one of the nearby poles and tried to forget his memories of the movie *Vertigo*. Looking up, he still couldn't glimpse what lay at the top of the artifact. Too many twisting planks still hid their goal from sight.

Katerina came up behind him. "Anything wrong, Martin?"

"I'm just wondering what'll happen if we do find the aliens. Before we entered this artifact I hoped every 'miracle' they'd performed from terraforming planets to manipulating matter, energy, and gravity could be done if they only had sufficiently advanced technology and knew a few more laws of physics than we do.

"I know it's silly, but I fantasized we'd find the humongous super-scientfic machine inside here they've been using to do all those amaz-ing things. Then we could study it and learn enough about their science to turn it against them—like spunky earthlings routinely did in those old-time SF pulps. Or maybe we'd be like James Bond and his sexy Russian counterpart breaking into the secret citadel of the latest world-conquering megalomaniac, finding his doomsday device, and pushing the big red button on it marked 'Press This to Save the Earth.'"

"That's not realistic, Martin."

"Obviously. But if the aliens are so advanced they can send us back through space and time over four billion years, they're way too power-ful to fight. The only 'weapons' we can use against them are our own words. But how do we figure out what to say when we don't know how the aliens think—and when we can't even be sure what their motives are or what they want from us?

"Heck, we've been calling them 'aliens' all this time—but we really don't know *what* they are!"

Katerina studied the intricately interweaving planks and beams above them. "I don't know either. But if we do find the aliens, remember that our first priority is to save the Earth. If there's no other way to do it, each of us is expendable."

"I know, Katerina. I hope this isn't a suicide mission—but if I have to I'll throw myself on the grenade."

"I'm not talking about that. You pointed out before that the aliens are angrier with me than they are with you. If the only way to save humanity is for me to give up my life to appease them, then you're going to have to let me do it."

"I'd never let them do that, Katerina! Okay, I know I really couldn't stop them if they made up their minds to kill you. But if they try, I'll do everything I can to save you or die trying!"

"Don't be foolish, Martin! If we both die, who's going to save Earth? If something happens to me *you* need to stay alive to convince the aliens to spare humanity! Promise me you won't do anything that might endanger you too!"

Martin said nothing. He resumed their upward trek as if he hadn't heard her. But after they'd climbed together for several more minutes Katerina thought she heard his voice whispering inside her helmet.

"I'll cross that bridge when I come to it."

Martin scowled. "End of the line, Katerina."

He shook his head at this final obstacle at the top of the spiraling stairway. Below them the network of interlaced metal planks they'd just climbed filled most of the artifact's lower three one hundred-meter tall cubes and its quartet of side cubes. The horizontal plank they now stood on was twelve meters higher than the upper opening of the square shaft running vertically through the center of the artifact. The plank extended to the outer edge of the middle of one of the shaft's eight-meter-long sides. There it connected to a final short beam slightly less than two meters long that angled downward at forty-five degrees, forming a short ramp pointing toward the dark bottom of the shaft far below.

Directly in front of them at the same height, another long horizontal plank like the one they stood on beckoned to them from eight meters away across empty space and the open mouth of the deep shaft. At that plank's near end another shorter one angled downward, mirroring the ramp attached to the beam they were trapped on. At the other plank's far end a vertical metal ladder five meters high led to a meter-square opening in the gray metal "ceiling" above them, formed by the otherwise solid flat base of the artifact's highest cube. Bright pale light emanated from that opening, from the interior of what promised to be a new chamber inside the uppermost cube.

Martin grasped the vertical rod at the end of his horizontal plank for balance and studied the similar beam eight meters away across a black abyss. The plank on the other side had a rod set perpendicular into its end that looked similar to the one that he was using as a handhold. He muttered, "All these hundreds of beams and girders inside here—so why couldn't the aliens make one more so we'd have a bridge to the other side?"

Katerina sidled up behind him. She held the rod just behind his and studied the scene. "I know how we can get across, Martin."

He slipped the coil of rope off his shoulder. "So do I—but I don't like it."

Martin formed a slipknot in one end of the rope and whirled his lasso with flair worthy of a young Hoot Gibson. On his second try he snagged the post on the other side and pulled the rope as hard as he could—tightening the loop circling that post and satisfying himself the metal rod wouldn't pull free under the strain he'd soon be putting on it.

The rope was just long enough to do its job. With barely a meter of it to spare Martin tied his end of the rope tightly to the base of the post by his feet. The rest of its length was stretched taut across the dark chasm as a makeshift, shaky bridge. He said, "If I make it across I want you to stay here until I see what's inside that opening over there."

"No, Martin. I'll go first. We don't know how much tension that rope can take before it reaches its breaking point. I'm lighter than you and the rope is more likely to hold my weight than yours."

After several heated moments of arguing Martin finally accepted that he couldn't argue with the laws of physics or an obstinate Katerina. She slipped past him and sat on the edge of the plank with her legs stretching along the much shorter one angling downward. Both of her gloves reached up to grasp the rope tightly. Then she carefully eased herself down the short ramp until her whole body dangled over emptiness.

Katerina's arms stretched up vertically clutching the rope. She kept both knees bent and legs close together to stabilize her body and minimize any bobbing or swinging. Her front palm slid forward along the rope, pulling the rest of her behind it in repeated jerky motions toward the beckoning ledge on the other side.

Martin's heart pounded as he watched Katerina reach and then pass the halfway mark on her nerve-racking journey. As he focused on her assiduously shifting hands gripping the rope he sensed a flickering in his uppermost field of vision. He glanced up—and felt an ice pick of terror puncture his heart.

The previously solid rod anchoring the rope on the other side of the abyss shimmered out of existence. The loop encircling that now-vanished support hung suspended in mid-air for an instant—and then Katerina's mass on the rope pulled its newly freed end down. Martin watched petrified as she swung back toward him still gripping the rope. Katerina arced out of his view like the weight on a pendulum as the length of rope in front of him collapsed onto the short ramp just below where he stood. The ramp hid the far end of the dangling rope and kept him from seeing whether she was still holding onto it—or had been flung off to her death.

Another instant and Martin snapped back into action. He leaned to one side and peered toward the far end of the rope. Relief and fright flooded his brain as he saw Katerina clutching the rope with both hands a meter from its dangling looped end. Her body twisted and rocked as she struggled to keep her gloves from slipping lower on that tenuous lifeline.

Martin watched helplessly as her hands slid even lower on the rope until she managed to damp her body's oscillations and steady herself. He yelled, "Don't try to climb up the rope, your gloves might slip! Hold on tight and I'll pull you up!"

Martin reached down and grabbed the length of rope just beyond where it was tied to the pole beside him. Carefully, trying to keep Katerina from slipping or swinging again if he tugged too hard, Martin gradually pulled the rope toward him over the short ramp's far edge. There was a fine line between pulling the rope so slowly she might become too tired to hold on versus jerking it too fast and making her lose her grip. As more rope accumulated at his feet he hoped he was tugging it at the right speed—and that the edge of the ramp wasn't sharp enough to cut into and fray the rope.

After an eternity compressed into seconds Martin gasped in relief as the top of Katerina's right fist, clutching the rope, peeked over the far edge of the short ramp. But as her left hand reached up for an instant to paw at the ramp's smooth slick surface he realized she'd never get a handhold firm enough to raise herself up onto it. And the vertical position of her body and the ramp's angle made it impossible for Katerina to get her elbows and enough of her upper body on the ramp so he could pull her up along it with the rope.

Martin's mind raced through his limited options on how to save her. He rapidly considered and rejected sliding the rope to one side and off the edge of the short meter-wide ramp. In theory that would let Katerina swing to a position directly below the side of the long horizontal plank where he stood at its junction with the ramp. If he was strong enough he could pull her up vertically from there until she could grasp the edge of this long plank—then he could grab her wrists to jerk her safely onto it. But what if she swung too violently and lost her grip—or what if he couldn't hold on to the rope with her unsupported weight on the other end—or what if he lost his balance and fell with her into the pit below—

Martin swiftly studied the rod beside him, the rope in his hands with Katerina at the other end, and the short ramp in front of him. Maybe if he'd had more time to think he would've realized this plan probably wouldn't work either—but he had to do *something* to save her!

"Hang on, Katerina! I'm coming to save you!"

Still clutching the rope in a death grip Martin lowered himself to his knees. His upper body descended face down towards the ramp's metal skin. Finally he was lying prone with his face pointing toward its far edge. He scooted his chest down the ramp's slightly less than two meters long surface while simultaneously inching his hands up the rope—keeping it taut so that Katerina remained hovering just below the ramp's edge. Then he turned his ankles until his boots were locked behind the rod set near the edge of the horizontal plank he'd been standing on. He kept both feet at right angles to the rod—anchoring him and preventing him from sliding off the ramp's far end where Katerina dangled.

The ramp was just short enough for Martin to stretch his left arm out over its edge and grasp Katerina's right wrist. In one swift motion his right hand let go of the rope and lunged out to grab her left wrist. Then he jerked her numb fingers off the rope she'd been holding for much too long. Now he was her only support—just like a circus trapeze artist hanging down with knees bent around the bar after catching his somersaulting partner in mid-air.

Martin braced his boots against the rod far behind him and kept them locked around it. He tried with all his strength to use his knees and torso to scoot back up the ramp with Katerina in tow. But the ramp was too steep and he wasn't strong enough to pull her up onto it. Maybe she should grab the rope again while he figured out what else he could do—

But that was no longer an option. Sometime after he'd grabbed Katerina, the rope she'd been holding had slid to the side and off the edge of the ramp. Now it hung along the ramp's right side out of reach of either of them.

As Martin tried pulling Katerina up one more futile time the loud cries inside his helmet he'd been ignoring until now finally resolved into words. "This won't work, Martin! Let go of me before you fall too!"

"No, I won't! I have to save you!"

He felt Katerina struggling to free herself from his grip. But his hands grasped both her wrists even tighter as she shouted, "You have to stay alive and find the aliens! Only you can save the world!"

"No, I have to save you first!"

Gritting his teeth, Martin braced himself to push the top of his boots once more against the rod they were locked behind and use the rest of his body to pull both of them up. Then in a horrified heartbeat he realized his boots weren't locked behind anything.

Though he couldn't look behind him Martin pictured the rod he'd been using to anchor himself shimmering and fading out of existence— like the rod on the other side of the chasm had done. Then his prone body was scooting with tortoise-like speed down the short ramp as Katerina's weight pulled him down. Another few seconds and he'd slide off the end of the ramp to join her in a final fall together and an end to every problem—

"MARTIN! LET GO OF ME!"

Suddenly he stopped moving. Martin lay still along the cold metal surface with his chest hanging halfway over into empty space. Eventually his brain registered where his palms were—clutching the sides of the ramp to halt his downward slide. As his hands methodically worked their way back up the ramp helping him scoot back to safety, teardrops dampened his forehead. The only sound within his helmet was a single sobbed word.

"Katerina."

Martin stood safely back on the long horizontal plank Katerina and he had shared only moments ago—staring down into the crushing blackness where she'd fallen toward the floor nearly three hundred meters below. Only wordless static came from his radio.

He watched dully as a long metal plank shimmered into existence. This new beam connected the one he stood on with the horizontal one on the other side—bridging the gap over the shadowed abyss at whose bottom Katerina's broken body lay. The plank felt solid beneath the testing tip of his boot. Then he was striding stiffly across it like a walking corpse—wishing it would disappear with him halfway across so he could join his dead beloved far below.

No—not yet. It'd be easier to die—but he had to live long enough to make her death mean something. Martin choked down the wrenching agony inside him and reached the long plank on the other side of the chasm. He grabbed the ladder at the plank's far end and climbed mechanically toward the bright opening above him. If he did find the aliens in that uppermost chamber it'd be hard to keep his grief and anger under control. But for Katerina's sake he would even grovel and plead in front of her murderers if it'd fulfill her last request to save the Earth.

As he ascended the ladder Martin glimpsed the golden cross still hanging from his neck and wondered if it was too late to pray. Reason and skepticism had been enough when life was happier and still held hope. But when existence turned into tragedy those modes of thought gave little consolation.

And if Katerina was right and miracles weren't always just delusions created by the devout, the gullible, or the wounded heart—he needed one now.

Martin peeked cautiously through the meter-wide square opening on the floor of the artifact's highest cube. He scanned its brightly lit surroundings—and blinked.

The chamber's walls were lined with what looked like obsolete mid-twentieth-century computer equipment. Tall steel monoliths studded with multicolored flashing lights and jerking reels of magnetic tape surrounded him. They stretched up several meters toward a flat ceiling one hundred meters above him.

Martin pulled himself up into the room and wandered from one archaic mainframe to another. The room resembled the set from the old *Time Tunnel* TV series—or a compact transistorized version of Multivac. But what were these electronic antiques doing here?

He walked toward a large typewriter-like printer sitting on a wooden stand. A sheet of paper stuck out of its carriage. There were two black words printed on the sheet.

WELCOME MARTIN.

He roamed further—exploring this museum of forgotten technology. The aliens must've created these machines from his memories. But why—

Then Martin noticed writing etched onto the machine in front of him—and lost his last sliver of self-control. His palms lashed out and struck the dinner plate-sized red button on the computer's panel marked "Press This to Save the Earth."

Martin screamed, "So you jerks think this is a big joke! Play with the funny little humans until one of them breaks and then taunt the other one until he goes crazy! I wasn't able to stop you from killing Katerina and I can't keep you from smashing Earth like Kane's snow globe! But if you're watching me, here's what I think of you!"

The glove made it hard to flex his fingers completely. But he managed to curl most of them and wave his right hand around the room at the unseen aliens.

At first there was no response to his words and actions. Eventually Martin stopped his tirade—drained of energy and any idea what to do next. He watched listlessly as the chamber's colorful contents blurred into an Impressionistic palette of softening hues. The artificial illumination within it faded away until he was immersed in a raven-black darkness he didn't want to leave. Stripped of hope—nevermore to see Katerina—oblivion would be a blessing.

Then Martin sensed something as empty of light and love as Satan's soul approaching him. He stood silent as it reached out toward his unresisting body. As that amorphous mass of Stygian blackness engulfed him he glimpsed a familiar scene within it. The setting Sun gently illuminated the habitation module Katerina and he had shared for several ecstatic months. The rocky russet ground surrounding their former home glowed with beckoning warmth.

With that last vision of paradise lost shimmering in his mind, Martin plunged gratefully into nothingness…

In his dream Martin stood by the ramp leading up to the open entrance of the habitation module. Fading sunlight glistened off its metal shell and bathed the ruddy soil around him. He could almost feel a gentle breeze riffle his hair through his helmet.

Martin pictured himself as the protagonist of *An Occurrence at Owl Creek Bridge*—falling with a last flicker of remembered happiness and hope an instant before the noose snapped his neck. Like that doomed man's last vision of his beloved wife, Martin saw Katerina stepping toward him with matchless grace and dignity. The plastisuit she'd worn at her death still flowed around her Grecian curves like a modest statute of Aphrodite. Her long auburn hair, released from the confines of the helmet lying discarded on the soil nearby, flowed gauzily behind her as she rushed to greet him.

Then Katerina's loving face was pressed against his own helmet. He saw this gorgeous phantasm's tantalizing lips form his name—her hazel eyes alive with tender love. Faint vibrations penetrated his plastisuit that resolved into muffled words...

"Martin! Take off your helmet!"

Her delicate fingers reached around his neck and released the seals bonding his helmet and plastisuit together. Martin gasped as the helmet came free and flew to the ground. His first gulp of open air was cut short by a kiss smothering his mouth. He reeled as two slim arms enfolded him and pressed his chest tightly against hers—

He dimly heard more words caressing his naked ear. "...and just as I was about to hit the floor I fell into one of those black blobs that the aliens use as portals. The next thing I knew I was standing here by the habitation module!"

With percipience rivaling Mortimer Snerd's, Martin stammered, "You're alive!"

After giving her fiancé another kiss Katerina sighed, "Definitely."

Martin hugged her tight. "I don't get it. The aliens nearly killed us again and again—then they bring us back here! Are they still testing us—and are they still going to destroy Earth?"

Suddenly Martin tensed with an uneasy electric sensation he'd felt three times before. His skin prickled and the hairs on his arms rose like when he'd played with the Van der Graaff generator in his college physics lab. His breathless body felt pressed in the tightening grip of an invisible vise. He separated from Katerina and looked around.

Several meters away a sparkling iridescent swarm of countless multi-hued pinpoint lights writhed with limitless irresistible power. From within that chaotic kaleidoscope of colors an uncountable number of beings perhaps older that the universe itself peered deep into the naked souls of the two humans.

Martin and Katerina stood side-by-side—waiting for the aliens to pronounce their Last Judgment on them and the human race.

Martin broke the simmering silence. "So you finally decided to show up."

A hollow genderless voice emanated from the luminous entities and wafted through the minds of the two flesh-and-blood creatures arrayed before them. *We are always with you. We observe your actions and read your thoughts. We know your feelings and fears.*

Katerina said, "Then you know how sorry I am for what I did. I was wrong to trick Martin so that we failed your test to see if he could change human nature for the better. Punish me if you must—but don't destroy our world because of my sin!"

We do not punish. We train and tend.

Martin's frowned. "How does repeatedly putting us in danger and threatening to destroy Earth do that?"

All that we have done was a test to determine if your species is suitable. Since the birth of time we have watched matter and energy coalesce into life with wide-ranging degrees of self-awareness. Simple forms of life are common. Complex beings with at least your level of sentience are rare. Your species possesses a combination of mental and physical abilities unmatched within this local group of galaxies.

We nurture all such exceptional creatures as you throughout this universe. We wish you to grow to your full potential. Your kind has the curiosity, intelligence, and rudimentary technology to venture off the world of your creation. We have tested you to see if your species has the other essential traits needed to expand throughout this galaxy. If the two of you with your great desire to explore and bring your species into space could not pass our test, there is no hope for others of your kind.

Katerina murmured, "And I made us fail your test."

You did not fail our test, Katerina Iosifovna Savitskaya. Until now it is you who have failed it, Martin Albert Slayton.

Katerina stared at the discombobulated expression on her fiancé's face. He sputtered, "Me? What did I do?"

It is what you could not do that would have condemned your kind to extinction. Both of you have forgone other goals and pleasures to come to this world. Each of you was willing to die if necessary so that your fellow beings might live. Such attributes make your species worthy to receive dominion over this galaxy.

But being worthy is not enough. You humans must also have the strength and will power to do whatever is needed to establish a permanent presence away from your native world. You must not only risk danger and death for yourselves. You must also be willing to endure any pain and suffering you must cause your fellow beings in pursuit of that goal.

Katerina said, "I don't understand. Most of our philosophies, religions, and traditions teach that it's wrong to intentionally inflict pain and suffering on others. Are you suggesting the end justifies the means—that it's 'good' to hurt others if it means reaching the stars?"

It is neither good nor justified. It is merely necessary. You performed such an act when you deceived your companion. You did not wish to hurt him yet you knew it would if he discovered your deception. You did it because you believed it was needed to protect your fellow humans. You were willing to accept responsibility for your actions though it caused you great pain.

The aliens focused their attention on Martin. *Until the end of our test your greatest concern was for your companion's safety and well-being. You accepted our gift to manipulate matter, energy, gravity, and time only to save her life. When you thought you could also use that power to help your entire species you renounced it because you did not wish to risk hurting her or only a few of your kind. You were willing once to risk your entire world being destroyed rather than let her die. When you finally chose to try to save your planet over losing her you passed our test.*

No further tests are needed for now. If enough of your kind are able to make such difficult choices, your species has all the skills it needs to fill this galaxy. We have encouraged your first steps by making your two neighboring worlds easier to reach and inhabit. Before we depart we will leave behind new artifacts on this and your second planet for you and those who come after you to explore. Studying these artifacts will help you acquire technology that will make travel within your solar system and galaxy much easier.

Katerina smiled. "This must mean you're not planning to destroy Earth after all."

On the contrary. Earth is doomed.

Martin shouted, "*What?* You said we passed your test! I even pressed that ridiculous button you made to save the Earth!"

By passing our test and pressing that button you have indeed made it possible for your world to be saved.

Martin glanced at Katerina, who looked as confused as he was. He said, "You've lost me."

If you had failed our test there would have been no further need to make you believe your world was in imminent danger from a collision with this one. We would have returned this planet to the orbit we previously gave it. We would have departed and left you and your fellow

264

beings alone to fulfill your destiny.

But if that had happened, your kind would have had no future. Within a century your current civilization will collapse. You will lose enough of your technology to make it impossible for you to ever live permanently beyond your world. You will condemn yourselves and your descendants to mere existence and eventual extinction.

Katerina said, "Then what have we accomplished by passing your test?"

You have proven you are capable of following a different path. Like many others we have observed and helped throughout this universe, your species has reached a critical point in its development. It must either grow into a galaxy-wide civilization or wither by confining itself solely to its world of origin.

Your population and technology is at a stage where your planet's limited resources and you yourselves are the greatest threats to your survival. To survive you must soon make use of the far greater resources of your own solar system and beyond. You must quickly transplant your kind and cultures onto new worlds.

Martin said, "You're preaching to the choir about that! But did we save Earth or not?"

If you had failed our test we would have done nothing more for your species. Because you passed it we have a final gift for you. We have seen that you humans find it difficult to look beyond your immediate needs, desires, and dangers. Our gift will motivate you to devote greater effort to venturing off your world so that your kind can continue and flourish.

When you pressed the button in our artifact it initiated a chain of events that will lead to either your destruction or salvation within a generation. The artifact is now returning this world to the more stable orbit it had until yesterday. In twenty-nine years our device will once again make this planet move gradually closer to yours. We have pro-grammed the artifact to make Mars and Earth collide one year later.

Katerina bit her lip. "It sounds like we've just delayed doomsday."

It is within your power to decide whether your kind continues to exist. You cannot return to the artifact you just explored. It has already reconfigured itself back into a spatial dimension you cannot reach at your current level of technology.

But other artifacts we will leave on your second planet and this one contain information that will allow you to regain access to the artifact you just left. Then you will be able to alter its programming to prevent your world's destruction and keep this planet in a stable orbit. That same information on how to move outside what you call space-time will also allow you to travel easily from star to star.

The aliens seemed to tower over the two humans. *Inform your leaders and people of what we have said. Tell them they must quickly send as many of you as possible to this world now and to the second planet when it becomes habitable soon. If you devote as much energy and resources as possible to colonizing your two nearest worlds, you will have sufficient time to find and explore the artifacts we leave there and save your own.*

Katerina said, "But what if our governments and people don't listen? What if they don't believe us and keep treating human space exploration as a frill—as something optional they can delay indefinitely?"

Then on June 6, 2066 every human on Earth and your moon will die. Even if a few of your kind are on the second planet that remnant will not have the resources to recreate a spacefaring civilization. Your sun is young enough that, with our help, sentient life could still possibly develop on one of its remaining worlds after your species is destroyed. If so, we hope that next one will be wiser than yours.

Martin said, "Sounds pretty drastic."

If your species does not care enough to ensure its own survival, then neither will we.

Katerina glanced at the golden cross still hanging from Martin's neck. She said, "In case we fail, I'd like to know if our deaths would have at least some meaning outside this life. It sounds as if you've been observing humanity since our earliest existence. Some of our major religions are based on the belief that specific events and miracles have actually occurred. Tell me—is my faith or the faith of others in vain?"

We have seen the events that inspired your beliefs and those of other humans. We know what is fact and what is myth. But it would not be helpful for any of you to believe what we could tell you. You would only be exchanging faith in your different conceptions of deity for faith in us.

It is better for you to consider what is beneficial and useful in your beliefs, even if you cannot be certain of them. Keeping the possibility that some of your beliefs are true may bring you greater comfort and inspire you to greater things than knowing their truth.

Martin said, "I have a simpler question. You've moved planets, put Katerina and me through the wringer with these tests, and hopefully given humanity the kick in the rear it needs to get our space programs into high gear. What I want to know is—why have you bothered to do it? Why do you care what happens to us?

"What's in it for you?"

The aliens hesitated. Then they said five final words—and vanished.

After the end of that longest day two spacefarers wearing blue jumpsuits stood holding hands beneath a clear night sky. Myriad multihued stars beckoned the young couple across the vast gulf of space, inviting them to come for a closer look.

Distant Deimos shone as a bright speck of light sewn into that celestial tapestry. Dazzling Phobos arced a more rapid path from west to east. But both moons paled compared to the azure orb that shone with a steady glow twenty-five million kilometers away. There word of the aliens' warning and challenge was spreading from NASA's Mission

Control and the Russian Space Agency through a burgeoning number of nonplussed government leaders. Soon, whether announced through official channels or leaked to the press, humanity would learn that the clock was ticking towards its destruction—or its self-created salvation.

"Do you think our leaders will listen, Martin?"

"Let's hope so for everybody's sake, including us—and any children we'll have."

Katerina frowned pensively. "I wonder if it's right to bring babies into a world that could be destroyed in a generation if we all fail this last test. But if we do pass it, someday our descendants may be scattered among the stars.

"I'd rather be an optimist. After we return to Earth next year and get married, I think we should make some descendants."

Martin grinned. "Sounds good to me! But first NASA needs to land another ascent vehicle here so we can return home. It's a good thing Mission Control wasn't too upset about us taking the other one out for a joyride and crashing it. I guess hearing we'd pushed the potential end of the world back from one year to thirty years distracted them from focusing on what else we did. And thanks for not telling them about my pushing that button and starting the countdown to doomsday."

"You're welcome. And there's something else I've been thinking about, Martin. I think I know who the aliens are."

"For a while it seemed you thought they were devils tempting us to destroy humanity. Don't tell me you've decided they're really guardian angels practicing the ultimate in tough love!"

"No, they're probably not supernatural. But I remembered some passages in Genesis that may fit. 'Let us make mankind in our image and likeness, and let them have dominion over the fish of the sea, the birds of the air, the cattle, over all the wild animals and every creature that exists on the earth.' Then later, 'The Lord God took the man and placed him in the Garden of Eden to till it and to keep it.'"

Katerina touched the golden cross hanging from her neck. "Change a few words and perhaps those verses describe the aliens and us—only *they* are Adam and Eve, and *we* are one of the kinds of animals they're tending in a universe-wide 'Paradise'!"

Martin decided to say nothing. Though he was skeptical of the theological implications of her analogy, the aliens' last words made him wonder if there might be a speck of truth in what Katerina said. She probably interpreted their farewell as a vindication of her faith that existence had both a human and divine meaning. But to him those nearly omnipotent aliens' five parting words held mystery—and a little fear.

We too are being tested.

Epilogue

The starship flashed back into normal space-time on the edge of an unexplored star system. Sensors gathered information as the ship's transphotonic drive propelled it sunward.

The survey's initial findings were encouraging. The system's sole star was medium-sized and not long past the middle of its projected useful life span. Its retinue of gas giants was located too far away from that sun's habitable zone to interfere with the orbits of any planets within it.

Soon the ship entered orbit around the only world in this system capable of supporting more than microscopic life. It had a breathable atmosphere and temperate climate. Large bodies of liquid water covered most of its surface.

Biosensors released from the ship searched for any types of life that had evolved on it. They found its ecosphere supported lush vegetation gathered mainly into dense jungles. A great diversity of creatures filled the world's oceans, land, and air. None of them showed signs of being sentient or having anything approaching a civilization. But several species showed enough potential that perhaps, in millions of the world's years, they might evolve into intelligent beings.

And that meant this solar system could not be used for colonization. Disappointed but hoping the next system they reached would be suitable, the starship's crew finished their survey. Its chief planetary scientist pondered the system's relative scarcity of small rocky worlds and the unusually great distance between the orbits of that life-bearing planet and the largest gas giant.

Perhaps it had something to do with the pair of well-populated asteroid belts located between them. The mass of debris in the inner belt *was great enough to have formed at least one or two reasonably sized planets. Instead even the largest body there was only a small fraction of the second planet's size.*

The scientist's computer simulations gave a tragic answer to that puzzle. Not long ago in astronomical terms, when this system's sun was about halfway through its main sequence evolution, a disaster occurred. Within the wide gap between the orbits of that second planet and the gas giant located third from the sun, two worlds there had suffered a catastrophic collision. All that remained of them was a vast collection of lifeless asteroids and dust.

The crew held a solemn memorial ceremony for whatever life might have perished on those worlds when the end came, long before their own species evolved. They locked minds in telepathic meditation, with each crewmember's middle arms outstretched and all fourteen digits intertwined in prayer. Then the starship flashed to the next star system on their survey, leaving the life they'd found on the second planet to follow its own path...

Dr. Alexander Stone jerked as a hand gently touched his shoulder. He blinked and focused on Nancy Kelley's face. She said, "You were groaning in your sleep."

Stone grimaced. "Hopefully that dream I just had was a nightmare and not a premonition."

Nancy smiled. "Martin and Katerina just contacted us. They're now ready to go exploring again if the orbiters find anything that looks like a new artifact. For a change, they don't have any medical issues for you."

She laughed. "In fact, after all those medical miracles the aliens did the other day, lots of other doctors don't have much work to do right now either. You've been here for nearly three straight days. It's time for you to go home and take a well-deserved rest."

Stone stroked the stubble on his cheeks and yawned. "I suppose you're right."

He checked his wristwatch. "It's about midnight in Moscow now anyway. I'll come back after I get some more sleep and freshen up. Then I'm going to call Petrovitch at the RSA. Maybe this time he'll listen to me."

"About what?"

Stone frowned. "The aliens said we have thirty years to find their artifacts and save the Earth. I hope we, the RSA, and other space agencies will work together to send as many people to Mars and eventually Venus as we can. Even if the Chinese and others decide to go it alone, an old-fashioned 'gold rush' to find artifacts will still give humanity a chance of passing the aliens' latest test.

"However it plays out, there'll be a huge need to train lots of people right away to go on those missions. It'll be easier to use people who've already had experience being in space than training new recruits."

The physician sighed. "Maybe that'll be enough to make those jerks in the RSA finally change their minds. I convinced them two years ago to hire Valentina as a trainer for new cosmonauts. After pleading with them for fifteen years, I hope they'll finally listen to me and let her back in the flight program. It won't change anything that's happened, and she'll probably still hate my guts. But if she does get to join one of the crews going to Mars, at least I'll have done the best I could."

Nancy nodded sympathetically. "And I'll put in a good word for her again too. Who knows, maybe she'll be the person who finds the artifacts that save the world!"

Stone snorted. "Yeah. Who knows. Just so somebody finds them."

He stood up and stretched. "I wonder what'll happen if we do pass this new test. Maybe the ones they put Martin and Katerina through, and now this one for the rest of us, are just the beginning—the 'easy' tests. I suspect the aliens aren't through with us yet—and the tests are only going to get harder."

Epilogue

After saying his goodbyes, Stone walked out of Mission Control and into a sunlit March afternoon. A bit unsteady from lack of sleep, he fumbled his cell phone from his pocket and dialed a familiar number.

As he waited for his call to be answered the physician thought of Martin and Katerina, and all the happiness he hoped they would share together in the years ahead. Thinking back over his own life, he told himself that any planet where love and caring existed still had room for hope.

Then he heard the voice of the most important person to him in the world murmuring from his phone. Alex Stone, husband and father, smiled and said, "Hi, Donna. I'll be home soon."